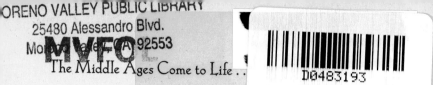

The Middle Ages Come to Life . . .

A PLAY OF PIETY

"[*A Play of Piety*] entranced me just as her books about Dame Frevisse did . . . This book abounds in authentic detail and intriguing, vividly fleshed-out characters. It gave me a sense of being carried back to medieval times. The precarious existence of traveling performers is realistically portrayed, and Joliffe is an engaging and resourceful protagonist. Without being archaic, the dialogue somehow rings true. The plot builds to a satisfying ending. All in all, this is a superb historical mystery." —*Historical Novel Society* (Editors' Choice 2011)

"Margaret Frazer depicts the Middle Ages with such ease; there is nothing awkward about the setting or speech of the characters, giving an overall familiar feel and a strong sense of place." —*The Mystery Reader*

A PLAY OF LORDS

"Will entertain and confound you with its intricately plotted mystery and richly detailed writing . . . Ms. Frazer knows the fifteenth century and it shows . . . You'll want to rush out and get the previous books in this wonderful series." —*The Romance Readers Connection*

"[An] amazing wealth of historical detail. While the mystery is compelling, and rooted in a fascinating historical period, it's the details of everyday life that make the story and characters leap off the page . . . Will appeal to readers who enjoy historical mystery and historical fiction." —*CA Reviews*

continued . . .

A Play of Dux Moraud

"Deftly drawn characters acting in a stage of intricate and accurate details of medieval life."
—*Affaire de Coeur*

"A meticulously researched, well-written historical mystery that brings to life a bygone era . . . Historical mystery fans will love this series."
—*Midwest Book Review*

"Wonderful . . . As always, the author provides a treasure trove of historical detail . . . Good, solid mystery."
—*The Romance Readers Connection*

A Play of Isaac

"In the course of the book, we learn a great deal about theatrical customs of the fifteenth century . . . In the hands of a lesser writer, it could seem preachy; for Frazer, it is another element in a rich tapestry."
—*Contra Costa Times*

"Careful research and a profusion of details, especially those dealing with staging a fifteenth-century miracle play, bring the sights, smells, and sounds of the era directly to the reader's senses."
—*Roundtable Reviews*

"A terrific historical whodunit that will please amateur sleuth and historical mystery fans."
—*Midwest Book Review*

continued . . .

THE CLERK'S TALE

"As usual, Frazer vividly re-creates the medieval world through meticulous historical detail [and] remarkable scholarship."
—*Publishers Weekly*

THE SQUIRE'S TALE

"Meticulous detail that speaks of trustworthy scholarship and a sympathetic imagination."   —*The New York Times*

THE REEVE'S TALE

"A brilliantly realized vision of a typical medieval English village."   —*Publishers Weekly* (starred review)

THE MAIDEN'S TALE

"Great fun for all lovers of history with their mystery."
—*Minneapolis Star Tribune*

THE PRIORESS' TALE

"Will delight history buffs and mystery fans alike."
—*Murder Ink*

THE MURDERER'S TALE

"The period detail is lavish, and the characters are full-blooded."   —*Minneapolis Star Tribune*

THE BOY'S TALE

"This fast-paced historical mystery comes complete with a surprise ending—one that will hopefully lead to another 'Tale' of mystery and intrigue." *—Affaire de Coeur*

THE BISHOP'S TALE

"Some truly shocking scenes and psychological twists."
—Mystery Loves Company

THE OUTLAW'S TALE

"A tale well told, filled with intrigue and spiced with romance and rogues." *—School Library Journal*

THE SERVANT'S TALE

"Very authentic . . . The essence of a truly historical story is that the people should feel and believe according to their times. Margaret Frazer has accomplished this extraordinarily well." —Anne Perry

THE NOVICE'S TALE

"Frazer uses her extensive knowledge of the period to create an unusual plot . . . appealing characters and crisp writing."
—Los Angeles Times

A Play of Heresy

Margaret Frazer

BERKLEY PRIME CRIME, NEW YORK

THE BERKLEY PUBLISHING GROUP
Published by the Penguin Group
Penguin Group (USA) Inc.
375 Hudson Street, New York, New York 10014, USA

Penguin Group (Canada), 90 Eglinton Avenue East, Suite 700, Toronto, Ontario M4P 2Y3, Canada
(a division of Pearson Penguin Canada Inc.)
Penguin Books Ltd., 80 Strand, London WC2R 0RL, England
Penguin Group Ireland, 25 St. Stephen's Green, Dublin 2, Ireland (a division of Penguin Books Ltd.)
Penguin Group (Australia), 250 Camberwell Road, Camberwell, Victoria 3124, Australia
(a division of Pearson Australia Group Pty. Ltd.)
Penguin Books India Pvt. Ltd., 11 Community Centre, Panchsheel Park, New Delhi—110 017, India
Penguin Group (NZ), 67 Apollo Drive, Rosedale, Auckland 0632, New Zealand
(a division of Pearson New Zealand Ltd.)
Penguin Books (South Africa) (Pty.) Ltd., 24 Sturdee Avenue, Rosebank, Johannesburg 2196,
South Africa

Penguin Books Ltd., Registered Offices: 80 Strand, London WC2R 0RL, England

This book is an original publication of The Berkley Publishing Group.

FIRST EDITION: December 2011

Library of Congress Cataloging-in-Publication Data

Frazer, Margaret.
    A play of heresy / Margaret Frazer. — 1st ed.
        p. cm.
    ISBN 978-0-425-24347-3
    1. Joliffe (Fictitious character : Frazer)—Fiction. 2. Actors—England—Fiction.
3. Lollards—Fiction. 4. Murder—Fiction. 5. Coventry Corpus Christi plays—Fiction.
6. Coventry (England)—History—Fiction. 7. Great Britain—History—Henry VI,
1422–1461—Fiction. I. Title.
    PS3556.R3586P54 2011
    813'.54—dc22

2011032141

PRINTED IN THE UNITED STATES OF AMERICA

10 9 8 7 6 5 4 3 2

Dedicated to Justin and Sarah and Seth and Preeti—
the doers and watchers of theater in my family.

And to Deb Murphy,
who shared in the excitement of watching
the twenty-three pageants
of the Chester Cycle those three days in May.

A Play of
Heresy

Chapter 1

The day was dove gray, soft under low clouds, with the rain mist-gentle on Joliffe's face and beading silver on his horse's dark mane. His cloak was a long way yet from soaking through nor had he troubled to pull up his hood; the rain felt good against his face. Too, he judged by blue patches of sky showing in the east that clearing weather was on the way and there would likely be sun enough to dry his hair and cloak well before he came to Coventry, especially since he was making no hurry of his going.

After a month of doing much, he was enjoying just now not having to do anything in particular. He would get to Coventry when he got to Coventry. There he would soon be doing much and more, and so was content in this while to be simply riding, with England at peace and in plenty around him. For such as worked the land, these were the year's gentle days. The spring's hard work of plowing and planting was past; the summer's hard work of haying and sheep-shearing yet to come. This year even the weather was kindly, with sun and rain in their proper proportions and sufficiency, and all the mingled greens of hedges, meadows, trees, and fields were at their fullest, the yellows, blues, and sudden reds of wild-growing summer flowers in the long wayside grasses at their gayest. In the hotter days toward harvest time, the greens would weary, the flowers fade under wayside dust, but for now the world and all were burgeoned new and full of promises.

Some of which promises might even be kept, Joliffe thought. Then, if only briefly, he was ashamed of so unthankful a thought. He had nothing to be unthankful for. Or not much anyway. The bruised ribs were nearly well, and he would be in Coventry before nightfall, with work and his fellow players waiting for him there, ready to tell him how everything had been going with them these few weeks he had been wandering England's middle counties, seeming a minstrel for the sake of learning things his worship the Cardinal Bishop of Winchester wanted to know. That his skills at singing and the lute were moderate at the best meant he had not greatly prospered as a minstrel. On the other hand, he had learned interesting things enough among the lords and gentry of Warwickshire and other parts to please my lord of Winchester. Please but not satisfy; my lord of Winchester was not a man easily satisfied when it came to knowing things.

That—among other matters—Joliffe had learned these past two years and somewhat more since coming into the bishop's service. Still, for this while, he was done with serving the bishop in matters subtle. He had already passed along to someone else what he had learned and in Coventry would need to be simply a player. Or not so simply. There was nothing simple about the dozen and more plays that would be played through the town's streets in a few weeks time. They were played every year at Corpus Christi to show the citizens' great piety and (not at all by chance) to their great profit, because hundreds of outside folk came, both for the holy procession before and the plays themselves. This year of 1438, the sixteenth of the reign of King Henry VI, would surely be no different, except that this year Thomas Basset's company of players, Joliffe among them, was to be part of it all. To their *own* great profit, Joliffe trusted.

The horse and he were come to Warwick where his way met and crossed the high road that, southward, went by way of Gloucester to Bristol, while northward it would take him by way of Kenilworth to Coventry. Today not being a market day, there was no more than an ordinary scattering of people going about their business as he rode into the marketplace around the cross atop a deeply carved tower of pinnacled stone rising from three stone steps. The rain had stopped, and Joliffe thought he would, too, there being a tavern with a fresh ale-bush on the pole above its door. The ale proved to be good, and so was the small meat pie he had with it, but he stayed only for a single bowl of the ale and finished eating the pie as he rode out of town, minded that even though he need not make haste, he did need to keep steadily on to be in Coventry by day's end.

His first certainty that this simple plan was not going to go so simply came a few miles out of Warwick, at a crossroads where a tall wooden crucifix stood on a single stone step in the middle of the way. On the step a rat-faced man with straggling hair pushed back of his ears was sitting at his ease, leaned forward with his crossed arms on his knees, a tall staff in the crook of one arm and propped against a shoulder. He had all the look of someone who had been walking and was stopped here to rest, but he straightened as Joliffe neared him, and Joliffe, drawing rein a few yards from the cross but not dismounting, said, more surprised than unwelcoming, "Sebastian. What are you doing here?"

"Waiting for you, surely." When he did not choose to curb it, there was a slight Welsh lift to his voice.

"You knew I'd be coming this way and today?" Joliffe said, then caught up to himself. "No. You saw me in Warwick just now."

Sebastian's smile unfortunately tended to be a lifting of the front of his upper lip, increasing his likeness to a rat. It lifted now before he answered, "Aye. But you didn't see me, did you?"

"I didn't."

"That's because you weren't looking. You've been taught better than that."

Given that it was Sebastian who had taught him, yes, Joliffe had been taught better than that. Never come or go from a place without noting everyone and everything there was to see, on the chance that there might be something or someone that ought to be seen, and if you could go unnoted yourself, all the better. Today Joliffe just had not cared, and he let the justified chide go by and instead asked, seeing no sign of pilgrimage on Sebastian's hat or elsewhere to serve for excuse of travel, "So where are you bound that brings you here?"

Sebastian's face fell into lines of grieving worry. "There's my brother ill. I've hope to see him one time more before he dies."

Since Sebastian had a wide array of putative relatives

always on the point of death when he needed to be somewhere other than he was and, for one reason or another, a
claim of pilgrimage would not suit, Joliffe was unmoved, certain the imagined brother would live to die another day when
need be. He was equally certain that Sebastian would not
have troubled to meet him here without reason, and dryly
and distrustfully, he asked, "Where's your brother dying?"

Sebastian's worry and grief disappeared somewhat more
rapidly than a drop of water from a hot griddle. "Coventry.
Where you're bound, yes?"

Immediately more wary, Joliffe answered with a single
nod, then brought himself to add, "Now that I've given over
what I've learned these past weeks, I'm rejoining my company for the Corpus Christi plays."

"So there *were* things to learn," Sebastian said. "What?"

Since Sebastian was his senior and superior in the work
they shared and would likely have report of it anyway, Joliffe
answered readily, "With the Earl of Warwick gone to France"—
By the king's will, not his own, so word ran—"my lord of
Stafford"—Another earl, younger but with ambitions to
power—"is doing just what was expected. His people are still
smarting and muttering at how Warwick saw to Bermingham
getting back his manor from Chetwynd last year and are
ready to back any moves Stafford may make toward bettering
his power his side of the shire. He'll have to watch himself,
though, because if he pushes too far, he'll come up against
Lord Ferrers who doesn't look like being behindhand in gain-
ing what he can while my lord of Warwick is out of the way.
Neither of them has done much overtly yet, but there's shuf-
fling in plenty going on out of sight. I won't venture a guess
how long it will be until it's not out of sight anymore."

Sebastian accepted all that with a nod, showing ready, brooding comprehension. "You're done with that, then. You've made report, and you're bound for Coventry now."

"Yes," Joliffe said. "And so are you. Have you been shifted to there?"

"Me? No. I'm still centered in Bristol for this while. I'm only here because someone from Coventry failed his meeting with me in Bristol. I had to finish something there that couldn't wait. Now I'm bound to find out what became of him."

"He found something better to do?"

"He's a mercer. He was to be in Bristol to deal over something that would have turned him a profit if he'd been there when he was supposed to be. No mercer misses a chance for profit without at least sending word why he's delayed."

"Things happen," Joliffe ventured.

"Aye," Sebastian agreed glumly. "With him, though, whatever happened, it happened after he'd left Coventry."

"How do you know he left Coventry?"

"Asked a passerby, surely. Bristol to Coventry, there's always men back and forth, and mercers always know what each other are doing. You ought to know that well enough."

Joliffe let the jibe pass. Sebastian knew he knew it well enough. Coventry town was growing richer by the year on its ironworking and the weaving of fine cloth from Cotswold wools. The cloth mostly went southwestward to Bristol whose sea-trade spread down the Atlantic coast to Gascony, Portugal, and Spain. Coventry cloth went; dried fruits, oil, wax, leather, and other goods came back, to be traded out across the whole middle part of England. The iron for the widely traded ironwork came mostly out of the Forest of Dean beyond Gloucester, then by the same Bristol-Coventry road.

All of that meant there was constant travel of mercers and other merchants between Coventry and Bristol. The hearing of Coventry news in Bristol would have been no great trouble for Sebastian, but Joliffe asked, "So who did you ask and what reason did you give for wanting to know?"

"A Coventry mercer's journeyman, come on his own on some business that didn't need his master and grateful for someone willing to show him the ways of Bristol's worser taverns and better flesh-houses."

"And when the evening was well enough along that he likely wouldn't remember what you talked of, you asked him about your man."

Sebastian touched a finger to the tip of his nose, then pointed it at Joliffe. "You have it. The fellow knew Master Kydwa was gone to Bristol but didn't know quite when. I finally made out he must have left Coventry about the time he should have if he meant to meet me in Bristol when he was supposed to. Since he didn't meet me, where is he?"

"Likely he had a servant with him," Joliffe offered. "Maybe the servant robbed and killed him."

"I'd be happy if I could think that were it, but Kydwa wouldn't have enough in the way of money to make him worth his servant killing him."

"A poor mercer?" Joliffe said as if that were a jest.

"It happens," said Sebastian gloomily.

"Maybe he's a bad master, and it was for anger, not money, his man killed him."

"I've met with Kydwa twice before this. I'd not say he was a choleric man. His servant, too, had been with him a long while, was an older man, not likely to want to unsettle himself nor take a sudden turn to killing. No." Sebastian's gaze was brooding on the green and quiet countryside. "There's a murdered body out there somewhere, waiting to be found."

"Or two bodies."

"Or two bodies, aye."

"Plain robbery, you think?" Joliffe said. "And the bodies hidden better than robbers usually bother to do?"

"It would be simplest to think so," Sebastian said, plainly not thinking that at all. "But it will be Lollards. I feel it in my bone here." He jabbed a thumb against his doublet at the breast bone underneath. "Lollards sure as anything."

Since with Sebastian it always came to Lollards, Joliffe let that go, saying instead as he gathered up his reins, "I hear horses. I'd best ride on." Since they would do best not to be seen together.

"Right enough." Sebastian stood up, stretching, readying to walk again. "I'll leave Coventry to you for now since you'll be there anyway. Learn what you can about Master Robert Kydwa and what he might have found out that got him killed. He was going to bring me more word about the damned Coventry Lollards. He knew some. Now he's likely dead, and it will be them that did it. Take heed on that. I'll seek you out later to hear what you learned." He was walking away as he said that. It was over his shoulder he added, "Stay alive."

The road to Coventry was straight ahead. Sebastian had taken the right-hand road, his tread the weary one of a solitary traveler knowing he would get eventually where he was going. Joliffe's glare at his back was wasted and the coming horses sounded only the last bend of the road away, so he nudged his heels into his own horse's flanks, setting it moving again as a fresh shower of rain spattered down.

Chapter 2

He was shortly overtaken by a trotting line of pack-horses, their rope-bound bundles strapped firmly to backs and sides. Their rider at lead did not give him so much as a look, but Joliffe and the rear man shared friendly nods as they passed. The tittupping of hoofs faded, the rain gave up, and for a time Joliffe was alone on the road again, except companioned now by regret at how much of ease was gone from his day. He had been looking forward to being simply a player in Coventry. Now he was supposed to find out what he could about this Master Kydwa. And Lollards.

He did not know why it was always Lollards with Sebastian. The man worried at them like a dog at a bone it hated. Maybe a special charge from Bishop Beaufort had set him on, but Joliffe suspected it was the other way around—that they were Sebastian's own-chosen foe and Bishop Beaufort simply made use of an itch Sebastian already had. However it was,

Sebastian was hell-bent on his quest to find out Lollards and their complots, and that hell-bent sat uneasily with Joliffe. True enough, a goodly number of the wilder ones among them had made trouble hereabouts—seven years ago, was it now?—with an armed uprising. For a few weeks things had been chancy, and afterward there had been some hangings, but so far as Joliffe had ever seen, most Lollards were not out to make open trouble. Yes, they were known to gripe against the Church and the government, but who did not? They claimed they wanted to understand what they were told to believe, which was fair enough on the face of it, but what was their chance of it, given that scholars had been quarreling over how and what to believe for centuries?

From what Joliffe had heard, the core of Lollard gatherings seemed to be someone among them reading aloud from the Bible done out of Latin into English. Then they would sit around telling each other what they thought it meant, sure they could do better at it than priests and scholars. Priests and scholars of course felt otherwise, but still the whole thing might have been no great matter if only there were not some Lollards who thought—convinced as they were of how right they were; after all, *their* name for themselves was "the True Men"—that they must do more than try to argue into the ground anyone who disagreed with them. More than once and not just seven years ago, hotter heads among them had wanted that "into the ground" to be literal, and they had risen in armed rebellion, meaning to put into graves those who refused to agree with them.

Joliffe granted that was a sure way to have the final word in an argument, but he objected to the arrogance that spawned such certainty of the right to kill because of beliefs that could never be proved, only be believed. Lollards called the Communion bread "Christ in a cake" and said there was no proof that the bread and wine changed to the actual body and blood of Christ in the Mass. Some of them had staked their lives and died for their right to refuse that belief. Joliffe, for his part, reckoned whether the bread and wine changed or not was a matter of faith, and without evidence weighted more heavily one way or another by more than pride-filled, quarreling men's words, he would make no trouble over it himself, thank you. To his mind, either way to take the sacrament of the Eucharist was a blessing and honor and therefore he took it gladly the one time of each year it was allowed to folk at large.

He did wish, though, that he knew why Sebastian had such great and apparently personal quarrel at Lollards.

Church spires let Joliffe see that he was coming to Coventry well before he was in sight of the town itself. With smaller places it was their church's tower that almost always showed first, tall above hedgerows and bends in roads. Larger, richer places often had spires atop their churches, and above Coventry two great spires thrust up against an afternoon sky no longer gray but blue and adrift with white fluffs of clouds. There was a third spire halfway built, its present stunted shape against the sky suggesting it might grow to be the tallest of them all but even now declaring with the other two that this was a town whose citizens readily used their wealth to the greater glory of God.

Undoubtedly a wise thing to declare and go on declaring after the mess and scandal of the Lollards seven years ago.

He had to wait outside the towered, stone-built gateway for a broad wain to rumble out over the cobbles, then rode through, into the wide street beyond. Tall, shoulder-to-shoulder houses lined both sides, their upper stories overhanging shops fronted along the street. Signs thrust out over the street from upper floors, well above the heads of riders passing by, telling what the shops had to offer, but Joliffe gave the shops no heed and only looked at signs until he saw the one painted with a rearing red horse that meant he had found the hire-stable where he was to leave the horse he had hired at the other end of his ride. Whatever the sign showed, his own particular mount had never showed even the slightest tendency to rearing, which assuredly suited Joliffe very well. He liked a peaceable horse and hoped, as he slung his bag over his shoulder and gave the gelding a final pat before walking away, that it had been as pleased to have a peaceful rider.

The day being well worn toward suppertime, many of the shops' keepers were swinging up the boards that served for displaying their goods in front of their open shop fronts during the day and as a stout shutter to close them for the night. Not being in need of anything at present except finding his fellows and being done with the day, Joliffe wove his way steadily along the street among a scattering of people homeward bound or on late errands, until he came to the wide meeting between his street and another. Satisfied he was well into the town, he looked around, saw the nearest tavern had a hanging sign of a canvas-wrapped, rope-strapped woolsack crossed by a pair of shears, and guessed that would be as good a place as any to ask his way.

The choice proved sound. In this supper-while before folk would gather in for the evening's drinking, only three men were there. Two were intent over a game of twelve-man morris, its lines and cups carved into a wooden tabletop where the light through the one window fell best. The third was behind the board at the back where piled cups and a pair of pottery pitchers waited for just such a willing customer as Joliffe. Told that one of the pitchers had red wine, the other ale, he took a cup of the wine, had a long, welcome swallow of it, told the tavern man that it was good, which it nearly was, then said, "I'm come to town to join my company of players. It's the guild of shearmen and tailors that's hired them. My reckoning is I'll easiest find them where they're practicing their play. Would you know where the guild's pageant is kept?"

"That'd be in Mill Lane, t'ward t'other end o' town," the tavern man said obligingly.

"Earls Mill Lane," grunted one of the men at the table without looking up.

"Everyone knows which one is which," the tavern man said with the easy good will of someone who would never be lost in his own town and assumed the same for strangers. To Joliffe again he went on, "You'll likely find your folk nearer than that, though. Master Silcok has the keeping of 'em and that's a lot closer than Mill Lane."

Joliffe put on all the brightness of a traveler receiving welcome news. "Master Silcok, is it? Can you tell me the way?"

"Just along Earl Street here." The man nodded toward the tavern's open door. "That's Earl Street. Cross it, go rightward maybe thirty paces, and you're there. You'll know the place. New glass window two floors up. Big one. Proud as can be of it, Mistress Silcok is, I hear."

One of the men at the table beside the tavern's notably unglassed window gave a snort in comment on that. The tavern man said past Joliffe, "Sniff if you want, Tad Faber, but there's those that work and get, and there's those that sit about playing twelve-man morris of a good weekday afternoon."

"Playing it badly, too," Tad Faber's companion said.

Tad Faber snorted again in answer to that and bent closer over the board.

Joliffe thanked the tavern man, finished the wine, picked up his bag from the rush-strewn floor—the rushes were due for a change, he thought—and went out. Earl Street was as wide and paved as the street by which he had come into town, the houses along it finer by what he could see of them in the gathering shadows under the day's last long slant of sunlight over the rooftops. He had no trouble telling the Silcoks' house among them, though. The new window was indeed a big one as windows went, wide across the housefront so that for much of most sunny days its many small diamond-shaped panes would glitter toward the street for the impressing of pass-ersby and neighbors while giving equal pleasure to the owner by flooding the room beyond with light.

Now, though, with the summer sun setting so far to the north, it was in shadow, and anyway Joliffe's greater interest was toward the gateway at one side of the house. The gate was standing partly open, not yet closed and barred for the night, letting him see into the narrow, paved yard beyond it, run-ning the length of the house, back from the street to another, shut gateway at the far end. Better yet, he saw, crammed into one far corner of the yard, the players' cart with its familiar red and yellow canvas tilt. Where their cart was the rest of the company must be, and with a heaved sigh of satisfaction, Joliffe went into the yard. An immediate welcoming cry of "Hai!" greeted him as Piers sprang up from a bench beside probably the kitchen door not far from where the cart stood. "Joliffe's here!" he shouted.

On the chance his shout had not been heard, he leaned into the doorway and called again, "Joliffe's here!" then pulled back, turned around, and said at Joliffe, "About time, too."

"If I'd known you were waiting so hard, I'd have taken longer," Joliffe returned, crossing the yard toward him, adding accusingly, "Are you taller than a month ago?"

"Grandda says it's him shrinking, not me growing, but it's not. It's me growing. Mam says so."

"No need to be so proud on it." Joliffe gave the boy a friendly punch on one shoulder as they met. "It's hardly your own doing."

"Ellis says they're feeding me too well and should starve me a bit."

"I've been saying that for years."

They were a company of six—or were when Joliffe was with them. Thomas Basset was their leader. Joliffe, Ellis, and Gil shared the playing with him, and his grandson Piers had up to now been useful as demon-imps and sweet-faced small angels and whatever else his size made suitable, while his mother, Basset's daughter Rose, had the often thankless task of seeing to their playing garb and feeding them all. Over the years they had been through good times and bad times together and were now again in good times, ever since Lord Lovell had become their patron and given them the protection of his name a few years past. Not quite so much to the good, perhaps, had been his putting Joliffe into the way of Bishop Beaufort of Winchester with word of Joliffe's skill at finding out things. The bishop was powerful and wealthy, uncle to the king and a rival for high place among other great lords around the royal court. Lord Lovell wanted no open part in those rivalries but was as aware as lowly players were of the use of having a powerful patron. Joliffe had been something like his gift to Bishop Beaufort for the sake of having the bishop's favor in his turn.

Not that Joliffe had minded. He had been given a choice and he had taken it, and for the most part he enjoyed the new skills he had been taught and the tasks he had been set. Besides, it meant that now the players had another patron, albeit one whose favor was hidden from view. What mattered were the coins that came in return for Joliffe sometimes having to go away about the bishop's business, as he had been gone this past month. But he was back now and glad of it as Basset came through the doorway into the yard, broadly smiling, reaching to clasp the hand Joliffe put out to him, at the same time sweeping a look down Joliffe's length as if to be sure he was all there and well.

Basset, as master of the company, had a somewhat better knowing than the others of what Joliffe did when he was away. He therefore worried somewhat more but rarely asked questions and assuredly had no chance for any now as Gil, Rose, and Ellis joined them with a mixture of welcomings and, from Ellis, "About time you showed your face."

"Not to mention the rest of me," Joliffe said. "How goes it with all of you? Except someone's been careless—there's assuredly more of Piers than there was a few weeks ago."

Rose looked at her son with the mingled affection and irk that Piers so often raised in those around him and said, "I've had to sew longer ties on his hosen."

"What I need is a new pair," Piers complained.

"Not until we're sure you're done spurting upward for a while," Ellis growled.

Enwrapped in the glad familiarity of them all, Joliffe laughed, threw an arm over Gil's shoulders, and said, "As the one closest to whole-witted here, *you* tell me how it's been going."

They all told him, of course, while taking him along the yard, past their cart to the yard's far corner and up wooden stairs to a room that—whatever its usual use might have been—was presently half given over to a long table piled with various cloths and scattered with scissors and pipes of thread and a small cushion stuck full of pins, and set about with stools. Out of the way of all the sewing that clearly went on there, the rest of the room looked to be given over to the players, with their bedding and pallets rolled and stacked atop familiar wicker hampers against the wall. Joliffe, having already gathered some things out of the happy talk around him, said, "So this is Rose's domain here."

"It is indeed," Basset said.

"Mine and Mistress Silcok's," Rose said, a little edged.

"You have her well in hand," Basset assured her and added for Joliffe, "Her husband is high among the tailors. She thought that gave her the right to be the same here."

"She's quite skilled at the sewing," Rose said, fair as always.

"But *you* know what will work best for players," Ellis said. He reached out an arm around her waist, to bring her close to his side so he could bend and plant a kiss on her forehead. "For which we thank you."

Rose smiled up at him. Her husband had disappeared

while Piers was a baby and never been heard of since. That meant there could be no marriage between her and Ellis, and for years she had resisted there being anything else. Those had been hard years for both her and Ellis and occasionally for everyone around them, but at last their care for each other had won out over the strictures of the Church: in every good way but law they were wed now, and everyone was the far happier for it.

Joliffe lifted the folds of a scarlet cloth at the near end of the table and was surprised by its weight and fineness. With open surprise, he said, "*This* is to be for the play?"

"For Herod," Basset said. He had taken one of the players' floor cushions from their pile beside the hamper and was easing himself down onto it where he could lean back against a wall.

"And the blue, the green, and the saffron yellow here are for the Three Kings," said Gil, going farther along the table where apparently partly finished robes were folded. With a wide smile, he laid a hand on the yellow and added, "This will be Ellis', so no matter what he says, he's happy enough about it all."

"Blessed Saint Genesius," Joliffe breathed. There was a good-sized fortune in cloth here, all for new playing clothes when the usual way was to be satisfied with over-worn clothing given by guild members for their company's play or, with the players, what could be had secondhand from those who sold such. Rarely was there the pleasure of something made new, let alone made new with cloth of this richness. "Of course it's the Shearmen and *Tailors* Guild's play," he said. "I suppose the tailors have cloth enough. Still—" He stroked the scarlet with an admiring hand. "All of this new at once?"

"It seems it was years since anything new had been done

for their play," Basset said. Pleasure shone from him. "The whole thing was showing its age and over-use—garb and pageant wagon and all. Many in the guild were already half-persuaded it was time to do it all anew. I persuaded them the rest of the way."

Moving along the table, Joliffe turned back the corner of clean sacking wrapping a bundle and gave a low whistle at what he saw. He looked back at Rose. "What is this?"

"Chainsil."

Joliffe shook his head to show that told him nothing.

"A most fine and costly linen," Rose said grandly. Here bleached to a shining white. "It's for the Angel's robe."

Joliffe covered it again almost reverently. "Saint Genesius," he breathed again. "We've fallen into a featherbed this time."

"*We've* fallen," Ellis said. "*You* haven't."

Joliffe looked to Basset. "No part for me?"

"Not in ours. There's been the usual contesting among the guildsmen for who will do which."

"Has not there just?" muttered Ellis. In a doddering voice, he mimicked, "I've always played the First Shepherd. The First Shepherd is *mine* and no one else can *ever* be the First Shepherd."

"It's that bad?" Joliffe asked of Basset.

"It was. Nearly."

"These days the fellow who says he's always been the Second King can hardly hobble even with a staff," Ellis said heatedly. "As for remembering his words . . ."

Gil had gone aside to where the players' large sitting cushions were stacked in a corner. He now threw one at Ellis, breaking off his grumble enough for Basset to come in with, "You know how it is with guildsmen and their pageants in these towns. They cling to what they think is 'their' part until both they and the part are creaking."

Rose, on her way to Ellis with her own cushion, paused to kiss her father on a cheek and say, "But you have wooed them out of it, and everything is better."

"Getting that way," Basset said, pleased and showing it. "New gear, new garb, mostly new men in the parts, some of them quite good, it turns out."

"With enough hard work by us to make them that way," Ellis muttered, but he let Rose pull him down to sit beside here, getting a kiss on his cheek in return.

"But no part for me?" Joliffe persisted to Basset.

"Or for me!" Piers said indignantly. "Gil is a Shepherd. Ellis is a King. Basset is Herod's Servant. *I'm* not anybody."

"You liar," Gil said good-humouredly, throwing a pillow at him. "You're a demon in the girdlers' play, leading a pack of other demons."

Piers threw the pillow back at him. "But I'm not in my own grandfather's own play!"

It was indignation for the sake of indignation, not even Piers serious at it. The pillow went back and forth another time until Joliffe snatched it in mid-flight, threw it on the floor, and sat on it himself beside Basset. Grabbing another pillow, Gil sat, too. Taking a small wooden recorder from his belt, he began to play softly, idly on it. Piers flopped flat to the floor with his head in his mother's lap, for her to stroke his curls while she and Ellis talked quietly together above him.

"So what am I to do if I'm not in your play?" Joliffe asked of Basset.

Chapter 3

"The other guilds have only lately begun to ready their plays," Basset said. "Word is out that the shearmen and tailors are set to spare nothing this year to make their own splendiferous beyond anything it's ever been before. It being the Annunciation and Nativity and . . ."

"And a half dozen other things, like jumble in a box," Ellis muttered.

". . . there are chances in plenty to fulfill their desire," Basset continued, ignoring him. "And I gather that the other guilds are taking up the challenge to rival whatever the shearmen and tailors are doing. So there's now something of a scramble for a greater leavening of skilled players among the general rout of once-a-year folk. Remember Will Sendell?"

Joliffe twitched his mind to follow that turn of the talk,

groped half a moment, and said, surprised and showing it, "As with the Will Sendell who used to be one of us?"

"That's him."

Yes, Joliffe remembered him. He had been one of Basset's company when Joliffe joined it, well before Gil's time. Sendell had shared parts with Ellis, they being much of an age and skill, and there had been another man, too, John Vicar who had been about to outgrow the women's roles he had been playing in the company. That was why there had been place for Joliffe, although that had made the company on the edge of being too large. To the good, Joliffe had shown skilled at changing their plays to fit the whole company into them, doubly earning his place. There had been prospering times then, before their then-patron turned on them. In the bad times after that, Sendell and Vicar had found the margin of the company's survival too thin, even for players, and had left—deserted was how Joliffe had thought of it then, before he stopped thinking of them at all. The company had struggled on, never quite dead although often just barely surviving, until Lord Lovell had decided to favor them. Now, with Gil joined to the company, they were thriving so far as players ever throve, and so thought of Will Sendell's desertion was not the irk it might have been, and Joliffe said, "He's here in Coventry?"

"He's directing the weavers' play for them. He says he could use someone's help with showing the folk he has to use how to do more than declaim and strut."

To have paying work and something to do here—something besides finding out murderous Lollards—would be better than not, that was sure, but Joliffe put off the acceptance he supposed he would give by asking, "What's he been at these years since he left us?"

"He took himself back to Lincolnshire where he came from, put together a company of his own, and swung along the east coast from there into Yorkshire and back. Then two years ago the company got caught in an outbreak of plague in Hull. Two of them died. The other two decided they were tired of a player's life and left to go back to whatever they had been before. Since then Sendell has been scraping by with what work he can find. I gather it's mostly been directing plays for church ale-fests."

Joliffe winced. That was catch-as-catch-can work for the most part and meant working with whatever folk and whatever play were to hand around the church for the sake of raising money by a day of merriment and drinking. With drinking the most important part of the day for all too many of the folk there.

"Now he's here," said Basset. "I've talked with him some. I think he can still do fit work when he has something and someone fit to work with."

"Which you say he presently doesn't," Joliffe said warily.

"That's what you'd be for," Basset said grandly. "You would be the hammer and saw and carpenter's plane he uses to shape the rough folk he has to something fine and worthy."

Ellis put in, "Better that Joliffe be the nail that gets hammered on the head."

"Ha," Joliffe said back at him, and to Basset, "The pay?"

"Good enough, I suppose, since there's the rivalry now for the guilds to out-do each other, and the weavers are one of the best-prospering guilds here."

"Seems a worthy way to pass the time," Joliffe granted. "At worst it's only for this couple of weeks. I'll find him out tomorrow. How often do they rehearse?"

"I don't know about him. With mine, I've talked our guild folk into letting me have the latter part of every third afternoon as well as evenings to work with one part of our folk or another."

Joliffe did not stop the widening of his eyes. "That much?" Players, with all their skills well-honed, could get by with a handful of practices when need be, but the town folk for the most part did *not* have well-honed skills and nonetheless too often seemed to think a play needed little more than for everyone to learn their words, stand up, and do it. To persuade merchants and craftsmen to give up time from their work for something they thought needed little work was a true accomplishment.

"That much, yes," Basset said dryly. "And it's needful. The ones I have in hand who've never played before don't know what they're doing. The ones that *have* played before need to be wooed out of all their bad, familiar ways."

Gil broke off his soft piping to put in, "It's not a simple play, either. There's the prophet Isaiah, Mary, Joseph, the angel Gabriel, the journey to Bethlehem, Christ's birth in the stable, the Shepherds on the hillside . . ."

"And sheep," grumbled Ellis.

"We're *not* having sheep," said Basset in a way that suggested he had already had to fight that out with someone.

Gil went on, ". . . a choir of angels, Herod and a Messenger, the Three Kings, the Bethlehem mothers with their babies . . ."

"*Not* real babies," Basset said, although given what happened to those babies that had probably never been at issue.

". . . and the Soldiers sent to murder the babies," Gil finished.

"All on one pageant wagon," Ellis grumbled. "Someone is going to be elbowed to death in the stage house."

"You'll never be in the stage house," Gil pointed out. "You're one of the Three Kings. You'll be on horseback. And the Shepherds start out under the stage."

"You'll be in the stage house when it's time you all change into the soldiers," Ellis returned. "Not to mention that you and Basset have to somehow convince your fellow shepherds that they don't have to be slap-my-thigh and fall-over-laughing on every speech *and* that soldiers should move differently than shepherds do."

"True enough," Gil agreed easily. "Meanwhile, all you need deal with are the other two kings."

"Meaning I'll be trying to make them understand that 'royal' is not the same as 'pompous ass,'" Ellis growled.

Rose leaned sideways and kissed his cheek. "Shhh," she said. "You'll wake Piers."

Although nothing but actual sleep was likely to keep Piers as quiet as he had been this while, Joliffe nonetheless eyed him distrustfully. Anyone who would add those several inches of height in hardly a month was likely to anything. Gil, seeing Joliffe's look, said, "He's been having a fine time running with Coventry boys."

Ellis had given up his grumbling in favor of kissing Rose, but she turned away long enough to say to her father, "I'm worried on that."

"Now Joliffe is here, he can take them in hand," Basset said comfortably.

"I beg not!" Joliffe protested.

But Basset went cheerfully on, "The girdlers have the Harrowing of Hell this year. I've suggested that an array of different-sized demons for Christ to send away in terror might not come amiss. I've likewise pointed out that Piers could be their leader, being practiced in the work in our company."

"Whoever is doing the Harrowing took to that thought?"

"The master girdler to whom I suggested it was quite taken with the thought," Basset said in a voice of pious virtue.

Gil laughed. "Given that two of his sons are some of the demons Piers is running with, Master Burbage was undoubtedly glad to find a use for them."

"I likewise offered your steadying hand to work with them a few times," Basset went on, beaming at Joliffe as if presenting a great honor.

"Hai!" Joliffe exclaimed.

Basset, choosing to take that for acceptance rather than protest, said, still beaming, "Good."

Joliffe bowed his head to him, accepting the inevitable and hiding his grin. A chance to order Piers to something and be obeyed at it was not to be missed.

Although there was a last lingering of light in the sky beyond the one window, the shadows were thickening toward darkness in the chamber, meaning it was time to lay out the sleeping pallets, the blankets, and the pillows. No one seemed ready, though, to disturb the resting quiet with that much effort just yet. Gil had returned to playing the small pipe in an evening-quiet sort of way. Ellis and Rose were whispering together. Joliffe, enjoying talk about playing as he had not been able to do these past weeks, asked Basset, "So other than Rose keeping busy with her days full of sewing, what are you doing with the rest of your time here?" Since he could not believe Basset would waste the company's time with idleness.

"A good many days we've been hired to play at one merchant's or another's house. The town is prospering and the citizens like to show each other just how rich they are. In between whiles we've tried doing a bit of nothing. We're being paid well enough we can afford that for this while." Which was a far crying from the days when the almost daily question was whether they would earn enough with their next playing in a village to buy some bread and cheese for a poor supper. "I've something for you to do, too, if you will."

Dryly, Joliffe asked, "Beyond the two things you've already found for me?" And not counting what Sebastian had charged him with.

Ignoring the dryness, Basset said, "I'm playing the Messenger to Herod in our play. The part is flat. He's mostly there for no more than Herod to bounce orders off him. Sometimes all there is on stage is Herod raving and the Messenger standing there like a block, dodging a blow ever now and then. I'd be glad of you having a look at the script to see what more might be done with him."

"Yes. Gladly," Joliffe said, meaning it. Even in the days when his playing was worth nothing better than next-to-nothing parts, he had earned his place in the company by his deft way with words, bettering what plays the company had, changing them when the company shrank or grew, sometimes even making an altogether new one when need be. He mostly enjoyed the working with words, expected he would enjoy it now, but said on a half-stifled yawn, "Not tonight, though."

Basset matched him with a yawn not stifled at all and agreed, "Not tonight."

"I'd best get my bedding from the cart then. By the by, where are Tisbe and Pyramus?" The company's two horses.

"Master Silcok is paying for their keep in someone's pasture outside the town."

"Master Silcok is being very good to you all."

"Master and Mistress Silcok are ambitious to stand large in Coventry. Part of that seems to mean being generous patrons to the players who will make their guild's play the best that's ever been seen here."

"Board and lodging for us *and* our horses. Very fine."

"Very fine indeed," Basset agreed.

Rose, readying to ease Piers' head from her lap so she could rise, said quietly, "Nor you've no need to go out. Your bedding is already here, over there with the rest of ours."

Joliffe, already on his feet, bowed his thanks.

Ellis, up, too, and heading toward the pile of bedding, added in his grumbling way, "After all, it took you long enough to come. We've been expecting you to show your face here any time these past few days."

Joliffe bowed again, to Ellis this time and mockingly, hiding how inwardly glad he was to be as "home" as he was ever likely to be.

Chapter 4

Since there was no peace to be had in the players' supper chamber once several women gathered to their sewing there with Rose, Joliffe spent the next morning cramped into a corner of the players' cart with the scroll of the Nativity (it being called that for simplicity's sake) play entrusted to him by Basset. Before seeing what might be done with the Messenger, he made a quick read through the whole play, this being Basset's copy and so all of it. Everyone else in the play would have only his own part and whatever line from someone else's speech cued each of his own speeches. That saved on ink and paper but could make confusion over what happened when and with whom until everyone became familiar with whatever play they were doing.

That, at least, would not be a problem here: the story was too familiar, and probably the whole play, too, it being done every year for Corpus Christi here, but that of course was a problem in itself—the play might be *too* familiar. How to make the familiar exciting nonetheless was the challenge Basset had taken up, and Joliffe read with that in his mind. The prophet Isaiah's single long speech at the play's very beginning was not a trouble. Besides giving the lookers-on time to shuffle about and settle to heeding what came next, once it was done whoever played Isaiah would be free to change garb and be someone else in the play. Next came the angel Gabriel appearing to Mary to announce the Christ child's coming. Angelic wings were always a problem, both for the wearer and for anyone around them, but they were a familiar trouble, and familiar, too, was the exchange between Mary and Joseph when, outraged and disappointed, he learns she is with child, only to be reassured by the Angel reappearing to calm him.

It was from there that Joliffe saw the worth of Ellis' grumbles about the play. Pageant wagons were never over-large. They could not be, since they were pulled through town streets, sometimes around tight corners, from playing place to playing place by a guild's journeymen. Mary, Joseph, and Gabriel would be no problem (even with the wings), but Joliffe quickly saw that for this play there would have to be some sort of stage house on the wagon, making the playing area smaller, and in that smaller playing space Joseph and Mary had to journey to Bethlehem, go into the stable— beyond doubt the stage house in this case—where Mary stayed while Joseph went in search of a midwife. He presumably closed a curtain to hide Mary, because with him gone, three Shepherds were to come on, meeting each other supposedly out in the hills somewhere to talk and eat and drink and then be awed by a suddenly appearing star and then by Angels singing.

They were still there, being awed, as Joseph came back to the stable to find (putting aside the curtain Joliffe supposed would be there) that the Child had been born. The Angels were then to tell the Shepherds to seek out the Child. They would go as they were bid and afterward leave the stage, while Joseph had to close the curtain again because now Herod and his Messenger were to come on for Herod to boast of how great a king he was. Loud music was called for, to accompany him when he went off. Then the Three Kings were to appear "in the street," the script said, to show they have come from afar, but they were to join Herod and Messenger on the stage. Having ordered them to find the Child, Herod and Messenger were to leave, while the Three Kings went the perforce very short distance to the stage house to present their gifts to the Child. Warned afterward by the Angel to escape Herod, they then left, and Herod and Messenger came back on for the Messenger to tell Herod the Three Kings were gone. Helpfully, the script said that Herod was then to do his famous raging not simply on the wagon but in the street as well, ending by ordering his Soldiers (come on from somewhere) to kill the children in Bethlehem. Herod, Messenger, and Soldiers then had to all go somewhere out of sight because the Angel reappeared to warn Mary and Joseph to flee, which they did as the women of Bethlehem came on, singing to their doomed children until the Soldiers returned and slaughtered the Innocents, the play then ending with Herod learning the holy family had fled to Egypt and violently swearing he would follow them.

Joliffe wished Basset luck with it. In the wrong hands, it would be a wallowing beast of a play.

Fortunately for the play and its guild, Basset's were likely to be the right hands, because whoever had first written this play had had skill at both words and stagecraft. It *could* be made to work beautifully, and Joliffe saw why Basset was pleased to have it. With the wealth and ambition of the shearmen and tailors behind him, he would surely make the most of its possibilities, would turn it into something rich and rare.

Always supposing he had men who could play the parts well enough, not strut like idiots and mangle the language past hope.

Still, Basset had seemed unworried about that part of the business, so maybe he was in luck there, too.

Joliffe rolled back through the scroll to Herod and the Messenger. The latter's part was nothing much. The writer had probably seen little point in troubling to do much with only a messenger when it was Herod's rage that everyone was waiting to see. Joliffe had yet to watch a Herod who did not thrash and rage all over the stage in over-played fury. It was what Herod, any Herod, was expected to do, and all the lookers-on were waiting for it, ready to laugh and jeer and cheer. Whoever had written this play had understood the Messenger was there only because someone had to report one thing and another to Herod so Herod could fall into one and another of his expected rages.

Nonetheless Joliffe could see possibilities and began to scribble on a scrap of parchment on the slant-topped box that served him for a desk and held his quills, stoppered bottle of ink, and such paper and parchment as he had. By the time his belly told him that the morning was well gone toward dinnertime, he was satisfied with what he had so far done. With no qualm about leaving it for later finishing, he put everything away and crawled from the cart. Stiff with having sat still for so long, he stretched and bent and stretched again, careful of his bruised ribs but not careful enough. He straightened with a wince, and behind him Basset said, "What's that for? That wince?"

Putting an easy smile on his face, Joliffe turned to him. "Just a bruised rib or two. I bumped into something harder than I am." Or, more correctly, the pommel of someone's sword had been driven hard against his side. Not that he much complained about that: if Joliffe had been less quick to close with him, it would have been the blade in his side. A little carelessness in his questioning about why Lord Ferrers was gathering such a large affinity of men had made one of Lord Ferrers' men suspicious and then angry at Joliffe one drunken evening. It had come to blows, but since it was the man who was drunk and Joliffe not, nothing worse had come of it than bruised ribs and a need for Joliffe to leave that particular place before the next dawn. None of that being something he meant to tell Basset, he went lightly on, "I must learn to stagger less when I'm drunk."

"Taken to heavy drinking, have you?" Basset said dryly, letting his doubt show but not pressing the matter, saying instead, "How goes it between you and my Messenger?"

"Your Messenger is become a wry-witted man who knows very well what a fool his master is and lets the lookers-on know he knows it, while all the while seeming nothing but respectful to his king."

Basset brightened. "Yes! Good! I can play that more easily than the flat nothing he's been. Are you ready for your dinner?"

Joliffe looked along the yard toward the kitchen door from where good smells and an occasional bustling servant were coming. "Here?"

"Not for you, I fear. I spoke with Mistress Silcok this morning. You're welcome to sleeping space with us, but since you're no part of the play, she does not feel it right they do more. You're on your own for meals."

Joliffe had foreseen that. The last of yesterday's bread and cheese from his belt pouch had done for today's breakfast, and he had coins enough to see him through for a goodly while to come. Besides, going one place and another around Coventry for his meals would give him chance to do more of what Sebastian had wanted. So he shrugged easily and offered, "Shall I take you out to dinner, then? My paying."

Basset gave him a half bow. "I've always taught that a player never turns down an offer to be fed. To be true to my teaching and set you a proper example, I must perforce accept your offer."

Joliffe half bowed in return. "You are most kind, as well as faithful to your word."

"Also," Basset added briskly, "I know where Will Sendell is likely to be dining."

Joliffe committed himself to no more than, "Ah," being still uncertain how he felt about meeting up with Sendell after all this while.

Out of the yard and into the street, they turned the opposite way from the tavern where Joliffe had stopped yesterday. A slight early morning rain followed by a clearing sky had Coventry shining in warm summer sunlight, and the scattered crowd of various folk bustling about late morning errands or heading home or elsewhere to their own dinners seemed in a general good humour. Weaving their way among them, Joliffe said as much to Basset who agreed, adding, "This is their time of year, as it were. With Corpus Christi coming and the weather promising to go on as it has been, there'll be hundreds of out-comers pouring into town for the plays, spending money to make the merchants, innkeepers, tavern-holders, and everyone who works for them joyous with prosperity."

"And us."

"I am already joyous with prosperity," Basset said. "They can only make me more joyous."

They turned into a narrower street than Earl Street, well-paved between scrubbed doorsteps of shop-fronted houses, then soon turned again, down a short passage into a cobbled yard set about with benches beside a few trestle tables. One table, set across one of the doorways into the yard, had a servant man standing behind it, pouring something from a leather jack into a wooden cup held by a man across from him. Perhaps a dozen other people were scattered among the tables with cups and food. Basset, with no apparent need to look around, turned toward a table and two men in the yard's nearest corner. Both men were sitting with hunched shoulders, their hands wrapped tightly around the cups on the table in front of them, seemingly brooding into their cups' depths as if there were their last hope on earth before damnation took them. They both looked up as Basset and Joliffe came their way. One of the men was altogether unfamiliar. The other . . .

Will Sendell had not aged well in the years since Joliffe had last seen him. Never a sturdily built man and already begun to lose his hair all those years ago, he was well toward bald now and as weathered away and roughened as an old gatepost beaten on by too many seasons of bad weather. He had always been someone full of thoughts and forward-driving ambitions, who would sit leaning forward beside the players' fire in the nights, debating with Basset across the flames what the company should try next, where they should go. In the days before times turned to the bad, he had strode along roads with his head up and a readiness for whatever the next town or village or manor might offer.

Here, now, he looked only aged and tired.

And defeated? Was that defeat instead of only weariness in the slump of his head and shoulders?

At any rate, there was nothing there of him as Joliffe had last seen him, setting off on the road away from the company with no backward look or wave, a man just coming into the fullness of his life and ready to face all. Presently he looked ready to face nothing, including the effort of raising that cup to his mouth.

That Joliffe knew him immediately despite all that was as disconcerting as the rest. How much did a man have to change before someone who had known him would fail to know him again?

Just as disconcertingly, Joliffe found he was asking the question about himself.

"Will!" Basset said heartily. "Here he is. I said he'd finally show himself. Joliffe, sit you down. I'll fetch ours."

Basset veered away toward the serving table. Joliffe, feeling abandoned, sat himself down on the nearer bench beside the man he did not know, across from Will Sendell who had raised his head at Basset's greeting and now stared at Joliffe as if he were trying to care he were there. Joliffe had more than half thought he would be drunk, but he was not. His gaze was fuddled with misery maybe, but not with drink.

Clear-voiced enough and even with a kind of welcome, he said, "Joliffe. After all this time. Who would have thought it?"

Remembering what Basset had told him about Will Sendell's past few years, Joliffe thought better of asking him how things were with him; instead said, "Who would have thought it indeed. How goes this play I hear you have in hand?"

Sendell's face twisted into wry bitterness. "It's a bastard of a play. Endless talking and nothing else. Worse, I have to find a half-grown boy who can look like holy Christ and not gibber his lines. Much luck may I have at *that*."

"There's Powet's nephew," the other man said. "You might as well try him. Powet says he's likely to do if there's none other."

"I may have to," Sendell said, much as if admitting need to have a tooth pulled, but his gaze had stayed on Joliffe, and he now demanded, "Ever got around to telling anyone your whole name?"

From the first, Basset had made a jest of Joliffe never telling his whole name and over the years gave him various names in place of the missing one, with "Joliffe" sometimes first, sometimes second, keeping the jest going and no one else in the company caring except Will Sendell. For him the whole thing had grown into some kind of offense. It still seemed to be, but when Joliffe answered, deliberately lightly, "No," Sendell unexpectedly grinned and said, albeit with a bitter edge, "That's the way. Don't give away more to the world than you have to. Lesson well learned."

Basset returned, a thick-pastried pork pie on a wooden plate balanced on top of the two cups he carried. Setting it all on the table, he said to the man beside Joliffe, "Master Burbage. How goes the world with you?"

"As ever. And you?"

"As ever and all the better for Joliffe being here." Basset shifted around to sit beside Sendell, across from Joliffe. With his belt-hung dagger, he cut the pie into reasonably equal quarters and handed a piece to Joliffe while asking Sendell, "So. Think you can find a use for him?"

"Probably. Better than letting him wander around with nothing to do." Sendell and Ellis had always shared a belief that Joliffe needed watching.

Joliffe, taking a first sip from his cup, made a surprised sound. He had been paying heed to Basset and Sendell, not to the ale he expected. Now he held the cup away from him, peering into it as he said, "Wine? When did we rise to heights affording wine?" He looked around the yard, with all its seeming of an alewife's place, and added, "Coventry is so prospering that they drink wine where the rest of the world can only afford ale?"

Basset laughed at him, and Master Burbage answered, "Master Dagette is a wine merchant here. This is wine that suffered enough in its travels that he doesn't think it good enough for his high-paying folk. So he gives it over to his wife for this that used to be her ale shop. We get it not too highly priced, which makes us happy, and she and Master Dagette make a profit on it after all, which keeps them from being too gloomy." He took up his own mostly-eaten pork pie from the table and added, "A while back, for good measure, Mistress Dagette decided the cookshop down the street was making money she would rather have. So she added food to what she sells here."

"That can't have pleased the cookshop," Joliffe said.

"She buys it from the cookshop, then sells it to us for

dearer than she paid. But the wine is here, so here we are, too, with no need to go anywhere else from day's beginning to day's end if we don't want to."

As he bit heavily into the pie and chewed away, Basset belatedly said by way of proper introduction, "Joliffe, this is Master John Burbage of Bayley Lane. Master Burbage, this is our straying player, come to roost. Likely he's going to share the honors with you in Master Sendell's play."

"He can have my share and welcome to them," Master Burbage said thickly around a mouthful of pie.

"Supposing Master Sendell is indeed taking me on," Joliffe said.

"Oh, aye," said Sendell. "No reason not to." He brightened a little. "Likely you can have a try at leading Eustace Powet's nephew toward being more Christ and less a Coventry street-brat."

Seemingly much cheered by that thought, he set about finishing his own piece of pie as if food suddenly interested him. Joliffe went warily at his own, only to find it was richly savory. Nor was the wine bad, either. On the whole and aside from Sendell and his apparently despised play, he thought that, given the chance, he could get fond of Coventry. What pity he had met Sebastian on the way to here. Sooner or later, like it or not, he would have to give some manner of heed toward the questions Sebastian wanted asked. The trouble with those questions was that Joliffe could hardly, out of nowhere, ask someone, "Know anything about a Master Kydwa?" or—even less possible—"So. What do you know of Lollards hereabouts?"

That left him willing to suppose the best he could do for now was let the matter ride its own way. Here and now the wine was good, the pie was good, and he switched his mind back to the other men's talk, with Sendell presently saying, "Aye, Basset. You'll do well with the Nativity and all. I'm glad it's you that got it. You're someone who'll make the most and more of what's there. But what am I going to do with Christ at the Temple? There's nothing there!"

Master Burbage nodded ready agreement. "A whole play of nothing happening. It's painful, is what it is. Other years all the lookers-on have taken the chance to go to a tavern while waiting for it to move on and the next play roll into place."

Sendell looked at Joliffe. "Do you know the play?"

Caught with his mouth full of pie, Joliffe shook his head that he did not. Not as it was done here in Coventry anyway.

Like a man who has to keep picking at a sore or digging at an itch, Sendell said, "Prophets. It starts with two prophets. They stand there talking about everything that was in the play everyone just saw. Basset's play, that'll be. Speeches and speeches of talking about what everyone has just seen."

"That's when people start going away to the taverns," Master Burbage offered.

"The prophets finally finish, and then Simeon comes on, and *he* talks," Sendell said.

"And talks," Master Burbage added unhelpfully.

"Then Ane comes on and she and Simeon *both* talk. She leaves and an Angel comes and talks, telling Simeon what will happen next."

"Angels can save a play," Basset offered.

"Or at least slow its sinking like a holed ship," Sendell returned. "That's the best I can hope for here. I've some thought of keeping things afloat with some celestial music. Hire someone with a portative organ."

"That could well be useful," Basset agreed. A portative organ, with its short board of keys and single or double rank of pipes and easily carried, could well be used for a play.

Joliffe, swallowing, nodded matching approval. "That's a good thought. Basset, you're not having other than singing, are you?"

"Just singing by my angels and the cradle-song by the Bethlehem mothers."

Sendell went on, "The Angel goes away and Simeon talks to his clerk. Then the Angel appears to Mary to tell her to take the Child to the Temple, and there's a long bit between her and Joseph, with Joseph doing the foolish-old-man business that everyone expects of Joseph. Then the Angel appears to *him* and after that he and Mary take the Infant Christ to the Temple where everybody talks and Simeon does his Nunc Dimittis."

"Which is no surprise to anyone," Master Burbage said. "Those that are still there."

"Then," Sendell said gloomily, "it's suddenly twelve years later, and Mary and Joseph are losing the twelve-year-old Christ at the Temple and finding him with the scholarly Doctors there. Talking."

"Lots and *lots* of talking," Master Burbage agreed. "I'm Primus Doctor."

"Then it's over," Sendell said, "and everybody who hasn't been listening to us comes back from the tavern and the pageant wagon is hauled on for us to be tedious at the next site."

Joliffe could not deny that it was certainly tedious in the telling, but for something to say to the good, he tried, "Have you started to rehearse yet?"

"We read through the thing yesterday evening," Sendell

said. All too openly, that had given him no joy. "The trouble is that everyone knows the play. So, except for Master Burbage here, all among our good citizens who are any good at playing have chosen to go into other plays if they could. I'm left with a pack not fit for anyone else to take."

"That's not all to the fair," Burbage protested. "There's Eustace Powet and Ned Eme. They're fit enough. That's three of us."

"And me," Joliffe said with forced brightness, hoping to give an upward turn to the talk.

"And you," Sendell granted. "Do you still play women's parts?"

"Not much anymore, but I still can." Joliffe was no longer as suited to playing maidens and fair damsels as when he had been a barely bearded youth. Those were Gil's parts now, but he could still play an older woman if need be.

Sendell brooded at him. "I could use you for Ane the Prophetess maybe. Nobody wants to be her. I'd rather have you for the Angel, but there's no hope of pulling Ned loose from that."

"He won't be shifted," Burbage confirmed. "Fancies himself in flowing robes and those high wings too much. He could have my Second Prophet, though, and welcome."

Sendell looked at him, surprised. "You'd give it up?"

"Willingly. I have the demons in the Harrowing of Hell on my hands, remember, and could do with less here. I'll stay a Doctor in the Temple, and Master Joliffe can face off with Richard Eme." He added to Joliffe, to explain that last, "Our Richard fancies himself giving those great, long prophet-speeches."

"Fancies himself altogether too much," Sendell muttered. "I may have to start the organ playing even before the Angel comes on, just to drown his droning."

Basset clapped him on the shoulder. "Heart up, Will. Have Joliffe look at your script. He's done some bettering of mine. There might be something he can do to yours."

"Like turn it into a different play," Sendell said. He stood up. "I'm off to talk with Master Grynder, to see what money the weavers are willing to put toward this thing. I've hope of prying some more out of them than they've muttered about so far." He gave Basset a one-sided twist of a smile. "They're a bit worried about what they're hearing the shearmen and tailors have in hand for the Nativity and all."

"Tell him you've heard talk they're dealing with the gold-smiths to have real jewels and better than well-shined brass for the Three Kings' crowns," Basset said.

Sendell stared, startled. "Are they?"

"No, but just now you *heard talk* of it."

Sendell's smile came back and spread into a fox-grin so that he looked suddenly something like the high-hearted ras-cal Joliffe remembered he had been. "I have, haven't I? Just now I have indeed *heard* talk."

Chapter 5

Before he went his way, Will Sendell offered to come for Joliffe late in the afternoon, to take him where his company (said somewhat scornfully) would have their practice. He added, "If we're somewhat before the others, you can have a chance to look through the script, to see if there's aught to be done with it."

True to that, he came for Joliffe just past Vespers. Plainly he had been at the Silcoks' before: he came up the stairs to the players' chamber as if familiar there and was greeted easily by everyone, even Ellis, who had spoken the harshest about him at the company's breaking up. The women who had spent the afternoon sewing with Rose were long since left to see to their households' suppers, and the players were just readying to go to their own in the Silcoks' hall. "We'll buy ourselves something on the way," Sendell told Joliffe, sounding in far better spirit than he had been earlier, before saying triumphantly to

Basset, "The guild masters did not like hearing what I'd 'heard by the way.' They've turned most of the money they had set aside for new banners toward their play instead!"

"Well done!" Basset enthused. "White samite for Christ then?"

Sendell laughed. "Probably not, but finest white wool maybe. There'll be gilt and gilding for Simeon and the Doctors anyway, and that will help. At least there's hope of us *looking* good now."

Some of his high spirit faded when he and Joliffe had left the others. As they stopped at a cookshop for small pies, he said, broodingly, "There's still the script. There's not much to be done with that, I fear."

"We'll see," said Joliffe, giving over coins for his pie and Sendell's as well. "I remember you were good at finding more in a part than looked to be there at first."

That was truth, not simply flattery, and Sendell agreed to it with a nod but said as they walked on, pies in hand and eating as they went, "One thought I've had is about those two Prophets at the beginning. There's something I want to try. Couldn't hope to have it work with the two townsmen I have. For one, Richard Eme has decided prophets are as stiff with dignity as a bishop's crozier *and* already made it plain he's someone who knows how to play a part better than I can tell him and won't shift no matter what I say to him."

Joliffe made a wincing sound of sympathy. Those kind made poor players and worse playmasters, if ever anyone was benighted enough to give them power.

"But since Master Burbage is willing to give up playing Second Prophet, I'm thinking to shift Richard Eme from First Prophet to Second, set you for First, and have you play it as if all the 'news' you're giving at such length about the star and the kings and all was actually *news* indeed and you're all brim-full with the excitement of it all. Then Richard Eme can be as much like a post as he wants and it won't matter."

"Because he'll be a counter-weight to me and the piece all the more diverting for it," Joliffe said, easily seeing the possibilities. He grinned. "Almost in despite of him."

"Yes! Saint Genesius, it's good to talk with someone who knows what I'm saying!"

That was said so from the heart and with an edge of desperation that Joliffe wondered how long Sendell had been on his own, laboring forward in grief and defeats since his company died. Just staying upright under that double burden could wear a man down to nothing under the plain weight if the struggle went on long enough; no matter how great a man's courage was, it could not save him if he had no strength left to make it good. Bleed a man dry and all the courage in the world would not be enough to keep him going. How close to bled dry by grief and defeats had Sendell come before he came to this chance here in Coventry? And how much longer could he keep going if this chance failed him?

Making no hurry of wending their way among the traffic of carts and others afoot, Sendell was saying, "We turn here. Mill Lane," when someone called out, "Master Sendell," and Sendell looked around and called in return, "Master Powet."

The man crossing Earl Street toward them pulled up short to avoid being knocked over by a bustling woman laden with a market basket on either arm, then came on, cutting around the back of a trundling cart. Sendell, paused to wait for him, said low-voiced to Joliffe, "One of mine," and, louder as the man joined them, "Master Powet. Well met. How goes it with you?"

"None so bad as it might and never so good as I wish," Master Powet returned with an edge of grumble instead of lightly as he might have. He had likely been a goodly-looking man in his youth and none so bad in his middle years, but he was well-withered toward elderly now and no longer what he had been. The look he gave Joliffe was sharp enough, though, and Sendell answered it with, "Master Powet, this is Master Joliffe. He's usually a player in the company that's seeing to the Nativity, but he's late-come and they've no place for him, so he'll be with us instead."

"Another cast-off, eh?" said Powet. There was no mistaking the grumble in that. "Mind the stones," he added.

Indeed, not much around the corner that they were just turning a half dozen or so flat paving stones were stacked almost to toppling while two men in the street's middle, at risk of being stumbled into by a careless passerby or run over by someone's horse or cart, were levering the broken pieces of other flat stones out of the shallow, stone-lined gutter there, slanted with the street for water to flow into it and away rather than toward house fronts and doorways.

"Mending it at last, and about time they were at it," said Master Powet somewhat more cheerfully as he led the way around the piled stones. "I said, Master Sendell, didn't I, that you'll see all the streets being cleaned and mended to a fare-thee-well these last days. Shop signs are being new-painted everywhere, and every rush-strewn tavern and inn floor will be fresh-rushed by the end of next week when folk can be expected to start arriving. By then all the usual troublemakers will have had the bailiffs' hands laid heavily on their shoulders and suggestion given that they change their ways for this while or, better yet, leave town."

"Will they?" Joliffe asked. "Change or leave?"

"Some will. Others, without the wit to do one or the other, will find themselves locked all together in someone's cellar for the few days that matter."

"It's this way every year?"

"When the mayor feels he has a strong enough hold over things to make it happen. It's good for the town when he does. Having the streets mended is never a bad thing anyway, Corpus Christi or no."

"Here we are." Sendell went leftward through a wide gateway. Joliffe and Master Powet followed him into a wide paved yard surrounded by a three-floored building, stone-built below, of timber and plaster on the upper floors. "The pageant wagon is there," Sendell said, pointing to double doors at the yard's far end. "We'll have it out in a week or so, to begin readying it. Today we'll be at practice here in the yard, but my room is above, if you want to have sight of the script before the others come."

"If there's time," Joliffe said.

"If you read fast," Sendell returned.

"I'll bring out the benches," Master Powet offered.

Sendell said thanks for that as he led Joliffe up a tired wooden stairway with a single thin bar for railing, to a door he paused to unlock before opening it into a room above the pageant's place. The room was bare of comforts. There was a stuffed mattress with one pillow and a disheveled blanket on the floor against one wall. A cloak and a bag of probably Sendell's belongings hung on wall pegs. Otherwise there were only a joint stool beside a table with a roll of parchment and a candle in a plain candleholder. The wooden floor was bare. So were the plastered walls. The shutter was slid down from a small window high up in the west wall, giving the room some afternoon light. The rest of a day the place would be fairly dark unless the door was left standing open.

"It was all they offered me," Sendell said in answer to nothing Joliffe had said. "It serves, it's free, and saves me the cost of paying for somewhere better. No meals given, except when one or another of the guild or someone invites me to one. Here's the script." He took up the parchment scroll from the table and handed it to Joliffe. "You look through it. I'm going to see about the benches being set the way I want them. Bring this when you come."

He went out, and Joliffe sat down on the joint stool, unrolled the scroll at its beginning, and began a rapid read toward its end. He quickly saw that Sendell's unsparing moan about it being all words and little doing was generally true enough. He hoped they had someone well-voiced for Simeon. For Ane the Prophetess, whom he was apparently going to be, he saw very little he could do except be there. He had only got to Christ and the Doctors when a boy put his head in at the door to say, "Master Sendell says you're to come now and bring the script when you do." Rather than retreat then, as he might have done, his message given, the boy waited, only starting down the stairs just ahead of Joliffe and asking as they went, "Are you truly a player? All of the time, not just for now?"

"I am. All of the time." One way and another. "Are you one of the angels, or will you be Christ?"

"One of the angels," the boy said disgustedly. "I want to be Christ, but I sing too well, so I have to be an angel, Master Sendell says, and my da says I have to do what Master Sendell said."

"Your da being?"

"One of the masters of the Weavers Guild."

"So you're an apprentice weaver, I suppose."

"I am that. Would rather be a player, though. If I could do something besides play angels."

"Angels are hard," Joliffe said in sympathy, knowing that was not what the boy had meant.

"That they're not," the boy protested. They had reached the stairfoot; he turned to face Joliffe. "All angels do is stand there, say something, and sing. Or just sing—I just sing. Then they go away. None of that's hard."

"It is if you sing like I do," Joliffe said cheerfully. "But it's the *looking* like an angel I've always found hardest."

"That's not hard," the boy returned scornfully. "You're put in a white robe, and they put wings on you, and you're an angel."

Joliffe slumped his shoulders, shifted to stand hipshot, and cocked his head to one side. "There. Imagine me with a white robe and wings. Would I look like an angel now?"

The boy laughed. "Not standing like that you don't. Angels don't stand that way."

"What way do they stand?"

With hardly a thought, the boy twitched his own shoulders back, straightened his spine, centered his body on itself, and raised his chin. Then he looked startled at the difference. He raised his hands uncertainly, as if they suddenly did not belong to him. "These," he said. "Where do I put these?" He answered himself by pressing them together prayerfully. "Like this?"

"I don't know," Joliffe answered. "Try different ways and see what feels best."

Sendell called, "Hew, time to be over here."

A cold sickness slid down Joliffe's spine and into his belly. There had been another Hew who wanted to be a player, and the memories there were not good. This Hew, though, left off being an angel to obey Sendell's call and headed toward the benches now set in a U-shape and sat upon by a variety of men and another boy. Joliffe, following Hew, saw him make to sit beside the other boy, but a strong-featured older man said, "Hew," and pointed to a space beside himself. Hew grudgingly sat himself there while Sendell, taking the rolled script Joliffe offered him, said to everyone, just as he had to Master Powet, "This is Master Joliffe. He's usually a player in the company that's seeing to the Nativity—" A few good-humoured hisses answered that. "But they've no place for him as things are now, so he'll be with us instead."

"Who's he to be?" a tall, fair youth demanded. As it happened, Joliffe had sat down facing him, fully open to his suspicious stare.

"Ane in the Temple," Sendell said.

The youth eased.

Sendell added, "And one of the prophets."

The youth, who must be Richard Eme, the other Prophet, stiffened.

Giving no sign he saw that, Sendell went on, "Master Burbage will stay as Primus Doctor but has given over his part as a Prophet."

The youth eased again, openly mollified by that, until Sendell continued, "But Master Joliffe will now be First Prophet and you, Richard, will instead be Second."

Richard began an immediate bristling but got only so far as opening his mouth before Sendell smoothly cut off whatever protest was coming by saying, "I need you for that final speech, Richard. The one where the Prophet is alone on the pageant, speaking to the audience all by himself. That's why the change."

On the instant the youth's protest turned to preening. "I understand perfectly," he said. "I accept." He smirked at Joliffe.

Joliffe smiled blandly back, easily able to judge what Sendell was up against with him. For one thing, no sensible player ever told his playmaster that he "accepted" the playmaster's decision—not in that tone of voice at any rate.

"So if you'll give your script to Master Joliffe," Sendell went on, "and if Master Burbage will give you his, and here, Joliffe, is Ane's part."

The exchanges were made while Sendell went on, "Master Powet, I take it this is your nephew who may do for our Christ," nodding toward the boy wiggling on the bench beside Powet.

"Christ help us, yes," Powet said and gave the boy a light shove with an elbow. "Sit still, Dick."

Dick gave another wiggle but then tried to sit still, grinning first at his uncle, then around at everyone else. If it were granted that Christ might be slightly gap-toothed and very ragged-haired, Joliffe saw the boy might serve the part. Of course there would be the long Christ-wig to cover the hair and did Christ smile all that much? What mattered more was what manner of voice he had and if he could use it well, but Sendell put off such revelation as lay that way by saying, "You're welcome to our company, Dick. We'll see how you do when we come to your part. First, though, we're going to read through again from the beginning, now we have everyone. Ned and Hew, have you tried your singing together?"

"Already?" protested the young man who must be Ned.

With a patience that Joliffe did not remember in him years ago, Sendell said, "We've not that much time until Corpus Christi. You want to be better than only good by then. You want to be as fine as may be. We'll work together on it when we've finished reading through today. For now, just sing as best you can when we come to those parts. Master Joliffe, begin when you're ready."

Glad he had had chance to see this much of the script anyway, Joliffe began to read, pitching his voice to almost play-level, to be heard a wide way and the words very clear but holding back from the strength and excitement Sendell had talked of for the part. That could wait until he knew the part better and everyone was more familiar with him.

> *Great astronomers, now awake,*
> *With your famous fathers of philosophy,*
> *And to the Orient your heed take,*
> *Where news and strange sights be come of late.*

From the corner of his eye, he saw Sendell nod approval.

Chapter 6

On the whole the practice went well enough. Richard Eme, reciting the Second Prophet as if he were a particularly pompous Lord Mayor of London, would be simplicity itself to play off of. Joliffe's change from Prophet into the prophetess Ane should be no trouble: he would have the Second Prophet's long closing speech and Simeon's longer opening one to throw the Prophet's robe off, leaving him in a woman's gown worn underneath, and only a woman's cap, wimple, and veil to put on. Ane's own speeches were few and mostly brief, unlike Simeon's, so it was to the good that the man doing Simeon proved to have a deep voice that he used gravely, suitable to an aged priest of the Temple promised by God that he would not die until he had seen the Messiah. He sang his Nunc Dimittis—"Now dismiss your servant, Lord, according to your word in peace . . ."—already well-learned and from the heart.

The two angels—Ned and Hew—were a mixed bag at best. Ned spoke clearly and with suitable angelic dignity and grace, but Hew sounded as if he was not sure what words were for. Sendell would have to work with him.

The slender youth playing Mary was somewhat too soft of voice, but he at least seemed to understand the meaning of the words he was saying.

Richard Eme as one of the doctors who talked with the young Christ in the Temple played it the same as when he was a prophet. Joliffe had expected that, knowing Richard Eme's kind of playing. Any part someone like Eme was given he would make to his own size, changing the world to match himself, rather than taking on the challenge of changing himself to match the world, even the brief world of a play.

To the thankful good, both Master Burbage and the man who was playing Tertius Doctor had clear voices and some sense that who they played should not just be themselves with fancy words to say. With time and work on them by Sendell, they would likely do well enough.

It was Eustace Powet who took Joliffe by full surprise. As Joseph, Powet was better than only good. By voice alone, since they were only reading this evening, not up and moving, he caught Joseph's doddering age as well as his querulousness, yet somehow showed, too, the old man's deep devotion to his young wife and her son. He made Joseph both a figure for laughter, as he was supposed to be, and at the same time almost as heart-touching as—at best—he should be, too.

Powet's nephew Dick, on the other hand, made a very poor Christ. He had a clear voice and that much was to the good, but he seemed to have taken Richard Eme's style of playing for his own and that was *not* good. Why couldn't he have taken after his uncle instead? As it was, Joliffe silently wished Sendell luck with changing the boy.

Interestingly, what came clear as they read the play to the end was that its "bones" were surprisingly strong. True enough, it lacked the Nativity's possibilities for dazzling, and that showed in the flat looks among the men and dispirited rerolling of their scrolls when they were at its end, but Joliffe could see that, well-played, all the play's differences from the Nativity would be a goodly, needed balance to the excesses of Herod and the murdering of the infants of Bethlehem played just before it.

The catch was in that "well-played." The skills among the men and boys were very uneven. Much was going to depend on how far Sendell could bring them in the all-too-few days he had before Corpus Christi. That was surely in Sendell's mind as, starting to reroll the master scroll from its end back to its beginning, he said, "There's hope in it. Tomorrow we take it onto its feet. Joliffe, not then but the day after I'm going to want you to work with our Mary on how to move. So, Tom Maydeford, I need you to bring a dress you can wear for that."

"Why can't I just use what I'll wear for the play? I'm not likely to hurt the tired old thing."

"Because I'm probably going to use that tired old thing to wipe the stage clean. You can't wear what you'll wear for the play because we don't have it yet." Sendell paused, giving the men time to be puzzled by that, then said triumphantly, "I've talked the guild into money for some new garments and for fresh paint and a bit of gilt on the pageant wagon."

Glum faces brightened, and there were exclaims of "Well

then!" and "Hai-mai!" and "Not before time!" There was even some slapping of thighs and everyone in altogether merrier minds when they left the yard than when they had come. Only Dick was made unhappy by Sendell saying he wanted him to stay a while longer. The boy grimaced but, clouted on his shoulder by his uncle, granted he had nowhere to be just then.

"Except home to bed," Powet said. "Nay, he can stay, Master Sendell."

"It's that the whole last part of the play depends on the young Christ," Sendell said. "That's why I want us to work particularly at it, Dick. There's a while of daylight left. I won't use it all up. Let's sit here." He moved to the farthest end of the benches and gestured for Dick to join him.

Dick grumpily did. Powet sat down on another bench, well away from them. Joliffe, who had lingered for a chance to talk to Sendell, went to sit beside him. The two scrolls of his parts were still in his hand, and Powet asked, nodding at them, "You mind having just those for your parts?"

"Mind?" Joliffe echoed, surprised.

"You're the one of us does this for your living. You should be doing more than a dull prophet and a woman who's only there because the Bible says she is, not because she does aught that matters in the play."

"She gives Simeon someone to talk to besides himself. That's useful," Joliffe pointed out. "And, no, the size of the parts doesn't trouble me. Like always, I'll try to play them the best I can. That's what matters."

Powet made a humphing sound that neither accepted nor rejected any of that and shifted to stare at the cobbles in front of his feet. Mindful that the man knew Coventry better than anyone with whom he had yet had chance to talk alone, Joliffe said, in hope of drawing him on, "You're a weaver, then?"

"Nay. I'm a mercer of sorts, although these days I mostly stand front for my niece, she having the greater skill and her husband being dead and all."

"So the guilds aren't tight about who can be in their plays? Only mercers in the mercers'? Only butchers in the butchers'?"

Joliffe would have been surprised if that was the way of it. The plays were too important for the guilds to hobble themselves like that. He simply wanted to keep Powet talking, and the man obliged with, "Nay, nothing like that. They all just want the best they can get. Mind, if you're good and your guild has a place for you in their own play, that's where you go before elsewhere, but there's more who want to be in the plays than there are parts for, so those as direct have some chance to choose who they want. I've been in the mercers' play more than once in my day, but other guilds' plays, too. Good parts in all of them. Have been Christ twice. Pontius Pilate three times. The Devil more than once. Four times one and another of the Three Kings. God himself in the Doomsday one year. Like that. I was good enough to be wanted. Now—" He shook his head. "Now the knees are not to be trusted, and I've lost strength in my voice. Not fit for anything anymore but old, doddering Joseph, and soon I likely won't even be up to playing old and doddering. I'll just *be* old and doddering, no play about it at all. They all know I'm past my best. That's why I'm here in this play. Nobody else wanted me this year."

Mindful of how well Powet had read Joseph, Joliffe said carefully, "You need a new best. That's all."

"Oh, you're young. You don't know yet there comes a time when there's no more 'best' to be had. Only 'not so bad' followed by 'not so bad as it might be' followed by 'that's the end then.'"

Having long since learned there was never sufficient answer to "You're young. You don't know," Joliffe made none. The best he could hope for was that someday he would be old enough to say it to someone and irk them as much as it irked him now.

Powet went gloomily on, brooding at his hands twisting together between his knees, "Last year I was the prophet Elias and faced off with the Antichrist. That wasn't so bad, but I knew I got the part because I'm aging out of all the rest. Can't sing well enough to be Simeon, so there I am. Down to Joseph or nothing. Comic old Joseph." He looked at Joliffe and demanded, "Come. It *must* fret you, you being who you are—making your living by playing and all—to be cramped into little parts like your dull prophet and Ane."

Sensing a right answer might make great difference to Powet, Joliffe paused before trying, "I don't feel cramped. For one thing, what are called 'small' parts matter as much in a play as something large. What's hard to see from the outside is that 'small' parts can take as much skill as I have to make them work well." Not scrupling to choose someone Powet knew, he smiled evilly and added, "Just think how someone like Richard Eme can make a large part into something not worth spitting at."

Powet gave a barked laugh of both surprise and recognition. "Saint Swithin, yes! All you ever see of what he does is Richard Eme. Large part or small. Though God help whoever tries to give him a small part!"

"And I'll warrant there's no one so fond of Richard Eme—save himself and maybe his mother—as wants to see only him and nobody else in everyone he plays," Joliffe said.

"No!" Powet agreed on another bark of laughter.

"That's where what you did with Joseph, reading his part here, was so different and so good."

Sobering, Powet gave him a sharp look of mingled surprise and wariness. "You're saying that for kindness' sake," he challenged. His tone made clear how deeply he would scorn that manner of "kindness."

"I mean it. You didn't play him only for laughter at the old man. You added the sense that he's someone who cares for his wife and child and is maybe afraid he can't be good enough for them."

Powet regarded him with narrowed eyes, silent for a long moment before saying, "Aye. That's what I was trying for. It was there, then?"

"It was there, and it was very good. I don't make light of my craft to anyone. If I say it was very good, it was."

Powet held silent a moment, his eyes fixed on Joliffe's face, then made another sound in his throat as if he were halfway to believing Joliffe's words.

From the other end of the benches Sendell said, "That's it for tonight, then. The light is gone anyway. You work at learning your words, and we'll see how things go tomorrow."

Dick stood up with great readiness, rolling his scroll closed while saying to his uncle, "If you want to go on home, Uncle Eustace, that's well. I just mean to go around to . . ."

"You just mean to go home with me, that's what you mean, just as your mother said, or we'll both be in trouble." Powet stood slowly up with a stiffness that told how far to the bad his joints were indeed gone. "I don't mean to suffer her tongue-lashing for your sake, and you don't want another thrashing from Herry this week, do you? Come along." He started for the gate.

Dick, slouch-shouldered and scuffling, went with him, muttering, "I'll warrant nobody ever threatened to thrash Christ when he was a boy."

"*I'll* warrant there was never a *need* to thrash Christ when he was a boy," his uncle returned and was rumpling the boy's hair as they went out the gate.

Sendell and Joliffe looked at one another in the now silent and deeply shadowed yard.

"It's not hopeless, is it," Sendell said, not quite making a question, not quite daring to hope it was true.

"It's not hopeless by a long way," Joliffe said. "You've a very good Joseph, for one thing, and I think your Mary should come along well. There's no trouble with Simeon, the others are mostly sound enough, and of course your First Prophet and Ane are the uttermost of fine."

"Beyond doubt," Sendell said sourly. "Nor don't think I don't note you say naught about my Second Prophet or Christ."

"Your Second Prophet you'll have to keep a hard rein on," Joliffe granted. "Far too pleased with himself, is Richard Eme. Your Christ—" He did not finish. He and Sendell both knew young Dick was going to take much work.

Another moment's silence fell between them until Sendell tapped his rolled script on his knee and said, "Well, that's all there can be tonight. I'm for bed. Tomorrow I'll set to finding the new garb and seeing if there's much to be done with the old."

He sounded tired, as well he might. He had put in a good day's work, talking the masters of the Weavers Guild into spending on their play and then rehearsing with a cast hardly of his own choosing. But he also sounded halfway to discouraged just thinking about what came next, as if hope and effort were both almost beyond him, and Joliffe heard himself saying before thinking better of it, "Want me to join you over the garb? A pair of heads and two sets of eyes being better than one, as they say."

He felt Sendell nearly refuse him, then abruptly shift and say, "Depends on the worth of the second head and set of eyes, doesn't it?" with something of his old, cutting impatience before adding, "That would likely be helpful, yes. I'll come for you sometime in the morning?"

"I'll strive to be awake," Joliffe agreed and rose to take his leave.

"If you're not, a toe in the ribs does wonders. Can you find your way back?"

"Out the gate. Turn right. At the corner, not falling over the paving stones, turn right again and keep going until I see the Silcoks' gateway. Or a likely looking alehouse. Whichever first comes."

"You have it. Mind curfew," Sendell said and waved him on his way.

Joliffe left him still seated on the bench in the gathering twilight, maybe thinking about the play or maybe just summoning the strength—or the will—to get himself off the bench and up the stairs to his bed. It could be either, and Joliffe did not know which, only that Sendell was maybe as worn down almost as far as a man could go without finally breaking.

Chapter 7

The players were readying to bed when Joliffe came up the stairs. Someone—probably Rose—had already laid out his pallet, pillow, and blanket. When Basset asked how the practice had gone with Sendell and all, Joliffe said, "Not so bad as he feared. He has some players who will do."

"But then there's you," Ellis said.

Making show of ignoring that, Joliffe went on, "If he can better the others, he won't have a bad play on his hands. He'll have a good one, in truth. *And* the guild has given him leave to get better garb and will be painting the pageant wagon all new."

Basset was openly pleased at the news. So were Ellis and Gil as far as they cared at all. Rose, busy with washing Piers' ears and neck at the table beside the door where the pitcher of water, basin, and towel were, closest matched her father's pleasure, saying, "Oh, I'm glad for him, then."

All Piers offered was, "Yeow. That hurts, Mam!"

"Learn how to do it rightly yourself then," Rose returned with no noticeable mercy. "And more often."

Joliffe asked how their own play had gone. Their rehearsing being further along, there was more to tell, most of it to the good. By the end of that, they were all of them settled under their blankets, and the last of the long-lasting almost mid-summer twilight was gone, the chamber all in deep shadow. Basset made a last murmur about horses, and after that there was only a sleeping quiet into which Joliffe willingly slipped.

He and Will Sendell had some luck on the morrow among the fripperers, sellers of secondhand clothing. Besides that, their quest gave Joliffe chance to know Coventry better, with its wide main streets and the side lanes that curved off them and around and into one another in a maze that would take learning. Joliffe meant to wander the place when he had the chance, to see what there was to see and hear if there was any talk of Sebastian's missing merchant or of Lollards. Enough to satisfy Sebastian anyway. The merchant's disappearance mattered, and Joliffe would do his most there, but he lacked any great desire to hunt Lollards out from among ordinary folk. If they wanted to read their Bibles in English and find grounds therein to quarrel with the churchmen about which meant what, let them. God, Christ, and all the apostles knew the churchmen seemed to have been doing the same among themselves for going on fifteen hundred years.

Joliffe's guess was that it was not the poaching in their park the churchmen minded so much as that among the things Lollards found to challenge from their bible-reading was why they should pay either heed or—more importantly to some churchmen—tithes to men they thought unworthy of acting in God's name. Hitting priests in their purse and their pride was always a sure way to stir them up to fury like a prodded wasps' nest. Still, there was nothing new—or particular to Lollards—about any of that, and nothing the least fresh in their claim that the world needed reshaping, that those who were high but unworthy in both Church and worldly government should be brought low, and that the poor be exalted into their places—and likewise into the wealth rightfully forfeited by the high and unworthy along with their power. People had been feeling and saying those same things time out of mind, so near as Joliffe had ever learned. If someone was up too high, someone else wanted him down, and there were always reasons on both sides for why or why not this should happen.

Where the hotter-hearted among the Lollards earned the church and government's ire was in purposing to reshape everything and everyone to their desires by weaponed uprising and revolt to throw down not only such churchmen as they found unworthy, but the king and nobility and judges and all the civil government, too. The several times in the past few decades that some Lollards had raised rebellion toward that end had ended only in grief for the rebels and in black suspicion and distrust of all other Lollards.

Joliffe had to grant that the suspicion and distrust were fair enough. No one cared to have armed men trying to make good on threats to rob and kill you. Maybe the hotter-hearted Lollards should have heeded Christ's behest to "yield to the emperor those things that are the emperor's, and to God those things that are of God." At least then their more peaceful fellow Lollards would have been able to get on with their bible-reading and arguing without the hard eyes of spies on them, waiting to pounce at the first stirring of suspicion. And suspicion could be stirred by so very little.

For his own part, Joliffe's only reason to be wary against Lollards was that at least some of them had hauled up the old arguments against plays and players. False portrayals, mocking God's creation, and so on. That most folk took no heed of them about it kept it from being a great matter but still . . .

He was thinking about that as he and Sendell came out of a shop where Sendell had bought a long black robe with full hanging sleeves gathered to the wrists and trimmed with fur around the neck. The fripperer had said the fur was marten. Neither Sendell nor Joliffe nor how little Sendell had paid for it agreed with the claim, but Sendell was nonetheless pleased with it.

"It will do well for Simeon and perhaps one of the Doctors in the Temple," he said as they started along the street.

Joliffe, following the flow of his own thoughts, said, "It will indeed," and then, "Will, have you heard if there's any stirring here among Lollards against the plays?"

Sendell, busy counting coins into his belt-purse, answered easily, "None that have come my way. After the pounding they took hereabouts a while back, I doubt any would dare." He chuckled as he drew the purse closed with a tightening of the drawstring. "All the ones that were fool enough to stir trouble then met with the hangman. The ones that are left have wits enough to keep their heads down. Hai!" he added in greeting. "Master Powet."

It was indeed Master Powet coming along the street at a stroll that said he had nowhere in particular to be. He returned

Sendell's greeting with a surprised, "Good morrow," and veered from his way to come to them. Coventry was not so large that meeting someone known was all that unlikely, but while for Joliffe, having spent the past few hours among throngs of unfamiliar faces, a familiar one was unexpectedly welcome, it crossed his mind that maybe for Powet, all too familiar with Coventry faces, the welcome was in seeing their less familiar ones. Or maybe it was just curiosity, because eyeing the black robe folded on Joliffe's arm and the bag slung over Joliffe's shoulder, bulging with their other purchases, he said, "You've had some success at finding what you want, then."

"We have," Sendell said. He nodded toward the robe. "That's our latest. Will do for Simeon, I think. There's a large, faded place high on its front where someone tried to clean a stain and ruined the dye instead, but some wide collar and frontlet of rich stuff wide down his chest will cover it." And a different frontlet or something when it became a doctor's robe, he did not add.

Joliffe shifted the robe to show the faded place. Powet nodded, fingered the fine cloth, and said, "That should do well for Simeon, yes. For the rest?"

"Meaning yours?" Sendell asked with a grin.

"Aye, mine," Powet said with an answering grin.

"You'll have to wait and see with everyone else."

"Ragged old Joseph," Powet said with a sudden gloom and all jest gone from the words.

"Hardly," Sendell said, sounding as taken by surprise as Joliffe was at his change of humour. "I see Joseph as a prosperous carpenter. Fine green doublet and—oh, no, you don't! You're not tricking me into telling you more. You can wait and see along with everyone else."

Joliffe did not think it had been a trick; he thought it had simply been Powet still unhappy at being Joseph. But Powet had brightened, although perhaps not so much at Sendell's words as at whatever he was looking at farther along the street, because, as if a new thought had come to him, he said, "I know what may serve for Simeon's frontlet. Come with me."

The broad street was lined by tall, lean buildings, most of them of the usual half-timber and plaster and with a shop at their front, facing onto the street below the two or three out-thrusting stories that somewhat narrowed the sunlight into the street but gave added space in the rooms above and good shelter to passersby on rainy days. Powet led them toward one of the wider-fronted ones. Its shop window was open, the sturdy board swung out and spread with varied mercery. In the shop behind the board, a young man was presently taking a box from one of the shelves there, saying to a plump goodwife waiting outside, "This is from the same dye-batch as what you bought before. I kept some back, thinking you might need more." Taking a pipe of red embroidery thread from the box, he held it out to her. "You'll see it matches perfectly." Without turning his apparent heed from her or changing his level, soothing voice, he said as Powet neared, "Uncle, Mother is hoping to see you soon."

"That she will," Powet said. "Mistress Aylesford," he added respectfully.

"Master Powet," she said with matching courtesy, not looking up from comparing the thread she had brought with her to what she had been offered. The men waited until finally she granted, "Yes, this will do," paid for it, and went satisfied on her way.

Powet, going to the board in her place, said to Sendell and

Joliffe, "This is my nephew Herry Byfeld. He has mercer's blood in his veins and no doubt about it. Given the chance, he could sell coal to the Devil to keep the fires of hell burning."

"And you'd smooth-talk him into giving it back to you for nothing," Herry Byfeld said with open affection for his uncle but a questioning look at Joliffe and Sendell.

Powet said who they were. Herry said, "You're going to make a Christ out of Dick, are you? Luck with that."

"What we're here for," said Powet, "is that length of lampas-woven silk. You know the one I mean?"

"Surely." Herry Byfeld went to a far corner of the shop, shifted some things, and came back with a folded piece of cloth that he opened with a flourish across the board. There was hardly a wide yard of it, but it was richly made with red and gray silks woven in a pattern of pomegranates and vines.

"Yes," Sendell breathed. "That would be perfect." He made to touch it but must have remembered that was not the way to bargain, drew back his hand, and said with belated solemn consideration, "Perhaps. What are you asking for it?"

Powet named a price likely far too low, because Herry looked at him with badly hidden dismay. Sendell offered something even lower. Powet countered, and for far less than Joliffe guessed the cloth was worth, they had it. Herry, with a sidewise look at his uncle that said they would talk about this later, began to fold it again as Sendell laid the coins out on the board. Powet, ignoring his nephew's look, said, "Now you have to find someone to sew it."

Herry, gathering up the coins, said, "Cecily. She could do it for you."

"Well thought!" Powet said. "Is she in?"

"Where else?"

"Come then," Powet said to Sendell. He paused. "Unless you've someone else in mind?"

Sendell looked to Joliffe. "Rose?"

"She'd probably stick a needle in me if I offered her more to sew than she has."

"Cecily, then," said Powet and led them through the door standing open beside the shop into a stone-floored passageway and toward whatever rooms were beyond. As he went, he explained, "Cecily's family fell on hard times a few years ago. Or had hard times fall on them would maybe be the better way to say it. Mercers until things went bad for them. Now my niece rents them a room here—Cecily, her father, and brother—and Cecily helps for their keep while her brother tries to bring back the family's good fortune."

They came out of the passageway into a kitchen that Joliffe guessed also served as the heart of the house, because whatever chambers lay beyond the doors they had passed in the passageway or up the stairs, this looked to be where the family did much of their living. Besides the well-scoured work table and expected gathering of cooking things near the wide hearth against the room's end wall, there were a scattering of three-legged stools, one with someone's abandoned shirt tossed across it, and a tall-backed bench with a writing slate with what looked like a half-finished lesson lying on one end and, at its other, a sewing basket, a black-worsted hose hanging out of it with a half-mended heel.

Presently, though, no one was there but an old man hunched in a round-backed, tall chair near the hearth, staring at the floor, and a young woman, her hair bound up under a simple coif, tending to a large kettle hung over the hearth's low fire. Not a woman, Joliffe amended as she turned from the hearth.

A girl. The man did not stir in his chair but the girl, prettily flushed from the heat, looked with surprise at Sendell and Joliffe while she said to Powet with kind concern, "Have you had your dinner? There's pottage with lamb if you haven't."

"I'll want it shortly," Powet said. "Thank you, Cecily. First, though, this is Master Sendell who's doing what he can with this benighted play of ours, and Master Joliffe who's a player by occupation and going to show us how playing is properly done."

How much bitterness was under that jest? Joliffe wondered, while Cecily turned her kindness and a smile toward him and Sendell. "I wish you joy of it all," she said to them both and made to return to her cooking, but Powet said, "Master Sendell has a request to ask of you."

"A request for what?" a woman said, coming into the kitchen behind Powet, Sendell, and Joliffe. She had a covered basket on her arm, and Dick was behind her, carrying another basket.

"Help with the play," Powet said.

"Oh, Uncle," she laughed, setting her basket on the table. "From what you say, the only hope is for everyone to say their words as fast as may be and be done with it."

"That's maybe changing," Powet said stiffly. "These are Master Sendell who's already made it better than I thought it could be, and Master Joliffe who's helping and a player, too."

"But you'll still be Joseph and not happy about it," she said.

"My niece Mistress Deyster," Powet said by way of making her known, adding as Dick thumped his basket onto the table beside the other, "Her graceless brother Dick you already know."

The boy grinned. "I've started learning my words, Master Sendell. I've been saying them while we marketed."

"He has that, Christ help us all," Dick's sister said, beginning to take things from her basket.

Joliffe guessed she was not much older than Cecily, but there was sufficient difference between the plain-gowned girl at the hearth with her work-spotted apron and bare coif, and Mistress Deyster in her go-to-market gown of fine light linen and white, starched wimple, and many-folded veil to tell who was servant and who was mistress here.

"What we're in need of," Powet said, "is for Cecily to make a frontlet for this robe here"—he gestured to it, still hung over Joliffe's arm—"from this silk." Sendell held up the newly-bought piece. "Master Sendell will pay."

"There's other sewing we'll need done, too," Sendell said as Cecily turned from the fire, wiping her hands on her apron and looking interested. "Some garments to alter, some to make new."

"For how much by way of pay?" Mistress Deyster asked.

Sendell named a sum. Mistress Deyster looked ready to bargain on Cecily's behalf but was forestalled by the girl saying, "Yes. That's fair. I'll do it."

She was right—it was fair. Mistress Deyster gave a shrug and went back to putting eggs from her basket into a waiting bowl. Cecily said, "Dick, will you stir while I see what Master Sendell wants done?"

Dick obliged while Powet said to Joliffe, "We'd best shift out of everyone's way," and led him out the rear door into a short, paved yard between the blank wall of a neighbor's building and a two-storied rear wing of Powet's house. A well was cramped into the far corner of the yard near a low gate that gave glimpse of green trees beyond—likely the garden that went with most town houses—but Powet sat down on the stairs to the wing's upper floor, gestured for Joliffe to do the same, and said, "Let me ask pardon for my niece not being as welcoming as she might. She's had to put up with much these two years and more since her husband died and she had to come back to live with her mother and us and all."

"This isn't her house, then?" Joliffe asked, surprised.

"Nay. It's her mother's. Mistress Byfeld's. In truth Mistress Byfeld is my niece, as happens. Anna—Mistress Deyster, that is—and her swarm of brothers are my greats, properly speaking. Then there's old John that my niece—she being friends with his wife—took in when they lost all. But she's dead now, is his wife, God keep her soul, and old John sits by the fire with his wits gone and his daughter seeing to the cooking and not much more than the life of a servant to look forward to unless her brother can remake the family's fortune. He may do. He's a sharp young fellow. But my niece is not best pleased about the understanding that's been growing between him and Anna. She wants Anna to marry better than what he has to offer yet. But Anna married 'better' the first time and see how that turned out."

"Not so well," Joliffe hazarded, mildly interested.

"Not so well," Powet agreed. "Master Deyster was sound enough. My niece wouldn't make a mistake that way. But"—Powet suddenly dropped his voice low, as if there might be listeners lurking somewhere in the bare yard—"the trouble came from his son from his first marriage. The young fool got mixed into that Lollard business a few years back, and his father wrecked himself to buy him out of trouble. Then, wouldn't you know, the young fool goes and dies of lung sickness two winters later, and his father just gives up. By the time *he* dies there's nothing left but debts. To buy free of them, Anna had to sell off all that should have been hers except for one place she's held onto out of what should have been her dower." The portion of a man's property he gave at his marriage for his wife to use if she were widowed. He could leave her more in his will, if it came to that, but her dower property was hers no matter what, if things went as they were supposed to. "A shop and house near Gosford Gate. She rents it out, and there's her income she uses to build her share in the Byfeld side of things and all, and here she is and not likely to listen to her mother on who to marry next."

Powet shook his head, in a brooding sort of way, but Joliffe with studied indifference asked, "So Master Deyster and his son were Lollards?"

Powet snorted. "Deyster was never so dusty as that. He wouldn't have given the fools the time of day. My niece wouldn't have had him for Anna if he did. Nor did that son of his care half a pin for any of all they argue about. He just took to the chance to take up billhook and run about yelling and making trouble with other fools. Got more than they bargained for when Duke Humphrey came down on them all." He sounded both disgusted at them and satisfied by their fate.

So no Lollards in this household, Joliffe guessed. He was looking for an unsuspicious way to ask other Lollard-shaped questions, only to be forestalled by Powet changing away to what likely interested him more than family troubles, saying as he rubbed a hand on the shadow of gray along his jaw, "I've begun to grow my beard for Joseph. Likely there'll be something to show when the time comes. Save hanging a false one on my face."

Fortunate man, thought Joliffe. No Lollards for him, just the challenge of playing.

Still rubbing at his jaw, Powet made a tching sound and shook his head. "I should have been a player like you and Master Sendell. I did nobody any good staying here in Coventry all my days." He dropped his hands between his knees. "You truly think I can make Joseph into something more than an old fool to be laughed at?"

For Powet's sake as much as for the sake of Sendell's play, Joliffe said strongly, "It's maybe not there so much in the words, but you were finding it there last night." He poked Powet's near leg, friendliwise. "Next practice, just wait and see what I do with the First Prophet. That will show you how far you can play beyond the words."

Chapter 8

Joliffe enjoyed that evening's practice. Sendell's plan was that they read through the whole play again but this time on their feet, with him beginning to set their movements, the playing space of the pageant wagon outlined by the benches, the stage house with its stairs to an upper level at one end marked by other benches and Sendell saying, "The stairs are there."

He also warned, "I'll likely change some things later, but we'll make a start. We've a change already, come to that. Our 'Gabriel' wasn't here last night and today sent word he's had to drop out altogether. So, Ned, I want to combine your First Angel with Gabriel, make them both Gabriel for simpleness' sake. Well enough?"

Ned accepted with a glowing smile and a nod and a triumphant glance sidewise at Richard Eme, who frowned a little as if uncertain he was as pleased as Ned. What was that about? Joliffe wondered.

"Let's begin, then," Sendell said. "Prophets."

Scripts in hand, Joliffe and Richard Eme stood up. Sendell showed how he wanted Richard to come from the stage house and up the stairs to the upper level where he was to take the stance of a wise scholar contemplating the heavens.

"Or maybe just your own deep thoughts," Sendell said.

Richard nodded his approval of that, took his place and his stance.

"Now, Master Joliffe, you enter suddenly and excited. Play it large. You're not saying anything folk don't know already, so you have to make them want to listen."

Just as if he and Sendell had not already talked over how to play this, Joliffe nodded earnestly, understanding they were "playing" this part of it for the others, to let them see how directions were given and taken. From what would be the stage house, he burst forward onto what would be the stage with arms wide and exclaiming, "Great astronomers now awake, with your famous fathers of philosophy—" He broke off and looked around confusedly as if trying to find these astronomers and philosophers, then seeing Richard Eme "above him" on the yet-to-exist stairs, he brightened and continued grandly, "And look to the Orient-East where news and strange sights be come of late, affirming the saying of old prophecy"—By then he was pointing eastward and almost bouncing with excitement, and Richard Eme was staring at him in utter disbelief—"that a star should appear upon the hill of Vaus among us here!"

Richard recovered and began reading, "You brothers all, then be of good cheer, for those tidings make my heart full light." Far from being light, he was all stiff with leaden dignity. "We have desired for many a year of that star to have a sight and especially of that king of might—"

He sounded as if he desired it about as much as a pain in his big toe. On the other hand, Joliffe was now bouncing indeed and nodding with eagerness, making as if he wanted to break in with more speech of his own. Distracted, Richard Eme stopped and said at Sendell, "He's doing it all wrong. He's playing a fool. Aren't you going to stop him?"

"He's playing someone stirred by the most marvelous thing that's ever happened," Sendell returned. "Maybe overplaying it somewhat." He gave Joliffe a stern look. "But that can be fixed as we go on. No, you continue, and we'll see how it plays."

It played quite well for a first time through, Joliffe thought when they finished. Their fellow players' heed had not wandered. Given the length of time the Prophets talked at each other, that was to the good. Only Richard Eme, as stiff in his final speech as he had been in his first, was—if his violently red face and short, angry breathing were anything by which to go—displeased. Sendell, as if he did not see those signs, said, "Now, Simeon, as he starts off, you're coming on. You will exchange slight bows as you pass. You will go into the middle of the playing space and begin. No," he added to Richard Eme who had put up a hand and had his mouth open. "We'll save talk until the end. I want to get as far with this as may be this evening."

With Sendell keeping them moving, they reached Mary and Joseph finding Christ talking to the Doctors in the Temple before the light was too far gone for reading their scripts and he had to call a stop. "It's gone well. Even better than I hoped," he told them.

Joliffe thought the same. There was probably nothing to be done about Richard Eme's playing except match him to parts that matched his opinion of himself. He did those quite well enough, and his two fellow Doctors at the Temple gave promise of being able to balance his stiffness well. Burbage had grave authority without Richard Eme's stiffness. Master Smale, who served as Simeon's clerk earlier in the play, was like his name—small of stature with a light voice to match that worked well against the other two with their weightier voices.

The surprise for Joliffe in the evening was finding out that Ned was Ned Eme and Richard's brother. With his comely face and a grace of manner and voice very unlike his brother's, he was shaping well as the angel Gabriel, although there was a twinkling of mischief about him that suggested "angelic" was not his usual way of being. Hew as his fellow Angel was still awkward with his movements but aware of it and trying to better. That boded well for their days of work to come. Tom Maydeford as Mary was nowhere yet and would need help, but probably not so much as Dick Byfeld who looked likely to need most working with to be anywhere near good enough.

And then there was Eustace Powet. For all his disappointment at being Joseph, he was not stinting his effort, had already put more effort into his part than anyone else into theirs yet, and was well along the way he had tried for last night, finding the warmth and depth behind the laughter always aimed at Joseph.

"Now heed this, all of you," Sendell was saying as they gathered themselves to leave. "The sooner you can play without your script in hand, the better we'll be when the day comes. You can have tomorrow's evening, most of you, to work at learning your words instead of being here, because I want to work only with the Angels, Mary, and Joseph then. Master Joliffe, too. I'd like you here to work with Tom Maydeford on being Mary. Right enough? Good. I'll see all the rest of you the evening after that. With all your words learned."

A few good-humoured groans answered that as nearly everyone made for the gate. Only Richard Eme did not. Instead he was closing on Sendell with protest in his every lineament.

Joliffe unashamedly escaped out the gate, leaving Sendell to his fate.

Because he and Sendell had agreed that finding a gown for the prophetess Ane was something Joliffe could do for himself, he readied himself to spend part of the next morning at it. He tried to persuade Rose to go with him, but she flatly refused, saying she had too much to do. Piers showed willing, but Joliffe tousled Piers' curls in the way Piers hated and deftly dodged a kick at his ankles while saying, "My thanks, but no thanks. That much mocking I can do without," and went on his way laughing at Piers' general indignation.

Before the morning was done he had provided laughter in his turn to several fripperers, all of them taking his quest in good part once he had explained it, so that at the end he had what he thought would suit an aged woman visiting a temple: a plain-cut yellow gown with close-fitted sleeves and high collar to wear under a loose, sleeveless russet over-gown edged with a tired fur that the seller swore was not cat. Any dark, soft-soled shoe would suffice for the feet, and a wimple and veil would be small trouble to come by; some wife among the weavers would likely gladly loan her nearly-best if Sendell asked for the favor.

That duty done, the rest of the day he wandered around the town, spending time in various taverns and at cookshops, drinking not much and eating slightly but all the while listening and sometimes easing into talk with one person or another. So far as hearing any worries about any merchant presently late in returning to town or finding any likely way to ask about Sebastian's missing Master Kydwa, the day was a waste, but he made a good start at learning his way around the town, and at afternoon's end he felt free to tell himself he had done what he could for now and went cheerfully to the evening's practice, Ane's garb tidily bundled under his arm.

He was early and glad to find Sendell in a cheerfulness to match his own, greeting him with, "You escaped fast enough last night. It took me a goodly while to talk Richard Eme around to believing your foolery served to make him look noble and profound. If I can keep him believing that, we'll be fine. Did you find a gown and all?"

Joliffe had just time to unfold and shake out the gown and over-gown, and have Sendell's approval for them and agreement that, yes, asking for loan of a wimple and veil from someone's wife would probably serve and he would see to it, before Ned Eme and young Hew came into the yard.

"My brother is not best pleased with you," Ned said at Joliffe with light, mocking sternness.

"I grieve to hear it," Joliffe said, not troubling to sound grieved at all.

Ned laughed. Tom Maydeford arrived, bringing an old gown got from his mother to practice in as Mary. Sendell sent him and Joliffe to the yard's far end to work together while Sendell gave his own heed over to Ned and Hew.

Joliffe, not altogether unexpectedly, found Tom greatly uncomfortable with having to wear a woman's gown. It did not help that his mother must be both wider and taller than her son; Tom had to use his belt to gather in the excess and hitch the skirts clear of his feet. While he did, Joliffe put on Ane's over-gown, wearing it being the easiest way to begin showing how women moved differently from men. He was no longer surprised that something someone had seen every day of his life had gone totally unnoted in its detail. Made to look and think, Tom was likewise surprised to see how much he had to change not only in how he walked but in how he stood and sat and kneeled and rose to his feet if he were to seem a woman. The second time he tangled in his skirts and fell over when trying to rise from his knees, he lay on the cobbles, unhurt but unready to struggle free of his skirts as he asked somewhat piteously, "How do they *do* it, then? In skirts and *all* the time?"

"More gracefully than you just did," Joliffe said and offered a hand to help him up.

On his feet again and shaking the skirt free of his legs, the youth complained, "I feel a right fool dressed like this."

"Ah, but remember it shouldn't be *you* dressed like this there on the pageant and saying Mary's words. It should be *Mary* who's there. If it's you in the gown and saying her words, you *will* look a right fool, but if it's Mary there, then everything will be right."

"Well enough for you to say, but doing it is another matter," Tom said.

"How to do it is what we're here to learn. Look you, do you remember me being the Prophet yesterday?"

Tom laughed, which was answer enough.

"Remember me the day before that, when we sat and read the play, and how you've seen me here when I wasn't being the Prophet yesterday."

Tom drew down his brows in thought. "Yes."

"And now you've seen me here, in this gown of mine, being"—Joliffe deliberately shifted his stance, that had been his own, into that of a young and noble woman—"someone else again. And yet it's always me. That's the trick of it: to give the seeming of being someone else well enough that the lookers-on believe you, if only for that while. Now if you wear Mary's gown and move and sound like Mary, you will be fine. If you wear Mary's gown but go on being you"—he went into the slouch of a young lout about town, which Tom was not but Joliffe wanted the point made plain—"you will indeed look a right fool. You see?"

Looking satisfactorily thoughtful, Tom nodded slowly that he did.

"Then let's try walking, then kneeling, then falling over—er, I mean standing up—again. And just wait until you have to do it all while wearing a wimple and veil, too."

"Oh, Lord have mercy," Tom groaned, but gathered up his skirts to try again.

They had worked a while longer, and Tom was catching on quickly when Sendell crossed the yard to them, leaving Ned and Hew on their own for a time, to ask Joliffe, "I'm wondering why Eustace Powet hasn't come yet. Ned says he'll go to see what's kept him, but I'd rather keep Ned and Hew at work." He looked at Tom. "You could work on your own or on your words while Joliffe's gone, yes?" Tom shrugged that he could, and Sendell said, back to Joliffe again, "You know where Powet lives. I just need to know something hasn't happened to him, and if it hasn't, then for him to get himself here as fast as may be."

"Done," said Joliffe, already in the midst of pulling Ane's gown over his head. "You have your script with you?" he asked Tom. The youth patted the belt pouch at his waist. "Then work your words and at sitting down and standing up *gracefully* while I'm gone." He nodded at the nearby bench while taking up his hat he had set aside for the while. "I won't be long."

Nor should he have been. Nowhere was very far away from anywhere else in Coventry. He only had to go the short way to Mill Lane's corner and turn right into the street he now knew was called Jordan Well despite there was no noticeable shift or turn between it and Earl Street and then, not far along it, turn left into Much Park Street where he and Sendell had met Powet yesterday. He had no trouble remembering which house he wanted, either, despite the shop was shuttered closed. Somewhat early for that, he thought, given there was still much daylight left and others were open, but after all Herry Byfeld surely had some life besides behind his counter and maybe was gone off about it.

First sign that all was not well nor going to be simple was that the door in from the street was standing open, and the passageway beyond crowded with a huddle-headed hush of people who looked as if they thought they should do something about something but did not know what. Neighbors, Joliffe thought. Three women and a man and two skirt-clinging small children. Beyond them, the door to the kitchen stood open, and from there came the loud weeping of several women.

Something was gone very wrong.

Before he had decided between retreat and pressing forward, one of the women looked back at him and said, "The shop is closed. There's been a death, seems."

A somewhat too familiar tightness taking hold on his chest and throat, Joliffe said, "It's Eustace Powet I'm here to see. Is he . . ."

The man among them called over the head of the woman ahead of him, "Hai, Eustace, someone is here asking for you." He laid a hand on the woman's shoulder and added, "Come away. They don't need us here. There's naught to be done."

She gave to the pull of his hand, beginning a retreat toward the outer door. The other women must have agreed with him, and Joliffe pressed back against one wall to let them pass, one of the women saying to another as they went, "A shame and all that it's him. I knew his mother, God keep her soul."

"Aye. They're a family that's had no good fortune at all these past years," another woman said.

"She undid them, that's right certain," the man said grimly. "God's judgment."

"I'll tell you whose judgment," one of the women snapped as they went out the door, "and it wasn't God's. It . . ."

"Master Joliffe?" Powet said from the passageway's other end.

"Master Powet," Joliffe said low-voiced, going toward him, wary of the weeping but too curious to keep his distance. "I'm to find out why you didn't come to practice."

Powet's face was taut and twisted with distress. "There's been a death." He looked over his shoulder at whoever else was in the kitchen behind him. "My niece—my great-niece—Anna—her . . . not her betrothed, they hadn't said the words yet, but they meant to, when all was better—word's come he's been found dead. She's been waiting all this past week for him to come home and now . . . Oh, god in heaven and all the saints' mercy, old John will never survive this."

Now in the doorway beside Powet, Joliffe saw past him into the kitchen that had been so easy with ordinary family matters yesterday. Today there was nothing easy or ordinary. Close to the far doorway Dick and another boy enough like him they had to be brothers were crouched shoulder to shoulder, looking caught between a wish to bolt and the fixed watching of what they hardly understood. The girl Cecily and Powet's great-niece Mistress Deyster, were crumpled together on the bench beside the table, clinging to each other. The loud sobbing was theirs. Herry stood in helpless uncertainty which way to go midway between them and the old man still slumped in his chair beside the hearth, with now an older woman on one knee in front of him, leaning forward with her hands braced on the arms of the chair to either side of him, saying into his face, "Do you understand, John? Do you understand?"

"For the sake of pity, let him be, Mother!" Herry exclaimed like a man pushed to his limit. "Better he never understands. Leave him what peace he has left!"

The woman who must be Powet's niece Mistress Byfeld stood sharply up and turned on her son. "And when he starts to wonder where Robyn is, starts asking when he's coming home? What then? *Then* we tell him Robyn is never coming home?"

"Tell him anything then," Herry said back desperately. "It won't matter. He won't remember. Let him *be*, Mother." And to his sobbing sister, "Anna, *please*."

Powet snatched his hat off a peg beside the door with one hand while putting his other on Joliffe's chest, pushing him backward from the doorway, saying desperately, "There's nothing I can do here anymore. Let's go."

Joliffe went with him willingly, wanting escape from there almost as much as Powet did but even more wanting escape from the chill foreboding cramping at the base of his gut. He was never comfortable when Fortune, that treacherous goddess with her wheel that rolled you high only so she could roll you low, seemed to play suddenly into his hands. The mourning behind him was for a man expected home a week or more ago and now found dead, and Joliffe was afraid of the answer even as he questioned Powet, "Who's dead? Who is—who was this Robyn?"

Pulling his hat hard onto his head as they came out the door and turned up the street, Powet said, grief in his voice, "Robyn Kydwa. Robert. Old John Kydwa's only son. Cecily's brother. Never even got to Bristol, the sheriff said. Not to judge by how long he's been dead. All this while we've been expecting him home, and he's been dead. Saint Michael have mercy."

The cold in Joliffe clamped more tightly. So Sebastian's Master Kydwa was found, and he was dead, just as Sebastian had feared.

Joliffe was trying to untangle questions to ask that would not jar against the grieving he and Powet had just left behind, then was spared the need as Powet suddenly slowed out of his rapid walk, shambled to a stop, and stood shaking his bowed head side to side as if in denial of it all, saying, "The boy was trying so hard. No. No boy. He's only Anna's age, but he left off being a boy seven years ago. That fool mother of his took that along with all the rest. And now this."

"His mother?" Joliffe asked, truly perplexed.

Powet, grim-faced, started walking again but slowly now under the weight of his thoughts and grief. "His mother. She ruined them all. Thought herself a Lollard. Was always thinking herself one thing or another and then was friends with Alice Garton at just the wrong time. That's what did it when all the trouble came. You remember when some of the stupider among the Lollards thought it was time to throw over the Church and government and all?"

"I remember."

"Well, this Alice Garton was stupider than most because she should have known better. She and her husband both. They'd tried this same foolishness before, back in the late King Henry's time, God keep his soul. You remember then? No, you'd hardly been born then, if at all. It was bad. Let it go at that. The Gartons survived it when many didn't. Wealthy they were. Owned places here in Coventry and land outside it as well as being mercers and drapers, too. Ralph learned his lesson, but Alice—" He shook his head. "She didn't."

They were near where Much Park Street met Jordan Well. It would take very little time to be back to Mill Lane, so to give him more time for the talking he wanted to do, Joliffe took Powet's arm and steered him to the window of an ale shop, sat him down on a waiting bench, fetched two cups of ale, gave one to Powet, and asked, to keep him talking, "So this Alice Garton didn't learn her lesson and got mixed up with the rebels seven years ago and took Mistress Kydwa with her. Was that the way of it?"

"Fairly much. They didn't take to the roads or wave weapons about of course. But money—that's what they gave to help the rebels and didn't trouble to hide it. They cut off her head for it."

Joliffe choked on a mouthful of ale, swallowed it hurriedly, and said, "The rebels killed them? This Alice Garton and Mistress Kydwa?"

"Nay. Not the rebels. The government. The justices had to find her guilty—Mistress Garton, that is. When it was all over and the arrests began and then the trials. A bad time all around."

A memory turned over in Joliffe's head. Basset, believing the late winter rumors of trouble coming around Coventry and Oxford, had had the company well away to the southwest, into Dorset and Somerset, staying there until nearly autumn to be sure of keeping clear of it all. From that distance they had heard things only piecemeal and uncertainly and, yes, among the less likely rumors had been one that a woman was among the rebels executed.

"High treason," Powet said broodingly. "That's what the justices said it was and they had it right. As lawyers say, she had 'sought to encompass the government's overthrow' and this was the second time. That's what did it. They could have hung her, mind you. She wasn't noble. They could have, by law, had her drawn and hung and quartered. Seen that way, the beheading was a mercy. Quick and all. Never done to a woman before, so far as anyone remembered. Better than hanging if the man is good with the blade, and this one was. So it was a mercy. The others they hung."

Powet drank deep then, taking most of the ale at once. While he was wiping the back of his hand across his mouth, Joliffe took the chance to ask, "And Mistress Kydwa?"

"She wasn't so deep into it all as Alice Garton was. Not twice-guilty either, the way Mistress Garton surely was. John Kydwa beggared himself to pay lawyers and fines and bribes to get her clear. He'd been doing well as a mercer, but that finished him. It didn't help that his brother—his brother was a tailor—was among those who were caught and brought to trial and hung. He was right guilty, was Thomas Kydwa. There were witnesses to what he had done and no way to have bought mercy for him, but I think old John Kydwa thought maybe saving his wife had cost him his brother. Then not many months after it all, she died. Just fell ill and died. Or lost interest in being alive, some said. And there Kydwa was, left with a ruined business and no wife and no brother. He struggled on for a while, but you saw him there in my niece's kitchen. That's how he's been these four years or so. Now there's this."

Chapter 9

Powet stood up from the bench, held out a hand for Joliffe's cup, asked, "Another?"

Joliffe gave over his cup but said, caught between duties, "We should be taking ourselves to Master Sendell."

"We should that," Powet agreed and handed both cups back to the alewife without asking for more. "Let's go, then. I want my mind somewhere else anyway."

Joliffe did not and said as they started off, "It was good of your niece—Mistress Byfeld?—to give the Kydwas somewhere to stay."

"Aye. Her mother and John Kydwa's were friends of some sort. I remember hearing the two mothers even talked of marrying Johanna and John to each other, but in the end what looked to be better matches were found. Seemed better at the time anyway. Was for Johanna, any rate. She's a widow but with four children living and a good head for the business her husband and she built up. Nor it's no hardship having Cecily in the house. She does more than what's asked of her and is a fetching little thing. If Herry had sense that way, he'd be thinking of marrying her, but he's been inclined to the Emes' girl. Goditha. Pretty as she is foolish."

"Ned and Richard's sister," Joliffe said, in hope of keeping it all straight in his head.

"That's her. Not that Johanna or the Emes are likely to agree to anything that way." Powet lowered his voice and leaned a little toward Joliffe to say quietly, "There's just the whiff of the Lollardy about the Emes, look you. Not so much as to force the priest to take heed of them and nothing to have any of the family in trouble then or now, but it's there. We can be friends easy enough but nothing further. Johanna wouldn't have any marriage for Herry that way and I doubt the Emes want one, either."

Cautious to make his curiosity seem light, Joliffe said, "I thought I'd heard Lollards were against plays and players. Mockers of God's creation. Mockers of the divine. All that manner of thing."

"They wouldn't live long in Coventry crying havoc against our plays," Powet said easily. "Nay, it's only the worst of them that go that far with things. Same sort as think they can overthrow the king and lords and Church and all. I'd guess most have naught against it at all, just enjoy suchlike with the rest of us."

"Come to it, I don't suppose there are many Lollards left here," Joliffe tried, not supposing that at all but trying for what Powet might know. "Not after everything seven years ago."

"Oh, I think they're still here and about," Powet said. "It's the loud ones that suffered. The quiet ones go as they did before, maybe all the happier for being persecuted. Proves they're important, that they're persecuted. Don't see that fleas are persecuted, too, and still aren't anything more than a small-brained bother."

Come to the yard in Mill Lane, Joliffe had no time left for having more from Powet, but he was satisfied with what he had and shoved the gate open and strode in, announcing, "Found him and it's not his fault he's late, so pray let him live, Master Sendell!"

"That depends on why it isn't his fault and if he has any of his lines learned," Sendell returned.

"Tell them," Joliffe said, stepping aside to shut the gate while letting Powet go forward.

Powet gave his news curtly, making as little as might be of it. So Joliffe was taken by surprise by Ned Eme, slumped at ease on one of the benches until then, springing to his feet to exclaim, "Dead? What about George? Is he found, too?"

"Not a word of him," Powet said. "Seems only Robyn is found."

"It can't be George killed and robbed him!" Ned declared. "I'll not believe that!" His face shifted from startled to dismayed. "Holy Saint Michael, Anna must be beside herself in grief. Master Sendell, can you be done with me for now?"

Sendell managed, "For now, yes, but . . ." before Ned was away, jerking open the gate and bolting from the yard.

"Has always had a mind to Anna," Powet said glumly, by way of something like explanation.

"Who's this George?" Joliffe asked.

"George Wyston. Been servant to the Kydwas for years. Is all but another son to old John. Sure, he's not murdered Robyn. Ned's a fool."

"Could we come back to the play now?" Sendell asked with the patience of a director who did not want to be patient much longer.

The next morning, deliberately out and about in hope that Sebastian was somewhere near and looking for him, Joliffe had no surprise at all when someone in the jostle of the market crowd along Cross Cheaping near Coventry's market cross bumped into him from behind and slipped a scrap of paper into his hand. He did not look around. As he had been told when being taught the trick, "If you're not *both* subtle, then it's all a waste, isn't it?"

Besides, he had found no one more subtle than Sebastian and doubted that—even if he had looked around—he would have found him out of the crowd. Instead he turned into the first narrow side street and only around its first sideways jog paused and read what few words were on the bit of paper. St. Michael. St. Thomas' chapel. Now.

Well, that was clear enough. Joliffe swung around and headed for St. Michael's church with its tall, unfinished tower.

For a parish church, the place was huge. The nave was six bays long, with arcaded aisles along both sides, an aisled chancel beyond that, and any number of chapels with their altars and arrays of candles set about here and there. Joliffe wandered until he found St. Thomas' chapel. Sebastian was there, sitting on the stone ledge along the wall, seemingly with all his gaze and heed on the carved wooden screen and statues of Saint Thomas, Christ, other saints, and a few angels for good measure behind the altar. Being Sebastian, he was surely also aware of every movement within his range of sight outside the chapel. Never a trusting man was Sebastian. Ever. When Joliffe came in, he stood up, bowed to the altar while crossing himself, and left, all without ever seeming to look at Joliffe. Joliffe, never looking directly at him, either, went through the business of kneeling before the altar and making what could have been a semblance of brief prayer except, so long as he was there, he made more than a semblance, praying, "Bless this work we are about, if it is work that should be done."

After all, it hardly seemed right to ask God's blessing on work that should *not* be done. The trouble lay in having only notoriously fallible human judgment to use in deciding. But finding out a murderer was surely a thing that should be done, and Joliffe rose, bowed, crossed himself, left the chapel, and not unexpectedly found Sebastian propped on the splayed plinth of one of the pillars not far off, head craned back in seeming study of the paintings of saints and angels along the length of the nave's wooden ceiling. Because naves, like church porches, were places where folk commonly came and went, meeting friends and standing about in talk, there was nothing to remark in Joliffe pausing beside Sebastian and saying, pointing randomly at something on the ceiling, "Word came yesterday your missing man has been found. Was it you that did it?"

Nodding and pointing as if agreeing about the ceiling, Sebastian said, "It was."

Having hopefully set into the mind of anyone who might have noted them that they had met by chance and were simply in talk about the church, Joliffe looked fully at Sebastian for the first time. Whatever the man had been doing, it had not lately included a good meal and a long rest. His narrow face was more than ever toward rat-like, without the usual glitter to his eyes and a flat weariness in his voice as he went on, "I said I was going to look for him, didn't I? I found what's left of him under a thick pile of brush, cut last winter likely from a hedge there along a cart-track on the rear side of a hay meadow. The brush had kept carrion birds off the body. Otherwise they might have brought someone to see what they were at. He would have been found, though, when someone used the brush pile, and that would have been soon, I'm thinking, when the haying started in that meadow."

Joliffe nodded, seeing it. The women would have started carrying the wood away then, because no wood went to waste if it could be helped; well-dried wood from hedge trimmings could serve under any number of small cooking fires. "Likely it was too distant from the village for them to trouble with it sooner?"

"Likely. They'd know it was there and to be had when the time came, when they'd be at the field anyway. Whoever put the body there knew it would be found. Meant for it to be found. Unlike the servant's body," he added glumly. "That one wasn't meant to be found now or ever, I'm thinking."

"George Wyston," Joliffe said.

Sebastian's gaze, that had been drifting around the church with an apparent idleness that Joliffe knew was not idle at all, whipped back to him. "How do you know that? His name?"

Joliffe told how yesterday had gone and how he came to be on the edge of it all.

"So you know the family," Sebastian said. "Families, since the Byfelds are so linked to it. That's good. Very good. Lollards are they?"

"Not on the Byfeld side of it, from any talk I've heard. The most I've been able to hear yet about Lollards is a neighboring family with a 'whiff of Lollardy' about them. Not enough to trouble their priest, and since they've two sons in one of the plays here, I doubt there's anything there."

"There's always something there if they're Lollards," Sebastian said. "What were they doing seven years ago?"

"Nothing, it seems. Not that their neighbor knows."

"Or knows but isn't saying."

"He talked about them freely enough, it seemed to me. He talked freely about the Kydwas, too. But you already know about them."

"I know about the woman. Mistress Kydwa. The rest of the family was never much part of her foolishness and are well over it. That's why Kydwa was helping us."

"And must have found out something."

"Or been found out. We need to talk, you and I. More than we should here. There's an alehouse off Palmer Lane. Go by way of Ironmonger Row, turn into Palmer Lane, and just across the river turn into the first alley on your right. Soon as you can after me." He ended with a laugh, slapped Joliffe friendliwise on the shoulder, and strolled away toward the near door with every look of chuckling to himself about something as he went.

Joliffe, widely smiling as if they had just shared a fine jest, strolled off the other way, admiring the church as he went, circling the nave until he was come around to go out the same way Sebastian had but well after Sebastian was gone.

He had no trouble finding the alley and alehouse with its bush above the door, was interested to see the alehouse's rear must be on the river, giving another and less likely way in and out of the place. He had learned from Sebastian to value places that gave various ways to come and go, and despite he had never had any desperate need of such as yet, he was strongly aware that "yet" might happen any time.

The day's overcast had gathered into spattering rain while he was coming from St. Michael's. As he approached the alehouse, the several men who had been seated outside were shifting themselves inside. He did not see Sebastian among them, but when he followed them inside, Sebastian was already there, sitting at ease and alone on a bench against one wall, with a fat chunk of bread thickly laid with sliced meat in one hand and a pottery cup in the other that he raised at sight of Joliffe, calling, "Hai! There's someone I'd not thought to see here! Come and sit and tell me how it goes with you." Adding as Joliffe came toward him, "You here for the plays?"

"I am that," Joliffe said, no more troubling to keep his voice down than Sebastian was, nor particularly raising it. Just two acquaintances meeting by chance. He took up a filled cup from the table beside the alewife, laid down a coin, and sauntered over to sit beside Sebastian. The bench was near none of the others in the room nor to either of the doors or the front window; was in fact in the most shadowed part of the room without being blocked from either of the ways out and altogether too well-placed to be by chance, which told Joliffe this alehouse had not been a random choice. But then Joliffe had never for a moment thought it was and said as he sat down, taking up their talk about where it had broken off, "So Kydwa's servant is dead, too. Someone said yesterday, when word came that Kydwa was found, that his man couldn't have done it, that he was someone who'd been with the family forever."

"No one thinks it likely then that he conspired toward Kydwa's death with someone, then was betrayed?"

"Not from what was said about him, no. Practically another son and all that."

"I've known sons that couldn't be trusted within arms' length of anyone in their family," Sebastian said darkly. His eyes narrowed with thought, he took a long drink, then said, "Still. I doubt that's the matter here. What it looks to me is that someone wants it *thought* he's guilty. Kydwa's body was sure to be found, being where it was. The other fellow was shoved under an under-cut stream bank and then the bank pulled down to bury him."

"Which could mean their murderer . . ."

"Or murderers."

"Or murderers," Joliffe granted, "wanted people to think his servant had killed Kydwa and was fled, and the only reason to take that kind of trouble would be to steer suspicion away from Coventry . . ."

"Not the only possible reason but the most likely one."

". . . which suggests the murderer or murderers are from here."

"Or just thorough in muddling their trail."

"Thorough would have been to shove both bodies under that stream bank and hope neither was ever found," Joliffe said dryly.

Sebastian acknowledged agreement to that with a show of his teeth in a tight smile and a silent jerk of his body that was nearest to a laugh Joliffe ever saw him come. "You have it. So their murderer is someone who wanted to keep suspicion turned away from Coventry, yet wanted it known Kydwa was dead. But not until it would seem this George Wyston was too far escaped for search for him to be of use."

"Cunning," Joliffe said. "And cold."

"That, yes, but clumsy into the bargain. Whoever did it had small skill at killing."

"There's a comfort if we end by going up against him," Joliffe said dryly.

Dryly never worked with Sebastian. He simply looked at Joliffe with his flat, rat eyes for a moment as if deciding how seriously Joliffe meant that, then said, back to where he had been, "The bodies were far decayed. Some things about them were hard to tell, but by what I could see of wounds, neither of them look to have defended themselves."

"Taken by surprise. Or sleeping."

"I judge they were upright when stabbed. So taken by surprise. From behind. The servant was stabbed in the back, either first or while he was trying to escape. I'd guess first. Kydwa was stabbed in the side, maybe as he was turning around, given the way the blade went in."

Joliffe was grateful he was not the one who had had to handle well-decayed bodies enough to find that out. "Sword or dagger?" he asked.

"Dagger."

"Unuseful." If a sword had been used, there would have been at least somewhat a lessening of who to look at, but nearly every man not a monk wore a dagger.

Sebastian nodded agreement to that and went on, "Both blows were poor. Whoever did them did not know his business. Not even with the second one to Kydwa, given after he was down to be sure of him." Sebastian sounded annoyed at such poor skill. Joliffe had not had occasion to see Sebastian's blade-work but supposed it was as well-honed as every other skill he had so far shown.

"Meaning his business, generally, isn't murder," Joliffe suggested.

"I'd say not. The servant may even have been still alive

when pushed under the bank and it was pulled down on him. Probably not aware, though."

For what comfort there was in that, Joliffe thought bitterly. He was starting to very much dislike this murderer. He drank the rest of his ale in a single long draught while Sebastian continued, "I'm seeing it as either their murderer came on them unawares or else was someone they knew and didn't mind having at their backs as they went along together. The servant was probably behind Kydwa and was stabbed first. As he suddenly went down—maybe cried out—Kydwa started to turn around in surprise and was stabbed in his turn. He went down and was stabbed again, finishing him. Then it was a matter of hiding the bodies."

"First of moving them," Joliffe pointed out. "It wasn't done where you found them, was it? It sounds too far off the road for Kydwa likely to have been there on his own."

"No way to tell. Maybe he was there to meet this man—or men—secretly. Maybe he was there to learn something. Or betray something. Me, maybe. Maybe he had turned his coat to the Lollards, only they weren't as grateful as he hoped and killed him."

"But you weren't betrayed."

"No." Sebastian granted that almost grudgingly. "So maybe it's that the Lollards had found him out as a spy and simply killed him to put a stop to it."

To move Sebastian away from Lollards, Joliffe asked, "How long since they were killed, do you think? And where? How far from Coventry?"

"A day and a half's ride out of Coventry. Almost three weeks ago, I'd judge."

"They were on the straight way to Bristol, I take it."

"Aye."

"So their murderer could have followed them from Coventry on purpose to overtake them, or gone before and been waiting for them. Supposing he was from Coventry at all."

"We have to start with thinking he's from Coventry. Or else from Bristol."

And if that doesn't play out, we'll have to think about combing through the whole middle of England for him, Joliffe thought, knowing there was little hope of success in that. Sebastian did not help by going on, "There's always the chance, too, that he went on—or else back—to Bristol and took ship and is long away." Which was altogether possible: Bristol was a large city *and* a port from where ships were away to Ireland and down to Portugal and Spain and Gascony, let alone a steady traffic of all manner of boats and ships to Wales and back. For leaving the country, Bristol was as good a place as London or Hull.

There being nothing to be done about that—if their murderer was that gone, he was gone past finding out or overtaking—Joliffe said, "The time that's passed is against us. It will be hard to trace who was gone from Coventry then."

"That will be for you to do. I'm for Bristol. The murderer might have been someone from there, heading out and meeting Kydwa on the way. Or maybe he was someone from Coventry but on his way home from Bristol. You'll need to find out who came back to Coventry about the right time, as well as who was gone."

"I'm to find out who *wasn't* here and who *came back*? Among how many thousands of people that live here in Coventry?"

"Bristol is bigger," Sebastian retorted glumly.

Chapter 10

With both of them mutually silenced for the moment by those thoughts, Joliffe took his empty cup and Sebastian's to have them refilled. Sitting down again and handing Sebastian his, Joliffe said, "It would be good to know if the murderer encountered Kydwa by chance or on purpose, planned ahead to kill him or simply used the moment as it came. And what happened to the horses Kydwa and his man were riding?"

"Sold somewhere well away from the Bristol-Coventry road," Sebastian said. "For the other, it would help to know, yes, but we're unlikely to until we've caught him. What I'd want to more immediately know is whether or not the fellow was out from Bristol. If it was someone who knew Kydwa was supposed to meet me and came out of Bristol purposefully to stop him, that'd not be good." Because it would mean Sebastian was known for what he was by someone dangerously ready to kill, however unskilled they were at it. "There's those that would needs be warned if that's the way of it."

That put Joliffe in mind of something about which he had wondered. "I don't suppose this Robert Kydwa, or Robyn as his people call him, was the only man spying in Coventry, was he?"

"Ha!" Sebastian scorned. "In a money-pot like this, with its trade in wool and cloth and iron making a wide web to west and south and north? There's more than our own lord master"—his usual way not to say Bishop Beaufort's name aloud—"want eye and ear to what goes on here. The more so with this present stirring of gentry and lords into new contentions now the Earl of Warwick's hand hereabouts is lessened for the while. But you know more about that part of it all than I do." Sebastian cocked an eye at him, inviting him to talk. Joliffe looked blank. Sebastian barked one of his short laughs, approving, and went on, "But me—I'm our lord master's huntsman after Lollards, God rot them, so Kydwa was the only man I needed to know here."

Joliffe never altogether accepted any claim of ignorance from Sebastian but outwardly always seemed to and only asked, "What, then, if I need help here or . . ."

"Best you don't need any."

". . . or want to pass on word about anything?"

"Wait until I'm back. Or if I don't come back, take it you know to where." He stirred as if about to rise. "Now I'd best set way back Bristol-ward. No use to my lingering hereabouts."

Belatedly thinking of it, Joliffe asked, "What about you as first finder of Kydwa's body? Won't you be wanted here?"

Sebastian shrugged. "Some fellow with a dun yellow beard and a ragged-edged hood paid a boy here in Coventry to take a sealed message to the crowner. The boy was to say the fellow didn't have time to find out the crowner himself and that's why he'd paid the boy to do it."

"Then you followed the boy to be sure he did it."

"Surely."

"And the fellow in a dun yellow beard and a ragged-edged hood won't be seen again."

"Not here in Coventry," Sebastian said with great satisfaction.

The one thing that Joliffe had been able to show him was the usefulness of skillful disguise. Sebastian had taken to it warily at first but quickly found out its usefulness and was become good at it. Joliffe suspected it was the added layer of deception that pleased Sebastian most: he was not someone who wanted to be known by anyone in any way.

They both rose, done here and making ready to leave, except Joliffe asked with another belated thought, "It was only Kydwa's body you reported. Nothing about the servant. That's to let the murderer think he's got away with his hope the servant will be blamed, yes?"

"That's it," Sebastian agreed. "Let the stinking Lollards think they're safe and maybe they'll be enough careless we can find them out. I mean to learn what I can of their stirrings in Bristol while I'm finding out who was there from Coventry one side or the other of the murders. A link there could lead back to any Lollards thinking about making trouble here."

Joliffe nodded despite he was not as altogether ready as Sebastian to assume Lollardy was the reason behind it all. He knew too much of what else was going on among lords and gentry now the Earl of Warwick's hand no longer held so tightly hereabouts to be altogether ready to let them go by the way in this. That meant a double watching out for anyone who might not want him to know more, either about Lollards *or* what some lord or other might be into.

They paused in the tavern doorway, Sebastian eyeing the heavily clouded sky that promised the present pause in the rain was only momentary, and a sudden other question came to Joliffe.

"About that brush pile where you found the first body and then the stream bank—were those just luckily there for the murderer when he happened to need them?"

"I suppose so, ye—" Sebastian broke off that *yes*, his eyes abruptly narrowing to a glare at Joliffe. "Or maybe not. And if not, then—"

He stopped, looking as if he were mentally chewing over his thoughts. Joliffe said them for him. "Or did the murderer know of the brush pile and the stream bank aforetime and plan to make use of them?"

"They were nowhere near any road or lane," Sebastian said. His eyes were shifting swiftly side to side as if he were trying to catch hold of all his thoughts as they sped past. "So if he knew of them, he must be someone of the place. Or else someone with reason to be familiar there."

"Or else a stranger who took the time and chance to search around," Joliffe offered.

Sebastian shook his head against that but granted aloud, "Maybe. That will be the sheriff's look-for. He'll almost surely ask around about any strangers seen thereabouts a few weeks ago. Me—I want to know whose land it is, who's the lord of it. If one of his officers was there nigh the right time, that would be someone to have a long look at. Especially if the fellow or his lord is any way linked to Coventry or Lollards."

"Ask, too, who owns neighboring land."

"That, too. Aye. That, too." Sebastian was turning away as he said it, was walking away by the time he finished, not troubling with any farewell. But he never troubled with farewells. Joliffe had once wondered if that was because in the work they shared a "farewell" could all too easily be a last one. Had wondered it once, then refused to think on it again. Not that, going the other way from Sebastian now, the thoughts he took with him were any more comfortable. The murderer they now sought seemed not to be skilled at killing, seemed not to be someone trained to it. Still, he had been able to kill two men together, had seemingly had Fortune on his side all the way in the matter, able not only to kill them but then to hide their bodies without being caught at it.

What of the blood, Joliffe suddenly thought. With all of that, wouldn't the murderer have bloodied his clothing, and if he had, would not someone have noted that and now maybe remember it? It would be useful if someone did. Or remembered that someone no longer wore his familiar clothing or else suddenly had new clothing for no good reason.

No, that latter was too thin a tether to follow. When Kydwa and his man had been killed was not far off Eastertide, when those who could commonly got new clothing, after a winter's wear had worn out last year's garments. Or, if the murderer had truly thought well ahead, he could have simply got from a fripperer whatever he wore when he killed the men, then buried the bloodied clothing somewhere and never been seen in it at all. *That* would have been the way to do it. So had he?

Joliffe saw no likely way of finding out, one way or the other. Between them, he and Sebastian had questions in plenty and not much in the way of answers. Or, on his own side, next to nothing in the way of answers and no certainty how to start after them. On that account alone, he was glad he had something else to do this afternoon instead of brood about it all, having learned that often and often he got better answers out of himself not by prodding, poking, and worrying at a problem straight on but by letting a tangled matter sink down to behind his thoughts while he got on with other things.

Today at least that was just as well, because last evening he had agreed to spend some of this afternoon helping Master Burbage with readying his little devils for the Harrowing of Hell. He suspected that by the time he had finished with them—or they had finished with him—thinking about murder might be a pleasant pastime.

He curved back toward the now-familiar Earl Street by less familiar streets that took him past high-spired Holy Trinity church and toward St. Michael's with its unfinished spire that would surely challenge, if not out-top, Coventry's other two. The low-trailing clouds seemed close to skimming the point of Holy Trinity's spire, but the rain was only spattering down, untroublesome, as Joliffe curved around the east end of St. Michael's with its bow of tall, stone-traceried windows and headed down a lane he knew would bring him into Earl Street. He was hurrying a little, uncertain if he were somewhat late but meaning to take time to buy at least a meat pasty on his way. He was not minded to deal with Piers and the others on an empty belly.

A man coming out of a doorway a few yards ahead of him said with pleased surprise, "Hai! Master Joliffe!"

"Master Burbage," Joliffe said in return, adding as a boy

younger and smaller than Piers followed Burbage into the street, "Your son? One of the devils?"

Burbage gave the boy a slight, affectionate shake by one shoulder. "That's him. Son *and* devil, often as not." The boy grinned and let his father's hand stay where it was, not shrugging it away as Piers would likely have done, as they went on along the lane with Joliffe, to turn into Earl Street. Or was it already become Jordan Well here? Joliffe did not trouble to ask; it was enough to know they were bound for Mill Lane again. He did buy a pasty from a woman selling them from a tray along the street and ate it while they went on, Burbage explaining along the way how the smiths and girdlers and several other guilds had their pageant houses off a shared yard.

"That means there's some working around who can use the yard when," Burbage said. "Mostly it's the smiths who have it, what with them having the Passion and Crucifixion and Pontius Pilate and Judas hanging himself and Herod and all."

"Their Herod is really good," young Burbage said excitedly. "I mean good at being bad. He's been Herod for the smiths how many times, Da?"

"This will be his third and, yes, he's very good at it. Knows how far to go without he goes too far." He smiled at Joliffe over his son's head. "I've warned Basset he'll have to watch out for his Herod. He's one of them that want to go altogether mad."

"So Basset has said."

What Basset had said *in full* was "If I left him to it, he'd be on his back rolling around on the wagon, kicking his heels and squalling. I told him he can stomp and flail but if he tried more than that I'd put a bit, bridle, and reins on him until he learned better."

Joliffe had asked, "Is he the kind who will do what you say until he's got lookers-on and then do what he wants?"

"I've told him that if he does, I'll have his guild fine him to within an inch of his life."

"Did he believe you?"

"Oh yes," Basset had said grimly enough that Joliffe, for one, believed him, and very probably his Herod did, too. Or did if he had any good sense at all.

No one ever seemed put off that Herod was played by someone different in every play, with three or more different Herods rolling past as the pageants shifted from site to site. Not to mention all the different Christs, Marys, Josephs, and Apostles there were from play to play. The odd thing Joliffe had noted the time he had been taken as a youngling to see the Corpus Christi plays done at York, long before he became a player himself, was that having so many different Christs and all meant that instead of the lookers-on becoming attached to the player of Christ, they attached to the story instead, and to the meanings beyond the story.

Burbage was saying, "The rest of us with our plays can do our practicing well enough with someone's hall or house yard most of the time, until things get harried near the end, but there's no trouble with using the yard this afternoon."

"The Smiths Guild, they got in a player from London to do their play for them," young Burbage offered excitedly. He looked up mischievously at his father. "Last year they had to make do with my da."

"Oh, aye, and a sorry mess I made of it, surely," Burbage said good-humouredly.

"You didn't!" his son declared with fierce loyalty. "You're as good as that London fellow is. Every bit. Better!"

"I'll settle for as good," Burbage said, smiling.

They had reached the double gates to the yard. They were wide and high-arched, making rolling the pageant wagons out and in easier, Joliffe thought. They were closed for now, of course, but the small door set into the right hand one was standing open, and Burbage's son skipped ahead and in. Joliffe and Burbage followed him. Counting Burbage's son, five demons were already there, scattering from what had probably been a friendly scuffling at each other in the middle of the yard. Piers and another boy were just coming out of an alleyway at the yard's other side. Joliffe supposed, without much thinking about it, that it must go to whatever was behind the long shed that ran most of that side of the yard. It also crossed his mind to wonder what Piers had been up to. Not trouble, hopefully. No hunt seemed to be on his trail anyway.

Another open-sided shed made up a second side to the yard, while sheds with doors hung with heavy locks closed the other two sides. Four large wagons were backed into the open-sided sheds, bare yet of anything built on them for their plays. Burbage, maybe seeing Joliffe's look all around or maybe just still explaining everything, said, "They'll be hauled out into the yard next week and everything built on them then. What's needed for that is stored in the other sheds, along with such things as don't need better keeping and haven't been taken elsewhere. I've the key for ours if you want to start with the spears and all. Can haul out the hellmouth, too, if you want that today.

"Not today, no," Joliffe said. The hellmouth would be a

large monster-head, painted in colors suitable to Hell, its mouth gaping large enough for the Devil and his devils to go in and out, and eventually for the Souls called to salvation by Christ to come forth. Before dealing with that, there were other things to be done with the young devils, who had heard the offer of spears and, led by Piers, were setting up a chant of "Spears! Spears!" doubtless in eager hope of having weapons put into their hands.

Master Burbage settled them down, made Joliffe known to them, named each boy to him, and stepped aside, leaving Joliffe to it. Joliffe, bracing himself, said, "First, you have to learn to fall down. Stand a full five feet and more apart from each other." Which would serve to stop their present elbowing and shoulder-butting at each other. "Now, Piers, you've been taught I know . . ."

"Why do we have to know how to fall down?" demanded the boy who had come in with Piers. Burbage's older son, Joliffe had gathered. "We're devils!"

He started to prance and grimace, and likely the others would have joined him at it, except Piers for once proved useful instead of troublesome by saying as he came to stand beside Joliffe, "We have to learn to fall because Christ is going to strike us all down and we'll have to writhe and everything, only we have to fall down without hurting ourselves. Like this—*only don't do it until Master Joliffe shows you how*!" he ordered.

With that, he took a few steps back, raced forward, and threw himself headlong into a somersault. His hands never touched the ground, he landed on his feet, paused long enough to say, "Then you fall down like this," and sprawled backward as if he had been hit by a huge fist. It was not easily seen, unless someone knew how to look, how he caught himself so no part of him hit the paving too hard.

The other boys gaped. Burbage's older son exclaimed, "Are you hurt?"

"Of course not," Piers said, springing back to his feet without using his hands. "Because I learned the ways to do it *rightly*."

Joliffe, choking down mirth at how much Piers sounded like his grandfather, said mildly, "But we'll start with something simpler than that, I think."

Chapter 11

With Piers full of delight at showing off his skills and surprisingly patient at helping the other boys begin to learn simple tumbling, Joliffe had an easier time with the pack of them than he had feared he would. Whatever Piers had been doing these days of running wild in the town, he had plainly found an acknowledged place among these boys that made them willing to listen to him and follow his lead. Of course the thought of anyone following Piers' lead in anything was usually cause for alarum, but Joliffe was not about to scorn the present usefulness of it.

When one of the panting boys thought to question why they were doing this, Burbage said, "When Christ comes to open Hell's gate, and the Devil orders his demons to stop him, and Christ gestures at you, I want something better than the lot of you just falling down and scuttling off the stage."

"This is the force of Heaven striking the forces of Hell," Joliffe put in. "It should look like more than just a bunch of clumsy boys falling over."

"We should be blasted right off the wagon!" Piers exclaimed.

"I was thinking that, yes," Burbage said. "Have you all fall about, then flee the wagon in all directions and out of sight under it, to leave the Devil suddenly facing Christ alone."

"But all that will only work credibly," said Joliffe, "if you learn to fall and tumble well."

He kept them at it for a while longer and at the end justly praised them for how well they were doing, finishing with, "Piers will let you know when we do it again."

"Again?" one of the boys protested.

"More of this," Joliffe confirmed, "but also how to use your spears so you don't truly stab anyone."

An answering chorus of "Spears!" gave general approval of the spears at least. At Burbage's word that they were freed then, they started a general surge away toward the alleyway out of the yard, on their way to whatever mischief they could find next, Joliffe supposed as he moved quickly enough to catch Piers by one arm in his escape. Piers, twisting against his hold and looking up at him, complained, "Ahhhh, Joliffe. I . . ."

"My thanks for your help," Joliffe said without jest. "You made a large difference how it went with them."

Piers stared at him, so startled that even when Joliffe released him, he only stood for another moment, still staring, before recovering enough to say brightly, "That's because you need all the help you can get, surely," before taking to his heels after the other boys.

Standing with Joliffe to watch them go, Burbage said, sounding well satisfied, "After all that, I have to talk to Master Crowe. He has the rest of the play in hand and will be glad at the chance for some new thoughts on what can be done."

While he said that, he and Joliffe turned toward the gates and found Eustace Powet standing there, hands thrust into his belt, a distant look in his eyes as he gazed past them across the yard. At Burbage's good-humoured, "Ho, Powet, come to take deviling lessons with the boys?" he swung his gaze to them, a smile lightening his drawn-down face.

"Nay then. Only I was remembering when I twice played the Devil in the Harrowing. Five and six years ago might have been?"

"More like eight or nine, I'd say," Burbage offered. "You've been Pilate since then a few times."

"Aye. But the parts are dwindling away, just like me," Powet said as they all ducked through the door and into the street.

"There's nothing dwindling about Joseph," Burbage said, shutting the door behind them.

Deliberately decrepit, Powet croaked from the familiar carol, "Joseph was an old man and an old man was he when he wed Mary in the land of Galilee."

Burbage gave him a friendly slap on the back of one shoulder as they started along the street. "At least you aren't stuck with being one of the Doctors in the Temple. *There's* a part to dull a man to tears."

"Not when Master Sendell is done with you," Joliffe declared stoutly.

"Well, we'll see," Burbage said, but cheerfully enough.

"It's Dick he's going to have to see to," Powet said, not cheerfully at all. "He was one of the Harrowing's devils last year and had a fine wild time of it. You remember, Burbage?"

"Oh, I do indeed." Burbage did not sound as if the memory were an altogether happy one.

"Once he hears what they're at this year, learning to tumble and all, he's going to be even more set by than he already is. He says there's nothing but tedious in being Christ."

Joliffe felt what was coming next even before Powet looked at him.

"What say you, Master Joliffe? Would you have chance to work some with him? Help him to see the part better than he does now?"

For the form of it, Joliffe demurred, "By rights, that's Master Sendell's task. I don't know he'd care to have me over-step what's his." But the back of his mind was clamoring for what might be a chance to be nearer those who must have best known the dead Robert Kydwa and his servant.

"He's to his neck with seeing about everything else," Powet said. "I said something about it to him when he came to ask if Cecily will be able to sew for us after . . ." He fumbled briefly. "After things being as they are," he finished.

"Will she?" Joliffe asked, the matter of Dick momentarily put aside. The new and newly-refurbished garb was going to matter in the play almost as much as having a well-played Christ.

"Oh, aye. She said when Master Sendell asked her that without Robyn they would need the money now more than ever, her father and her. Of course the tears came again then, poor wight, but she'll do it. Look you, there's nothing else can be done that way, and that's why I've put mind to Dick and the trouble he's likely to be."

"I'd be willing enough to do what I could with him, Master Sendell not minding," Joliffe granted slowly while thinking rapidly. "The trouble is I'd want to do it at your house, to keep just anyone from blundering in and . . . embarrassing him at the work." Yes: that sounded almost likely. Putting apology and regret into his voice, he added, "But this doesn't seem a time for doing that, coming in on everyone's grief and all."

"Dick and I will welcome something besides grieving going on," Powet said in no uncertain terms. "Herry, too, I'll warrant. It's the women are at it most. Cecily and Anna. My niece some, too, her having known Robyn's mother all her life and all."

They were all stopped at the corner of Powet's street, trying to stay out of the way of people busily going one way or another. It was here they would part ways if Joliffe was going with Powet, but Burbage paused to ask, sounding as if he already knew the answer, "How is old John Kydwa taking it?"

"I don't know that he's taken it at all," Powet said. "You know how he's been these few years past. He moves when someone reminds him to. He eats. He makes his way to the privy and usually back again if he's helped, though sometimes he forgets. All in all, there's no telling how much reaches him. Certes, little comes from him to let us know."

Burbage nodded sad acknowledgement of that. "Well, give my sympathy to whoever may want it. I'll see you this evening likely?"

That was to both Powet and Joliffe, and they both agreed he would. Taking a quick look against running into anyone or being run over, he cut away across the street toward his own, leaving Joliffe and Powet to turn down Much Park.

"Will we find Dick at home?" Joliffe asked as they went.

"His mother told him off this morning for being an idle whiner and set him to spend the day helping Herry in the shop. For which Herry is duly ungrateful," he added with a grin.

"Not shaping to be mercer, is Dick?" Joliffe asked.

"Shaping to be a great lie-about, according to Herry. But it's early days yet, and every once in a while I remind Herry of how he was at that same age." Powet chuckled. "He then says that was all different. But that's what the young always say when they're that bit older."

"What does Dick say?"

They were nearly to the Byfelds' shop. Ahead, Joliffe could see Dick holding up a bolt of cloth while Herry explained something about it to a man on the outside of the shop board.

"Dick says he wants to be like his old great-uncle Eustace and wander Coventry all day to hear what he can hear what's afoot with other merchants and bring it home for my niece and Herry to know."

Joliffe stopped short. A few steps more, he and Powet would be too near the shop to go on with their talk. With effort he leveled his voice to ask with a seeming of no more than good-humoured interest, "Is that what you do? Spy out what other merchants are doing?"

"Oh, aye," Powet said easily. "It never hurts to know who's going to where and why, and who's come back and how they did. Twice or thrice I've been able to send Herry off to one place and another on a short word, to nip in ahead of someone where it mattered." Powet tapped the side of his head midway between eye and ear. "The wits still work fine enough. I'm not just an idle old man wandering through my days, waiting for the church-yard, like most folk think I am."

Joliffe laughed, both pleased at Powet's pleasured pride in himself and ready to make use of it. "So. Has Herry been away to anywhere of late to better the family fortune?"

"Nay. I've heard nothing worth his going for almost a year now. But I've been able to put him on to other things right here in Coventry that have turned to our good. I earn my keep."

"Unlike poor old John Kydwa," Joliffe led.

"Ah, there's as sad a case. Neither decently dead nor de-cently alive."

"And now his son is gone, too. What was taking him to Bristol? Do you know?"

"There was word a ship had come in there from Spain. He'd be late getting there, but whatever was left of the lad-ing he might get cheap enough to turn a profit on it here. If nothing else, there's always something to be had in Bristol to bring back here, if the Spanish ship came to nothing."

"Herry didn't see him as a rival?"

"Robyn? Nay, Robyn was a long way from being a rival to us. Truth was that Herry used him as a factor sometimes and would buy what he brought back if it suited. If he—Robyn—had ever got enough to dower Anna with, then there could have been a partnership as well as a marriage there." Powet shook his head. "It's all too sad past bearing."

He walked on. Perforce Joliffe went with him, all the while trying to see a way how he could ask more about who of Coventry had come and gone near to the time Robert—Robyn—Kydwa had been killed. And his servant, although no one here yet knew he was dead, too.

No one but the murderer.

He had too little time to find another question before he and Powet reached the shop. Dick was bundling the length of cloth the man had bought, and Herry was taking his coins. Powet and Joliffe stood aside the few moments until they finished. The man went off, giving a nod and "Master Powet" as he passed, Powet nodding back and saying, "Master Horsley," before going on to say across the shop board to Herry, "Master Joliffe here has said he'll spend some time with Dick if you'll give the whelp leave for a while."

Herry looked around at his brother. "You willing to be freed from one taskmaster to another?"

Apparently not one to consider whether he was leaving the frying pan for the fire, Dick said, "Surely!"

"He's done well today," Herry said to Powet and Joliffe. He took Dick by one shoulder and gave him a slight, affectionate shake. "Mind you do as well for them. Go on, then."

He gave the boy a push toward the door at the side of the shop. As Dick went through it into the passageway, Herry said, again to Powet but not so lightly, "Ned is here again."

Powet made an impatient sound. "He doesn't hear what's said to him, does he?"

"Seems not. Let be it's too soon on this side of things, any way you see it, what makes him think his people will take kindly to his wooing Anna when they didn't look kindly on my suit to Goditha?"

Powet had no better answer to that than a shake of his head. Dick came through the outside door into the street. Powet went to turn him back into the passageway.

"Ahhh," Dick said on the same note of protest Piers had used. "Can't we away?"

"The rear yard will do well enough," his uncle said. "Out of the way and all."

As Powet steered his nephew back inside, Joliffe, following, asked, "Goditha?"

"Ned's sister," Powet said, and farther along the passageway, when Dick had run on ahead, "Herry offered for her last year, but the Emes aren't for marrying outside their own kind if they can help it."

"Being Lollards," Joliffe said, to see what more he might hear.

"Being Lollards," Powet agreed easily. "But quiet ones, like I said before. Do just enough of what the Church wants to keep the priest happy and otherwise go their own way. Had no part in that foolery seven years ago."

Belatedly, Joliffe wondered why Sebastian had not known about the Emes' Lollardy. If it was so easily known, Robyn Kydwa had to have known of it, too, and surely should have told him. Or—and this thought Joliffe did not like at all— what if Kydwa had known and *not* told Sebastian? Then the question had to be why he had not. And had the telling—or the not telling—played any part in his and his servant's deaths?

Or—and this Joliffe could believe almost as readily as anything else—Kydwa had indeed already told Sebastian about the Emes, and Sebastian had simply chosen not to let Joliffe know how much he knew. That would be very much like Sebastian.

Joliffe followed Powet into the kitchen. Old John Kydwa was still in his chair to the far side of the hearth, looking as nowhere as the other times Joliffe had seen him. Cecily was standing at one end of the table rolling out a pastry crust while

Mistress Byfeld and her daughter were seated on stools at the table's other end, slicing strawberries into readied pastry shells. Ned Eme was straddling a bench on the near side of the table, helping himself to a whole strawberry from a basket and saying to Cecily before nipping off its stalk, "When will his funeral be? Is it determined?"

"Tomorrow," the girl said, intent on the pastry. "In the morning. There's to be a wedding there in the afternoon, but Father Anthony says we can have the morning."

Ned tossed the strawberry stem into the stem-filled bowl in front of Anna Deyster. She did not look up, but it was to her he said, gentle-voiced, "Anna, I'm sorry. You know I am. If I had waited and gone with him . . ."

"You've said." Her voice was flat and she did not look up from the strawberry she was deftly slicing.

"But if I had . . ."

Slamming the knife down on the cutting board, Anna sprang to her feet. *"You've said!"*

Ned in distress tried to catch her near hand. "Anna . . ."

She knocked over the stool behind her as she backed out of his reach. Ned started to rise, hand still out toward her. Anna turned away, crossed the kitchen in a rush, and fled up the stairs to whatever of sanctuary she might find there. As Ned moved as if to follow her, Mistress Byfeld said firmly, "I wouldn't, if I were you."

Ned stopped, then sank down onto the bench again, looking confused and hurt. "But if I *had* waited instead of going . . ."

"There's no blame to you that you didn't," Mistress Byfeld said. "No one knew any reason you should have waited, when need was for you to be away. *Now* is when you need to wait.

It's too soon to ask her to turn to you. We keep telling you that."

Ned sighed. "I know. It's just—you know."

Powet went to lay a consoling hand on his shoulder. "We know, lad. You've waited a long time and it's hard to wait longer."

As Ned nodded what looked like unwilling agreement to that, John Kydwa stirred in his chair. Everyone turned startled looks toward him. In a voice cracked and dry with un-use, he said toward somewhere on the floor beyond his knees, "All things have their time, and all things under the sun pass in their time. Time of birth and time of dying. Time . . . time . . ." His failing voice faltered over those words from the Bible. He bent his head upward from his stooped shoulders and seemed to look—supposing he saw anyone at all—at Ned. "Time . . . Time to slay, and time to make whole. Time . . ."

Cecily gave a gasp and started toward him, hope lighting her face, but Ned was nearer, saying as he took three strides toward Kydwa, "We don't need your bible-talk, old man! You lost your right to God's word. You . . ."

He was bending over to shout into Kydwa's face as Cecily reached them both. As Kydwa's head dropped, blank-faced again, she seized Ned by the shoulder, dragged him back a step and spun him around, then with both hands on his chest shoved him violently away from her father. She was shorter than him by half a head, but Joliffe had seen strength like that in women often enough. It came of all their carrying of full buckets of water and baskets of laundry, their shifting heavy cooking pots onto the fire and off, and their scrubbing, always scrubbing. That they rarely chose to use it against men was men's good fortune, Joliffe had thought before now. Men's good fortune and the Church's teaching that women should be obedient to men. His other thought was that if women ever decided not to bow to that teaching, it would go hard with all the unprepared men.

Ned was assuredly unprepared. He backed from Cecily's reach as she said angrily at him, "You leave him alone. You're not someone to be talking to anybody about God's word. You—you—"

Before she found what she wanted to call him, Mistress Byfeld said, quiet but firm, "Best you go now, Ned. As old John says, there's time for all, but this isn't time for you here. Later but not now. Go on."

"Come on, lad," Powet said, going to again put a hand on Ned's shoulder, this time to begin drawing him away toward the passageway.

Baffled and beginning to be resentful, Ned let Powet guide him but complained as he went, "It isn't me you should all be angry at. It's George, isn't it? Where is he? Run off with Robyn's money, that's where. Why be mad at *me*?"

"Because you're here, lad," Powet said. "That's all. It will be better later. Be patient. We'll see you at the funeral tomorrow, yes?"

Looking back and forth between Cecily's still-furious glare at him and Mistress Byfeld's encouraging, comforting nod, Ned said, "Yes. Tomorrow." And suddenly sounding the penitent boy, added, "I'm sorry, Cecily. Master Kydwa. I'm sorry."

Master Kydwa, gone again, did not stir. Cecily made an impatient gesture that might have been forgiveness or just a wish for Ned to go away. Joliffe saw him swallow heavily, as if choking down other words, before he spun away and left, disappearing into the passageway. Everyone waited. Only when they heard the outer door shut behind him did Cecily turn away to begin a fussing at her father, and Mistress Byfeld return to slicing strawberries. To Joliffe and Dick as if there had been no break, Powet said, "We'll to the yard now and to work, shall we?"

Chapter 12

The work with Dick went well enough, and Joliffe told him so. That did not keep the boy from bolting out the yard's rear gate as soon as Joliffe released him. Powet, watching his great-nephew escape, suggested they leave the same way. "So as not to trouble my niece, you know."

More likely to avoid being called to account for Dick's disappearance, Joliffe guessed, but agreed. His own motives were mixed and he regretted that. He liked Powet, understood somewhat the hurt the man was in, but beyond that he was not likely to have a better source than Powet for matters in Coventry and about Kydwa. That made of value every chance to talk with him and draw him out.

Happily, the latter was never hard to do. Beyond the back gate was not a garden, as Joliffe had expected, but a town orchard of the sort meant for the use of the citizens whose houses bounded on it. Powet led him slantwise among the trees to come to the rear door of an alehouse where they settled down at a table with cups and a pitcher of strong ale, and Powet, having worn out talk of Dick and the play on their way here, went on to the next thing that must be strongest in his mind. Without prompting from Joliffe, he said, "Poor Ned. I wish he'd put his mind all to the play and leave off with Anna for a time. No one can make him see it's too soon. He keeps coming to the house or, yesterday, he met her in the street and would not be put off keeping her company all her way home. Anna said afterward he hovered over her and she hated it."

"Hovered?" Joliffe echoed, diverted by the word.

Powet lifted his arms to the sides and moved them in imitation of small, rapid wing-beats. "Like a lapwing over its nest," he said.

"Or a hawk watching for prey," Joliffe returned.

Powet chuckled. He had already drunk deep of the ale and was becoming noticeably light of tongue and cheerful of wit. "Prey—that's good. See? Prey. Pray. Anna was coming from church. She'd been praying for Robyn. And there was Ned. Preying."

He chuckled some more. Joliffe chuckled, too, and then despite a twinge of shame at making use of him, asked with a slurring deliberately more than Powet's, "Poor ol' Ned. She's a pretty prize. He been waiting long?"

"Long and long and long and long." Powet stopped himself with apparent difficulty. "And long. It has to be love because even now he wants her and she's not even a rich widow, just a poor one."

"Not so poor, surely. Her husband maybe left her next to naught otherwise, but there's still a property from her dower, surely. Am I remembering that rightly?"

"There's that. Aye. A proper, prosperous, pretty p . . . p . . . p . . ." Powet fumbled, trying to find another "p" word. He settled for, ". . . place. If she and Robyn had married, they'd have moved there."

"Well, there's why ol' Ned is so willing to her," Joliffe said, feigning triumph at having the thought. "A house, a shop, an income, a wife he wants to have. Not bad for a younger son to marry into. Wants in before someone else comes to woo her."

"Oh, ol' Ned has wanted her since forever," Powet said, muffled by the cup he had raised to drink deeply from again. "There's nothing new about that."

Joliffe made show of pausing with his cup raised halfway to his mouth and said as if totally confused, "But he was going to travel with Kydwa to Bristol. Ned was on about it. Not like they were rivals for your niece. How if he'd waited, it wouldn't have happened and all."

"Business and profit are business and profit," Powet said glumly. "When it's something probably not worth Master Eme's or Richard's going, it's Ned they send. It was a minor matter in Bristol, so it was Ned they told to go. Happened Robyn was going, too. Joanna—my niece—was the one who said why didn't they travel together. I don't think either much liked the thought, and now we have to listen to Ned bellyaching about 'if only.'" Powet refilled his own cup from the pitcher between them, saying while he did, "Young fool hasn't thought yet that it might have happened to them both if they'd been together." He took a long swallow and went on, "Nor it's no blame to him he went on ahead. Old John Kydwa took one of his turns for the worse as he does sometimes. Robyn wouldn't leave his sister to cope on her own. Ned said his family would have his hide if he missed his chance in

Bristol and went off about two days before Robyn was able to. Got all hot with hurry and away he went. Didn't even take a servant. Just his good fortune he wasn't the one the thieves happened on."

"What of what he was saying about Kydwa's servant doing it? Is that what everybody says?" Joliffe asked.

"What else is there to say? Robyn is dead. George isn't to be found anywhere." Powet dropped his voice and leaned closer as if to give away a large secret. "But I don't think it. Nor does anyone who ever knew him. His body is somewhere. I don't know why it wasn't with Robyn's, but it's somewhere. He never did any harm to Robyn. Never."

Joliffe poured the last of the ale from the pitcher into Powet's cup and said as Powet drank deeply, "So is Ned in with a chance? Or does he have more rivals to Mistress Deyster's heart?"

"Nay, there's no one else of late, not once she made it clear Robyn was her choice. Between her and her mother, they frighted off the others."

"But not ol' Ned," Joliffe slurred, readying to take another apparently deep draught from his cup. "Ol' Ned hasn't frighted."

"Hasn't the sense to fright off marrying. Ah, he's a good lad, all in all. Comely and not a fool. He and Anna would do well enough together if she'd have him."

"Will she? In the end and all?"

Powet shrugged. "Who's to say? Women. I've never understood 'em."

"You never married."

"Did. She died. Just as well. She and Joanna never got on. Huh. Come to it, she and me never got on."

Joliffe frowned. "But you said his family and yours didn't favor his sister marrying Herry. Why would they favor him marrying her?" Which was muddled but Powet understood and nodded sagely.

"Younger son. Get him provided for by way of a wife with wealth, then there's more of the family's own can be left for the elder. Daughter is well-looking enough, they mean to make the wealthiest marriage they can." Powet leaned forward, lowering his voice. "Wealthy and a Lollard for her husband."

Leaning forward and lowering his voice, too, Joliffe said, "Anna—" Deliberately hiccuped and corrected himself. "Mistress Deyster isn't a Lollard."

"Nay. Never and a day."

"But then Ned's family—"

"Nobody thinks he cares about God's word one way or another so strongly he'll get into Lollard-trouble over it. Add that to his family being likely tired to death of him wanting no one but Anna, they'd settle for it. Get him married and off their hands. That's how it is with them."

"The black sheep son," Joliffe suggested wisely.

"Nay. Nothing so much. More the tedious son they're tired of listening to."

"And here I thought it was his brother we were tired of listening to," Joliffe said.

He and Powet laughed together over that and drank deep and soon after that got up to go their separate ways for the while. Joliffe waited until they were in the street before he made show of being taken by a sudden thought, laid a hand on Powet's arm, and asked with a slightly drunk man's rude curiosity, "*You're* not a Lollard, are you?"

Powet reared back a little in mock horror. "God and the saints forbid." Then he chuckled and said, as if imparting deep wisdom, "Here's what I say. I say let the priests tell us what to do and be done with it. Seems from what they say that by obeying them we've done our duty. So if they're wrong about anything, the fault and sin of it lies on *their* heads, not on ours, I say. Only fools like Lollards want to take the whole business onto their own heads. I say let it lie on the priests."

"Right enough," Joliffe slurred. "That's what I say, too."

They nodded to each other, pleased with their mutual wisdom, and parted company, Joliffe feeling a little guilty and worried over how befuddled or with headache to come he had left Powet. His time and coin had been well-spent, though. Or well enough spent. He had not learned much that was new, but had confirmed some of what Powet had said before and had better understanding of which way things went, at least with the Byfeld household and the Emes. There seeming not much more to learn that way, what he needed now was to delve deeper and find more in other directions.

He used what was left of the late afternoon to make his way between other alehouses and taverns. There were nearly always at least some folk talking about Kydwa's murder for him to overhear and sometimes join in. More than once, in answer to someone's right curiosity about himself, he had to explain who he was, why he was in Coventry. That he was a player and part of the plays was always answer enough. To that, he could add that since his company of players traveled nearly all the time, they had as much interest as any merchant in where they might run onto trouble, which gave sufficient reason for his interest and let him freely join in other men's talk.

Unfortunately, his efforts gained him nothing of use.

There was too much he could not ask. The furthest he dared press matters was to wonder who of Coventry might have been on the way to Bristol about the same time. "On the chance they saw something, heard about something, even saw someone that didn't mean anything at the time but could now," he said.

The most he got were questioning looks at each other among the men, followed by shrugs. Someone said, "Something for the sheriff to ask, surely." The other men there nodded and that was all.

Joliffe heard nothing at all about Lollards and chose not to ask, nor did anyone stir a suspicion in him that they might be a fellow spy. Although he had to grant wryly to himself that a good spy would not let himself be suspected at his work, would he? He assuredly hoped he went unsuspected by anyone.

Either way, he was glad when time came to give over the whole effort for the day and head back to spend a while with Basset and the others. He bought his supper as he went, intending that when they went to theirs in the Silcoks' hall, he would sit alone with his in their chamber, alone being very much what he wanted after the day's surfeit of people and talk and thought. Not that he had hope of stopping his thoughts. If nothing else, he would be thinking how tired he was of talk and ale.

He found the whole company gathered. Rose looked up from sewing a seam in a heaviness of cloth laid across her lap and greeted him with a smile. Basset, Ellis, and Gil were variously sitting or sprawled on the floor cushions while Piers was in the clear middle of the room, just finishing a forward somersault—hands to the floor and a flip of his body, ending with him upright on his feet—in apparent demonstration of what Joliffe had been teaching the other boys, because Piers said scornfully as he finished, "That. Simple. I've known how to do it since I was a baby."

"Nearly," Ellis said with laughter behind his words. "We did wait until you could walk before we taught you."

"Until then," Joliffe offered, "we juggled you. Tossed you around with the painted balls. Painted you, too, come to that."

"You didn't!" Piers protested scornfully. "You weren't even in the company when I was that small."

"Just as well for you," said Gil. "The way Joliffe juggles, you would have been dropped on your head, surely."

"Someone must have dropped him," Joliffe said. "How else did his wits get so addled?" He reached to rumple Piers' curls. Piers ducked away, and Joliffe went on before Piers' outrage turned into words, "But those other boys have never tumbled at all until now, so of course you're far better and that's why you'll surely be lead-demon when the time comes."

"Will I be?" Piers demanded, his wrath immediately diverted.

"How not?" Joliffe returned.

Piers immediately flipped forward into a handstand, flipped back onto his feet, was readying for more when his mother said, "Enough. Go to the yard if you want to do that," sternly enough that Piers stopped. Or maybe it was because he knew that when he disobeyed his mother, Ellis tended to give him the flat of a hand to the back of his head, one of the few things that could turn Piers from something he purposed.

They all went to supper soon after that, except Basset

hung back to say as the others thumped away down the stairs, "How goes it with Will Sendell and all?"

"Better all the time. He's making something worth watching out of what we all doubted."

"How is he handling his people?"

"Better than at least one of them deserves," Joliffe said, thinking of Richard Eme. "The others I think he'll get their best out of them."

"How are you and he doing together?"

"Well." Joliffe let his surprise show in his voice. "Better than ever we did when we worked together before. He knows what he's about."

"That can happen as we grow older," Basset said dryly. "If we're fortunate." He let go the dryness. "And you. How go things with you?"

Because Joliffe had kept to himself what else he was doing, he supposed the question had no hidden sides to it and answered simply, "I'm enjoying it all. It's satisfying work."

"Good," said Basset. "That's good." Rose called from the foot of the stairs for him to come on. He slapped Joliffe companionably on the shoulder and went, and Joliffe sat down to his own meal, ending with the treat of a berry tart.

He was somewhat behindhand in getting to rehearsal that night. Instead of being among the first, he was among the last. Not the very last, though. That was Hew, skidding out of a run into the gateway behind him, panting to Joliffe who turned to grin at him, "I'm late, aren't I?"

"Not yet," Joliffe reassured him. "Master Sendell is just coming down the stairs. You're doing well with your angel, by the way."

The boy beamed. "My thanks. Ned has helped me with the singing." He dashed ahead to sit on a bench beside Dick so they could shove elbows into each other's ribs until someone would tell them to stop.

Joliffe's choice of where to sit was between sharing a bench with Powet and Ned Eme, or another with Master Smale, Tom Maydeford, and Richard Eme, the latter bending the ears of his two companions with probably his usual talk about other parts he had played unbelievably well in other plays. He never seeming to wonder why, if he was so outstandingly good, he had been left to this play, rather than taken up by someone else. Caught between that and Ned Eme's probably moanings over Anna Deyster (if the woe-ridden look on his face was anything to go by), Joliffe reluctantly went to sit on Powet's far side in time to hear Powet saying, "She's only just lost the man she thought she would marry. Let it rest a time. It's too soon to be wooing her to turn to another," and see Ned curl his fingers closed over a glint of bright metal—a brooch or maybe a gilt belt buckle or figured aglets. Something for Anna Deyster, anyway, Joliffe guessed.

Aggrieved, Ned protested at Powet, "Now is perfectly the time. When she's in most need. Before she finds someone else instead of me to turn to."

"I'm only telling you that to wait may gain you all." He pointed at Ned's hand. "That won't."

Ned made a face at him and turned away, sullenly fumbling whatever he held into his belt pouch.

The rehearsal went well. Tom as Mary would need more help but was beginning to find his way into—as it were—motherhood. Powet as Joseph was making stronger the man beneath the comic husband, a man as aware as Mary of the duty they had been given and trying to lighten the burden of her worry with his lighter humour but no less concern. Hew was still perhaps a shade too stiff but no longer rigid as a stone statue and there was no faulting his voice, while Ned had all the grace of voice and looks that could be desired of an angel. Richard Eme was . . . well, he went on being Richard Eme, but that sufficed to give Masters Burbage and Smale clearer ways to their own Doctors, playing off Eme and to each other at Sendell's skilled direction.

Once, though, Sendell brought the practice to a stop, to ask of everyone not a Doctor in the Temple the why of their smothered laughter. Fingers pointed, forcing Burbage to confess he was copying the all-too-familiar voice and gestures of the senior priest at St. Michael's. Sendell frowned in thought, looked at the merry faces, and finally said, "Pull it in somewhat and lose it altogether when you begin to take Christ seriously. Yes?"

"Yes," Burbage agreed, and thereafter obligingly did. Having directed plays himself in other years, he likely understood there were few things someone directing a play loved better than a player who took direction.

The evening's high surprise was Dick's Christ. Dick was not easy in the part yet nor anywhere near to knowing his lines off by heart, but he was far better than he had been and was *working* at being better, which was more than he had done before. Sendell managed to keep both surprise and relief out of his voice at evening's end as he told Dick how well he had done, before dismissing everyone until tomorrow.

Powet caught Joliffe's eye and made a gesture of raising a cup to his mouth, silently asking if Joliffe wanted to go drinking, but added by a twitch of his head toward Dick that he would have to see the boy home first.

Joliffe's answer was forestalled by Sendell saying, "Master Joliffe, could you stay a time longer, please you?"

"Assuredly." He traded a regretful shrug with Powet but in truth sat back down on the bench willingly enough. Since he had probably drained Eustace Powet of all the information he safely could for the while, it was just as well to let him go now rather than risk more talk.

For his part, Powet probably did more than shrug when he realized Ned Eme was waiting at the gate for him, undoubtedly wanting more chance to bend Powet's patience with plaint about Anna Deyster. Joliffe was duly grateful for his own double escape as Sendell straddled the bench beside him, sat down, and asked, "What did you do to young Dick Byfeld today? He was almost good just now."

"Hai!" Joliffe protested. "He was well toward what you need him to be."

"Closer than he was last time I had to suffer through him mauling his lines," Sendell granted. "What did you do to him? I may have to do it to someone else sometime."

"I made him see that the Doctors in the Temple don't know the boy who shows up to talk at them is anything but a bold brat, that he has to charm them into listening to him because if some half-grown whelp came on all pompous at them, they'd simply clout him alongside his head and send him on his way."

"That did it?"

"Not quite. He still didn't quite have it. Not until I asked him if he meant to sound like Richard Eme being Richard Eme at his worst."

Sendell gasped on a surprised laugh.

"It made Dick laugh, too," Joliffe said with satisfaction. "That was when he finally started trying to say the words as if they were *his* words, not something painted a foot high on a church wall."

"Richard Eme as a dread example. I will remember that," Sendell said. "My thanks, Joliffe."

He said it so simply that for a moment Joliffe hardly understood, then said, trying to match Sendell's quietness, "You're shaping a good play here. I'm pleased to be in it and help as I can."

Sendell regarded him in such grave silence for a long moment that Joliffe added, "I mean it. It's shaping well."

Another moment passed before Sendell said quietly, "It is, isn't it?" And then, even more quietly, "I almost begin to hope," sounding as if hope were something he hardly recognized.

Chapter 13

A few days followed that were as near to ordinary as Joliffe was used to anymore. He worked twice with the young devils for Hell's harrowing. He firmed his lines as the Prophet and Ane into his mind. He strolled out once to see how Tisbe and Ramus were doing where they were pastured outside of Coventry. He spent time with Basset and the others, helping with their cart and gear, Basset having decreed that this while off the road was the perfect time to give a good tending to everything, from greasing the wheels and checking all the underpinnings and harness to laying out every one of their playing properties, to mend those that needed it and dispose of such as were past decent use. Basset set Joliffe and Gil on quest to find and buy what could be used in place of the latter, a quest which diverted Joliffe and Gil for most of a day and gave Joliffe chance to be in places around Coventry for which he might otherwise have lacked excuse. Not that he learned aught of notable use. Kydwa's murder was widely talked of, but he heard nothing new. Never any mention that Lollards were part of it or—come to that—anything about Lollards at all, beyond once an overheard mutter between other men at a tavern that old Master Kydwa had had no luck at all these past years, what with his wife and all. Then the talk had sheered away to the weather in a way that made Joliffe think it was not *to* the weather the men were going but *away* from old Master Kydwa's Lollard wife.

It was as they left that tavern Gil asked, "Hear anything of interest this time?" in a widely innocent voice.

Joliffe was both abashed and diverted at being caught out. "Um. Not really."

"Is it something particular you're hoping to hear?" Which was as close as Gil had ever come to asking about what the players somewhat knew he did when he was not with them.

Because Gil and the others had been so behindhand in ever questioning him, Joliffe answered more directly than he might have otherwise. "I don't know what I'm hoping to hear. I just listen to everything and see if anything fits with something else."

"Is it about this Kydwa's murder? The servant that did it?"

"Kydwa's family and close friends swear the servant never did it, would never have done it."

"You've somehow overheard them, too?" Gil mocked.

Joliffe poked him in the arm. "One of them is in Will Sendell's play with me." Two of them if Dick was counted, but he seemed to have naught to say about Kydwa's death, now Joliffe came to think of it. "I don't have to 'overhear' anything. I get told."

Gil nodded, either satisfied with that or sensible enough to let it go, and Joliffe tried to be more circumspect with his listening thereafter. He found himself wishing he could hear what other than tavern-folk were saying, women most particularly, and realized belatedly that he had the perfect place to do just that, given the women who presently spent hours sewing in the upper room with Rose. Not that Rose would let him in any way help with the sewing. His stitchery fairly well matched his juggling and neither was a pretty sight. That drove him to hit on the claim he wanted to sit in a corner and write at a thought he had for a new play, using a rainy day for excuse why he did not want to crouch in the cart for the work.

Since he had often enough written while the players' life went on around him, nobody thought a room full of women was an odd choice of place. Not that his afternoon spent listening to them did him any good. There was inevitably some talk of the murder, but since it had not happened in Coventry itself, the strongest edge was off it, the women having less to say about it than the men had and making not even sliding mention of Mistress Kydwa. They spoke with pity for Cecily, done out of any hope of marriage now, and with respect for Mistress Byfeld for taking in the Kydwas as she had, and with some sympathy for Anna Deyster, but as one woman said, stitching an embroidered band to the sleeve-edge of a king's robe, "After all, she could all along have had a better marriage than to Robyn Kydwa, and there'll surely be some other come her way soon enough."

Another woman's sly, "Oh, there's someone already," was met with the laughter of general understanding who she meant.

That was the sum of what Joliffe learned there. Unless their failure to speak of Mistress Kydwa at all told something in itself. There had not even been the almost obligatory "Thank the saints she did not live to see this day." Was it a continued wariness to talk of those brought down by Lollardy, even among women?

Joliffe caught himself. The matter was hardly a simple "*even* among women." Both Mistress Kydwa and her friend Alice Garton must have been known to these women to one degree or another. Remembering those women's fate could well be sufficient to curb their talk in that direction.

For Joliffe's purpose, however, absence of something said was not of much help—unless that utter silence was a worry in itself. Was it hiding something so deeply dangerous that no one was fool enough to talk of it?

Oh, please, he thought—please don't let it be Sebastian was right, and this is all, at the root, to do with Lollardy.

But since Kydwa's and his servant's deaths were not about plain robbery, what were they about, if not because of Lollardy, he wondered while sitting over a wooden bowl of good pottage at one of the inns along Earl Street on his way to practice that evening. That so much trouble had been taken to put blame on the servant had to mean that whoever had done it did not want anyone looking back toward Coventry, which meant whoever had done it was tied to Coventry in some way, and that might mean that Kydwa in his spying here in Coventry had learned something—very possibly about Lollards, Joliffe grudgingly granted—but been himself found out by someone determined to keep him from passing on what he had learned. And if that was the way of it, then there was no reason the murderer would not be willing to kill again to protect . . . whatever he was protecting.

Joliffe did not like that possibility. He had developed a strong dislike to anyone wanting to kill him, not to mention a truly *deep* dislike of anyone actually trying.

But what if Kydwa's death was *not* because of his spying? What if it was for something else? Thus far, Joliffe had heard no word against him from anyone. He seemed to have been seen by everyone as a pleasant, hard-working young man and nothing more. So why would someone take the trouble to have him dead?

Of course the first answer that came was—Ned Eme.

Who had been gone from Coventry at the right time.

Who could not hold off his eagerness to have Anna Deyster for even this while she was in worst mourning.

Who by marrying her would gain not only her but more freedom from his family than a younger son might readily hope to have.

Who, apparently unexpectedly, had money to buy a pretty piece of jewelry.

Damn.

Joliffe finished the pottage without the heed it deserved and went onward to Mill Lane, overtaking John Burbage along the way. With two plays to talk of, they had a pleasant time of it until at the corner of Mill Lane they encountered Richard and Ned Eme coming from the other way, their home being near Gosford Gate. For the short way farther to the yard, Joliffe had to keep up a lightness of talk he did not feel and hold off eyeing Ned too closely. Nor did it help that Burbage asked the youth how his wooing went.

151

"As ever," Ned said glumly. "Badly."

"He won't listen. I tell him he needs to hold off, but he won't heed," his brother said with a virtue ripened by unfaltering certainty of his own good judgment in all things. These past few practices he had taken to making suggestions to Sendell on how better to do things. He had finally grasped that how Joliffe was playing the First Prophet was a success, might even be drawing people's favor away from himself in that part of the play. His attempt then to lighten his Prophet to match Joliffe's had been as leaden as wayfare bread and immediately curtailed by Sendell. Eme had sulked through much the rest of that practice but unfortunately was undaunted for long. Yesterday he had begun to suggest how the Doctors at the Temple might be played better—meaning how his own Doctor could stand to the fore of the pageant wagon and Master Burbage's and Master Smale's not only be kept to the back but give up some of their lines to him. Their better lines of course.

So far Sendell had taken it with outward patience, although he muttered to Joliffe at the end, "His thoughts on it all are as dull as his playing."

"But his good opinion of himself remains sharp," Joliffe had returned and left Sendell snorting on smothered laughter.

This rehearsal Sendell's patience raveled to an end. When Richard Eme during one of his longer speeches—and against what Sendell had earlier carefully directed him to do—cut around his fellow Doctors and behind Christ, forcing Dick, Burbage, and Smale all to turn their backs to where most of the onlookers would be, Sendell roared, "Stop! What in the name of Saint Genesius are you doing, Eme?" Although he and everyone else knew very well what Eme was doing—making certain all the onlookers would be seeing him more clearly than anyone else at that moment in the play.

Eme, brought to an abrupt halt in the middle of a line, gaped at Sendell, momentarily startled by Sendell's shout, then drew himself up to dignity, and said, "I thought we should try how that worked. It played better than what you had, don't you think?"

Joliffe slapped a hand over his own mouth just in time to stifle a burst of laughter. Sendell, strangling not on laughter but barely in-held anger, said, "No. I don't think that at all. That's why I did not have you doing it."

"But . . ." Eme foolishly started.

"And don't do it again," Sendell snapped. "Now get back where you were and stay there. I'll tell you when and where I want you to move."

Red was a color that went well with Richard Eme's fair hair, but not when it was suffusing his anger-tightened face. At least Joliffe supposed it was anger, since he doubted Richard Eme had the sense to be rightly shamed. Still, he was holding in his apparent rage, had even begun to stalk back to where he was supposed to be, when Ned called out from the corner of the yard where he and Hew were working their Angels' singing with one of the town waits and his small organ, "Told off again, eh, brother-mine?"

Richard Eme whirled toward him. "You shut your mouth, loblolly-wit." Ned made a gesture toward him that could only be called rude. Richard returned it. Ned opened his mouth to answer, his eyes' merry glitter betraying he was about to say more mischief. But Sendell roared, "Enough!"

Startled, everyone—the Emes and all—looked at him.

He glowered at both Ned and Richard. "You can be

brotherly at home or in the street, but not here," he snarled. He shared his glare around to everyone else. "So back to Dick's last speech before Eme decided he knew better than I do what the play needs." He jerked a single nod at Dick. "Start."

Dick scrambled his first words, then steadied. By the time he reached the speech's end, Richard Eme was back in place and recovered enough to take up his own part, albeit with a certain stiffness of the jaw. Since he mostly spoke and moved in the play as if his joints were made of unoiled iron hinges, the little more stiffness made barely a difference. The practice went on. Dick would never play Christ to Joliffe's satisfaction. The boy lacked any deep place in himself from which to draw thoughts and feelings beyond his familiar ones, but Sendell was having some success crafting those familiar ones as best he could into what he wanted for Christ. Tom Maydeford as Mary and Powet as Joseph were settling into their parts—Powet warming into the loving husband trying to soothe with light humour his wife's passion for her son, Tom moving more freely as Mary with every practice. From the corner of the yard Ned's and Hew's voices rose and twined together in the Nunc Dimittis they would sing with Simeon. If actual angels did not sing so, they should, Joliffe thought, glad that the not-well-joined pieces of the play looked to be coming together into a whole that would be pleasing when all was said and done.

A few more days passed much the same. Joliffe worked another afternoon with Piers and his fellow devils, after which Burbage declared himself satisfied and ready to use them. Talk among Basset, Ellis, and Gil told their play was shaping the way Basset intended, and on the whole Sendell was pleased with his. All of that was something to set to the good against the fact that Joliffe's daily wanderings around Coventry got him nothing new of any use. Given that, he was uncertain whether he was pleased or not the morning in the market crowd along Broadgate he found Sebastian looking back at him over one shoulder, meeting his gaze only long enough to give a single sharp nod before melding out of sight into the crowd, leaving Joliffe to guess where to meet him.

The chapel in St. Michael's church was somewhat nearer than the tavern in Palmer Lane, but with all the talk they would likely need between them, the tavern was the more likely place, and Joliffe twisted around by way of Butcher and Ironmonger Rows, always with an eye out for anyone who might be following him but seeing no one until he paused to buy a handful of strawberries from a woman's basket, giving him chance for a careful glance around. He glimpsed Sebastian a few hayforks' lengths behind him, using a chattering pair of broad housewives as a moving screen. Joliffe moved on, eating strawberries, dropping the stems into the stone-lined runnel down the middle of the street to be washed away in the next rain, and giving no sign he had seen Sebastian. But when three apprentices, probably escaped from their duties and making the most of their freedom before retribution overtook them, came barreling down the narrow street, crowding and jostling among the shoppers, Joliffe took the chance of being briefly out of Sebastian's sight to snatch off his cap, thrust it into the front of his doublet, pull out another of a different color, and jam it on his head at a different slant than he had worn the first, at the same time spinning sideways to seem intent on an array of shoes laid out for sale on the nearest shop's board.

The man behind his goods looked at him, rightly startled by the cap-switching. Joliffe gave him a deliberately merry grin and conspiratorial shrug and twitch of the head toward the street behind him, to show he was playing some manner of jest. The man grinned back, accepting that, which freed Joliffe to watch from the corner of his eyes as Sebastian went past, craning to find him somewhere ahead but probably not worried, likely certain by now that Joliffe had to be heading for the tavern.

Sharing another grin with the shopkeeper, Joliffe changed back to his first cap and set off after Sebastian in his turn. The cap-switching was an old but simple ruse. Sebastian would guess he had done it as soon as Joliffe overtook him, but Joliffe saw no point in having Sebastian know what other cap—or anything else, come to that—he might have to his use. Not if there was no need of Sebastian knowing.

He nonetheless found himself a little startled at how deeply he had taken to the habit of secrecy, even with someone supposedly his ally. Supposing that a fellow spy was indeed to be thought of as an ally and not simply as a fellow spy.

There was something twisted around on itself about that thought. He supposed he would have to think on it later. For now, it was enough that he carefully overtook Sebastian just as Sebastian reached the tavern. As expected, Sebastian entered with a step aside from the doorway, that he not be outlined against the light and to have a wall at his back while he paused to make quick surveyance of who was there and to be on the flank of anyone who might follow him in. He must have momentarily wondered why he did not see Joliffe, but Joliffe in the same moment went past the doorway, turned, and thumb-shot a small strawberry off the side of his finger, past Sebastian's nose with the accuracy of a misspent youth. Sebastian spun to face him, starting into a crouch, a dagger suddenly in his hand that had not come from the sheath at his hip.

Seeing Joliffe, he swore, straightened, and disappeared the dagger. "Fool. I could have gutted you before I knew it was you."

"That's why I kept well out of reach," Joliffe returned lightly. Sebastian was the longer-experienced of the two of them, but that was no reason to let him think he could have it all his own way.

Or else every bit the reason not to let him think it.

Either way, they both threw a quick, shared look around the room to see who was there and had noted them. To their good fortune, only one man besides the tapster was there, on a bench in a far corner, peering at them in a bleary way that suggested he was somewhat too far into his drinking to be sure what he had seen. Trouble, or just two friends playing the fools? Something of the same doubt—but clearer—was warily on the tapster's face, and Sebastian laughed and slapped a hand down on Joliffe's shoulder, giving him a friendly shake and saying lightly, "Well enough. You win." As if there had been some merry wager between them. "I'll pay the penny this time around."

They got their ale and sat on a bench well away from the only other drinker, in a corner that would leave them private from anyone else who might come in, as inevitably others did while they drank and talked, looking outwardly at ease despite what they were saying to each other.

Sebastian began it, asking as soon as they had sat, "So. What have you learned? Anything to the purpose? Anything that shows Lollards are part of this?"

"Any Lollards here are lying quiet and very low."

"Like adders," Sebastian muttered.

"Even adders only strike when troubled or affrighted."

"Nobody was frighting them seven years ago."

"Ah," Joliffe returned, "but the fools that were making trouble then paid for their foolishness—many of them with their necks. The ones that are left want nothing more than to be left in peace."

"Until the fools still among them again start to think they have a chance."

Knowing this was not a debate he was likely to win—nor needed to—Joliffe let it go, settled for saying, "As that may be, I've found out nothing that warns they're stirring now. I'm supposing you knew Kydwa's mother was a Lollard."

Sebastian accepted that with a grudging nod and, "Ruined her family with it, yes. So. What else?"

Joliffe told him. When he had done, Sebastian at first said nothing, just stood up and took their cups to be refilled. Only when he had returned and sat again did he say, "That, then, is as far as you've got? This Ned Eme is your only choice for maybe guilty?"

Joliffe bit back the urge to snap a curt and angry answer to that, keeping himself to no more than saying somewhat dryly, "I've been somewhat over-busy with why I came to Coventry at all. The plays, remember. I've gone about, listening as much as I've been able wherever I reasonably can. There's been nothing to hear. It's only by chance I have anything at all. Have you got better?"

Sebastian gave the narrow twist of lips that served him for a smile. "What I've got is a better that's all the better because it matches with yours. I've someone in Bristol who watches for who comes and goes there, and when, and why, if he can learn that, too. Merchants and others worth the noting. There were several who came from Coventry in the while that matters. The next thing that mattered was when they left here, and you tell me about this Ned Eme that left Coventry several days before Kydwa did. Yet, according to my Bristol man, he didn't arrive in Bristol until the day I was looking for Kydwa to come."

"Kydwa was delayed in leaving here. I've learned that. Shouldn't you have thought to see him several days before then?"

"Kydwa could come to Bristol any time he wanted, so long as he was there the particular day set for us to meet. It wouldn't have mattered to me if he were there earlier, so long as he was there that day. He wasn't, of course. But likewise this Ned Eme, leaving here before Kydwa, should have arrived in Bristol sooner than he did. That lends to wondering why."

Joliffe granted that with a nod but had to say, "It's thin, though, and goes nowhere to proving anything. He could have had reason to linger along the way."

Sebastian's rattish eyes glittered. "But there's the other thing I learned. That manor where the bodies were hidden—it's held by a Coventry man named Master Eme."

Chapter 14

Joliffe took in that bit of information with a jolt deep in his guts and was still finding his way to some response when Sebastian said with less satisfaction, "Not that that suffices to prove anything. Even if we find out this Ned Eme was there, his claim would be he was simply seeing to something for his father."

"Which he might have been," Joliffe pointed out in fairness. "And there's the reason, all honest enough, why he was late in coming to Bristol."

Sebastian gave a grudging nod of agreement but nonetheless added, "That's not to say he didn't do the murders."

"No," Joliffe had to agree. "Even if he was there for an honest reason, it still gave him chance to know where and when he'd have the best chance to deal with Robyn Kydwa and his man with no one to see it happen."

Even as he said it, he remembered the surprising beauty

of Ned's voice twining with young Hew's in the Angels' song, and his hand gracefully outstretched in blessing when, as Gabriel, he spoke with Mary. To think of that hand murdering . . .

"And where to hide their bodies after it was done," he said, the feeling in his belly now of sickness.

"That, too. And where it was safe to hide them and himself during the day, since he likely would wait until dark to do the rest."

"Although that's not to say he did any of it," Joliffe tried.

"Found out someone else who was gone from here at the right time, have you?" Sebastian asked acidly. "And knew the place where the bodies were put? And had reason to kill Kydwa?"

"It's not much of a reason," Joliffe said. "Jealousy over a woman."

He heard the foolishness of saying that even as he said it. People stupid enough to murder someone were stupid enough to murder for jealousy as readily as for any other reason.

Sebastian matched his thought with a mocking laugh and, "It's as good as any other. Not that it may be the reason—or only reason in this." He seemed to grudge granting that. "You've said the Emes are some of your 'quiet' Lollards. What if they aren't? What if Kydwa found them out—them or some others of their kind—and had to be 'quieted' in his turn?"

"That's—possible." If nothing else, it gave a better reason—a reason that could at least pass for "better" than plain, idiot jealousy—for killing Kydwa and his man. Having gathered the various wide-ranging strands of his thoughts, Joliffe said, "Right enough, then. It's Ned Eme we have to look at more nearly. One thing, though. We've a week until Corpus Christi and doing the plays. Even if we get the full proof we need against him, can we hold off using it until after then? He's needed in the play I'm in, and there's no likelihood he'll run, since he has no thought of being suspected."

Sebastian regarded him with a look both dour and mocking. "We can wait. The servant can go on rotting as readily where he is as somewhere else." Joliffe winced at that as Sebastian had meant him to, while Sebastian went on, "Always supposing we find proof enough to satisfy a jury. Any thoughts how to do that?"

"None," Joliffe said. "I've made no effort to be friends with him. Mayhap I'll have to." Or—Saint Genesius forbid—with Richard Eme.

Practice that evening was strange from start to end for Joliffe. What he did outwardly had little to do with where his mind was, which was pity for more reasons than one, first and foremost being that Sendell had decreed they would run the entire play without stop for the first time, beginning at the beginning and going straight through to the end. "So we can see the shape of it. To see how well it plays as a whole," he told them all before they began, adding aside to Joliffe in an undertone, "To see if it plays at all."

Deep in work that had been going well, Sendell had been free of that manner of gloom these past days. Given the beating his life had taken these past years, for the gloom to come again now and again was no surprise, but Joliffe might have taken more note of it surfacing again if he had not been so wound into his thoughts and the effort not to show them.

Happily, Sendell was given no grounds for gloom. The two Prophets kept up the pace of their speeches, Joliffe having at last goaded Richard Eme into moving his words along instead of wallowing in them. Simeon in his turn gave his speech just the right weight that Joliffe should have time, when the time came they had their playing garb, to change from Prophet to Ane. His time with Simeon done, he returned to a bench, watched Simeon and his Clerk carry through their parts at a goodly pace, then had to school his face to carefully nothing but interest while Ned as the angel Gabriel spoke with Mary.

As Gabriel Ned was competent and smooth, not exciting but a very satisfactory angel. Tom Maydeford played Mary as sweet and strong, remaining humble before God's messenger while knowing the wrapped bundle of supposed child in her arms gave her high place in the world. The lighter word-play between her and Joseph made relief from the solemnity of what went before it, with Tom and Powet playing perfectly Mary's affection for Joseph and his love for his young wife even as he gently vexed her. It made more touching Joseph's honest complaint of utter weariness when he was left alone to find the doves they must take to the temple. But Hew as the Angel brought the small cage with its (false) doves to him and renewed his strength.

At the Temple, Simeon, Ane, the Clerk, Mary, Joseph, and the Angels carried through their parts almost faultlessly. Simeon fumbled one of his long speeches but recovered and kept going with no need to be prompted, and when time came for singing of the Nunc Dimittis, the soaring of Gabriel's voice in antiphon to Simeon's made Joliffe's chest clench. How could Ned, standing there with hands spread in blessing toward them all, singing with such piercing beauty, be guilty of what everything seemed to say he was? And yet . . . and yet . . .

Mary and Joseph left the playing space. On the wagon itself, they would go into the stage house, to wait out of sight while Simeon, Ane, and the Clerk finished and left in their turn, the town musician with his organ playing Temple-solemn music as they went but a moment later changing it to something merrier for Mary and Joseph to return, now with the young Jesus beside them, twelve years old and visiting Jerusalem for the first time.

Their going out would leave room in the stage house for Master Smale to be helped into a Doctor's long, full robe over his Clerk's garb, readying him to go out with Burbage and Richard Eme. That was going to take adroit shifting and some practice for all of them—including two Angels and their wings—to fit into the stage house's cramped space, but tonight there was no need, and as Mary, Joseph, and young Jesus moved into the playing space, Joliffe looked around for Ned Eme. Like it or not, time was come to strike up better acquaintance with him.

Not liking it at all, Joliffe had braced himself to suggest they go out for a drink tonight when they were done here, and so he was disconcerted not to see Ned anywhere in the yard. Thinking he was probably gone to the jakes, Joliffe watched Burbage, Richard Eme, and Master Smale readying to move into the playing space as the Doctors and forgot Ned for the while, the more easily because the Doctors were not playing as smoothly as they might have. Neither Burbage nor Master Smale were at ease with their words yet. Burbage missed out an entire middle part of one of his speeches, which threw Dick off balance for his own next one, it coming sooner than he was set for it. They fumbled and faltered but did not lose place entirely and, importantly, kept going, so that at the end Sendell said, "None so bad at all. Well done with your save, Dick." The boy stood straighter, glowing with the praise. "Burbage . . ."

Burbage, easily able to know what was coming, held up both hands in surrender. "I'll have every word fixed into my head by next practice. I swear it."

Sendell nodded his satisfaction with that and turned to give a wide smile around at all of them. They were waiting for what else he had to say and surely tomorrow he would have suggestions and corrections and additions to make, but for now he settled wisely on straight praise, saying, "It's coming together. We've a very good play despite it all. The tavern keepers are going to be very displeased with us." That brought laughter all around, as he surely meant it to, and he set them free, sending them home feeling good about themselves and their work.

But Ned Eme was not there, had not come back from wherever he had gone, and Joliffe went aside to Sendell to ask, "What happened to Ned? He disappeared well before we were done."

"Before we started he asked if he could leave when his part was finished," Sendell said easily. "I said if everything went well, he could. He went."

So much for hoping to strike up talk with him tonight. Joliffe did not hide his guilty relief from himself while asking Sendell, "Join me in a drink to celebrate we've made it this far and it's looking well?"

"I think that if we try," said Sendell merrily, "we might

even make it several drinks before curfew. I, at least, am in need of them."

They got their several drinks, and went their separate ways to bed, and on the morrow Joliffe spent the day doing nothing to Sebastian's purpose. He knew he might try to find Ned Eme but made no effort to think of an excuse he could give Ned if he did. Instead, tired of Coventry's streets and taverns and not wanting to meet Sebastian even by chance, he dug the horse brush out of the cart and went out again to see Tisbe and Ramus in their pasture. Both he and they enjoyed the while he spent grooming them, although Tisbe, as ever, showed her displeasure at having to share him with Ramus by butting Joliffe hard with her head and snapping at Ramus' flank. Despite she might have been grateful to share the pulling of the players' cart with another horse and despite the months they had been together, she never forgot there had been a time when she had had Joliffe's heed all to herself. Joliffe, to reassure her she was still the best of horses, spent a long time combing out her mane, talking to her all the while, leaving her mellow and drowsy-eyed when he finished.

He spent the rest of the day loitering along a stream among willow shadows at the pasture's edge, with a meat pasty he had brought on his way out of Coventry and his book of Hoccleve's poetry for company, although he read little, content with watching the water purling and listening to the day's small wind among the willow trees. He stayed until nearly suppertime and came back into the town by way of Gosford Gate, not all that far from Mill Lane. He got his supper at a cookshop and strolled on to the yard, coming somewhat early for rehearsal and regretfully bracing himself to the necessity of being particularly friendly with Ned.

He found the pageant wagon had been drawn out of its house into the middle of the yard. Sendell and Burbage were atop it, wrestling an upright post into place at its far end, to finish the frame of the playing house that—later hung all around with cloth for walls—would give the players somewhere to disappear when their parts were done and to change garb. The boards that would become its flat roof—to be set with the high altar of the Temple and likewise give the angels somewhere "heavenly" to appear—and the stairs that would go up to it were in a careful pile on the remaining long open bed of the wagon, with the wooden pegs to fasten it all together probably in the basket standing beside them. The steps that allowed players to come down from the wagon to the street and up again were already attached to the wagon's rear end, hinged so they could be swung up onto the wagon while the wagon was pulled from playing place to playing place through the town.

Delighted excitement stirred all through Joliffe at the sight. He had seen, once, the great pageant of plays done in the city of York. York, being larger and richer than Coventry, had more plays, beginning not in the New Testament but with the Creation of the world and running on through both Testaments and to Judgment Day itself. Besides the thrill of the stories, what had stayed with Joliffe through the years—he had been, what, eleven years old or maybe twelve the time his family made that almost-pilgrimage to see the plays?—was the flare of delight at the sound of one pageant wagon, its play finished at one place, rumbling away along the street to its next playing place while the following wagon rumbled up, pulled by laughing apprentices and journeymen of whichever guild the play belonged to. Each wagon had promised new and unforeseen delights, and something of that long-past gladness leaped up in Joliffe at simply seeing "his" wagon here. But if he was feeling that gladness again, then it was not long-past, was it? He paused on that unexpected thought. Did gladness last as surely in the heart as sorrow seemed to?

When great sorrow came, it always seemed to shatter all gladness there had been, but that was a false seeming. Somewhere in the heart and mind the gladness still was. Did sorrow so often seem the stronger because people dwelt in it, clung to it, rather than turn to the gladness there had been and hold whole-heartedly to it? Was sorrow easier to have than joy? It was sorrow's pain that gave sorrow such strength, he supposed. Pain in its first, terrible moments had a way of taking the mind away from everything else, and the worse the pain, the longer it held the mind. But to never let go of it? Never return to the gladness that still was if the mind and heart still held it?

There were things in his own life he would sorrow for until his death, almost all of them entwined beyond separating from some gladness that had gone before. Both were there in his heart and mind, so why let the sorrows outweigh the gladnesses? He had found all too terribly how sorrow could cling to mind and heart like a poisonous vine, but he had also found that treasured gladness could be a burning sun that withered sorrow, stopped its smothering growth. He would have his sorrows forever, yes, but he would hold to his gladnesses, too, treasuring them for their light and joy against sorrow's darkness.

And thinking of sorrow's darkness, he saw Cecily Kydwa

sitting on a bench against a far wall of the yard. All the benches that had outlined the playing space these past days were gathered there now, out of the wagon's way. Folded piles of clothing were set out along them, and Cecily was stitching at a seam in a length of dark cloth laid across her lap. Instantly guessing everything there was playing garb, Joliffe went to see it. The girl briefly looked up at him and quickly bent her head to her work again. She was not presently crying but Joliffe had glimpsed the swollen redness around her eyes and the strain of grief tightening her face. For her, alas, now was far too soon for any remembered gladness to be more than pain, he thought, but schooled his voice to ordinary curiosity as he asked, "So is this the last of the garb?"

"Most of them are only roughly together," the girl said, stitching steadily without looking up again. "For you all to try on tonight. Then if they're right, I'll finish them."

Voices from the gateway behind him told others were come in. For form's sake, knowing it was of little use to her, he said gently, "I'm very sorry for your brother's death."

"Thank you," she choked softly, still to her lap and hands, and Joliffe went to head off Hew and Dick and Tom crossing the yard to see the garb in their turn.

"We have to leave her alone," he told them. "Else she won't finish with what she needs to."

Sendell and Burbage had finished with the frame for the playing house and now demanded Joliffe and Master Smale come help with putting the stairs together, with Hew and Dick to hand over the wooden pegs and mallets for pounding them when need be. While they worked, the rest of the company came in, singly and by pairs, and were swerved from going to look at their garb by Sendell, still struggling with the stairs, immediately calling for them to come put up and fasten down the boards for the playing house's roof that would make the upper playing space. "Because I doubt our angels want to truly try hovering on air there," he said.

Sight of the pageant wagon and the promise of trying on their garb seemed to work on everyone the same glad way it had on Joliffe. They joined to the work eagerly, and maybe Joliffe was the only one to notice that neither of the Emes were there yet. Only as the last pegs on stairs and boards were being knocked into place did Richard Eme stalk into the yard and over to the wagon.

"Here at last, are you?" said Sendell, tossing his mallet into the now-empty basket but not sounding particularly irked as he wiped sweat from his forehead. "You chose a good evening for being somewhat late. Where's your brother?"

Richard Eme frowned around the yard as if expecting his brother to conjure himself out of thin air. When Ned failed to, Richard said, very irked, "I don't know. I was hoping he would be here. Feckless as always, the fool."

Now Sendell was frowning, too. "This isn't the time for him to turn feckless if that's what it is. Ah! I don't need this now of all times!"

Powet put in easily, "Likely he'll show up soon. He's lost track of the time or some such foolery. He won't miss a chance to wear those wings, that's sure."

Sendell gave an unwilling laugh at that, recovered at least his outward demeanor, and said, "You've God's truth there. Come. Let's try the garb. No," he ordered, slowing everyone's surge toward the benches. "Keep your hands off it all until Cecily gives you what's yours. Prophets first. The rest of you after that as you come on in your parts."

By then Cecily had finished and folded the robe she had been sewing, had set it beside the others along the benches, and now, still with downcast eyes, began taking up garb to hand to each man and boy as they came forward. She had given Joliffe and Richard Eme and Hew their robes and was handing over Simeon's when a man Joliffe did not know came into the yard. He gave a quick look around, then crossed directly to Burbage, last in line, who did not see him coming until the fellow took hold on his elbow. Burbage startled. The man leaned near to say something close into his ear. A moment later Burbage snapped his head around, stared at him for one frozen instant, then veered out of line.

"I have to see to something," he said to Sendell.

Sendell, frowning, had been opening his mouth toward protest, but at the urgency in Burbage's voice, he closed off his protest and nodded acceptance of his leaving.

Spurred by Burbage's urgency and with no better reason than his perhaps damnable curiosity, Joliffe dumped his prophet's robe onto the one in Richard Eme's arms, said, "Here. Hold it for me. Thanks," and followed Burbage without even the courtesy of excusing himself to Sendell.

He briefly wondered if it was not an oversight on the theologians' part to have failed to include Curiosity among the Deadly Sins.

Burbage and the man who had come for him were going out the gate at a walk not quite a run. With his longer legs, Joliffe was able to overtake them in the street, asking as he did, "Burbage, what is it? Not one of your sons?"

Instead of Burbage, the other man answered, too rattled to keep it in. "It's Ned Eme. He's hanging on our pageant wagon."

Chapter 15

The smiths had begun readying their pageant wagon, too, but had yet to roll it out of its shed into the yard. Their shed being higher than the weavers', they had been able, so far, to work sheltered against the likely chance of rain. With the westering sunlight slanting low and long into the shed, Joliffe could see the steps from the wagon to the ground were already in place and that the stage house's frame at the wagon's far end was up. Deeply involved in his own work as he had been, he had not yet taken in much about other guilds' plays, but here a thick post fixed to one side of the wagon, a high crosspiece thrusting out to one side, could only be the "tree" from which Judas was said to have hung himself in his despair and guilt. That meant the smiths' pageant must be Christ's Passion and Crucifixion, that being the play that usually had Judas' death. When the wagon was rolled out of the pageant house, that cross-arm would thrust out over the yard and then over the street. Here it thrust merely toward a wall. And here and now it should have been bare, no more than an empty possibility of a gallows.

Instead a body hung from it.

The man who had come for Burbage had been gabbling all the way across the yard, saying he had come to measure for a new board needed to replace a broken one for the wagon's floor, that he'd swung the doors wide to have enough light, had seen the body hanging and thought it was someone's ill jest, a counterfeit man hanging there.

"Then I found it wasn't. It's Ned Eme. I swear it. I looked into his face. Even strangled, I could tell it's him, Christ have mercy and all the saints defend us."

He crossed himself, then fell abruptly silent as the three of them stopped together in the doorway, both he and Burbage apparently as unwilling as Joliffe was to go in. To go in was to take the first step toward everything that would come afterward, and everything that came afterward was going to be terrible.

But there was no going back from where they were. There was only onward.

Still, Joliffe held where he was, waiting for one of the other men to go first because it was not his place. He was an outsider, a looker-on to all these people's lives—and now death. And yet when Burbage finally went forward, Joliffe could not help himself but followed immediately on his heels. Burbage gave a backward glance at him but did not protest his company. The other man stayed in the doorway, probably having seen enough. Nor did it take long for Joliffe to see enough, too.

A strangled man's face was a mockery of his face alive.

Blackened and swollen out of shape with gathered blood, tongue thrust out, eyes in a glazed glare . . .

Despite all that, there was no doubt. It was Ned Eme hanging there.

"Christ have mercy," Burbage said in echo of the other man, as he and Joliffe, almost as one, signed the cross on themselves and stepped farther back from the dangling body.

From the doorway the man said, his voice shaking as the horror of it began to go deeper into him, "I should go for the bailiffs, shouldn't I? I should have gone for them first. But I knew you were just across the way. I thought . . . I thought . . ." He probably had not known what he was thinking, had simply wanted not to be alone in this, had wanted someone to know besides himself.

"Yes," Burbage said tightly. "This is for the bailiffs and the crowner." It was to be noted he did not say a priest. He turned sharply around to add, "But no one else. Not his family. Not yet."

"Yes. Right enough. Yes," the man agreed, already in retreat, then gone.

Left alone with the body, neither Joliffe nor Burbage immediately looked at it again, Burbage keeping his gaze outward to the yard, Joliffe looking elsewhere. He was beginning to remember the problems that would come from having let himself be a first finder of a corpse. By law, being a first finder laid certain duties on a man that could not be avoided. Sebastian would not be pleased. Or maybe, over all, he would be. If this was self-murder, their problem of bringing Ned Eme to justice for two murders was done. Except Sebastian's interest was not so much in justice as in Lollards.

Then Joliffe's mind tripped on itself and tracked backward. *If* it was self-murder?

"Should we take him down?" Burbage asked, still looking outward from the shed, then answered himself before Joliffe could. "No. Best wait for the bailiffs and crowner. If he's in town. The crowner. He might be. The bailiffs will know."

Burbage was talking to cover the dreadful silence of the hanging man behind them. Joliffe made some sort of agreeing sound, no more wishing to look at Ned than Burbage was. That did not stop him looking inward at other things, though, and that "if" was taking harder hold in his mind.

He understood well enough how Judas' hanging would be faked in the play. The rope would be already set, one end wrapped around a double-pronged hook on the upright, the other end with the noose looped back to lay along the crosspiece, held up by a plain hook so that all the man playing Judas need do as he said his final speech of despair and guilt was loose the noose and put it around his neck. "Demons" would be there, capering "invisibly" around him, mimicking joy at his damnation, one of them merrily helping him put the noose around his neck as if to hurry his destruction but in truth making sure it was safely fastened into the harness the man playing Judas wore under his clothing, a harness that kept the rope from truly throttling him as he flung himself off the edge of the wagon.

Had it been in despair and guilt matching Judas' that Ned Eme had put this noose around his neck, no harness to save him, and stepped off the wagon's edge? How far into despair and guilt did a man have to be for that, knowing neither the fall nor the noose would break his neck and he would slowly strangle to his death? And how great would his despair be if—having committed to such sin and agony—a man wanted, too late, to undo it?

As a man could have undone it here, Joliffe saw with an abrupt jerk of his thoughts. He looked around at the gallows and body to be sure. Yes. Here if a man's mind changed—if after all he had a last moment loss of determination to die, he *could* save himself. The cross-arm of the gallows-tree was short. If a hanging man reached out, he could easily grab the upright timber, pull himself to it, and wrap an arm around it, holding himself safe while he loosed the rope from his neck. Whoever played Judas of course would do no such thing, might feign a broken neck, would probably thrash and jerk a little to thrill the onlookers, then go limp in "death."

Ned, though, had put the noose around his neck, stepped or thrown himself off the wagon, and hung there without any last moment desire to live after all.

Joliffe heard himself ask aloud, "Why here?"

Burbage gave a shuddering shrug. "Is one place better than another to damn your soul to Hell? The true question is why did he do it at all?"

Joliffe offered hesitantly, "There's a woman who won't have him."

"When it comes to it, it's always a woman. Anna Deyster this time."

"It's not a secret, then, that he had hope of her."

"Not a secret he wanted her. I wouldn't have said there was much hope of it myself, but I gather he wouldn't be told." Burbage glanced over his left shoulder at the hanging body, jerked his gaze away, crossed himself. "Only, Christ have mercy, he must have come to believe it after all." Then with sharp urgency he exclaimed, "Christ's bones! You're going to have to tell Master Sendell he's lost his Gabriel!"

That jarred a different thought into Joliffe's mind. Saint Genesius, patron saint of players, how distracted was he to have thought first of Sebastian's displeasure and only now, belatedly, of what Ned Eme's death meant to the play? How much of himself had he lost with becoming Bishop Beaufort's man?

Or should the question be: how much of himself had he found that otherwise he might never have?

And was that finding a good thing or an ill?

But true ill was Ned Eme's soul damned to Hell for self-murder. Of course if Joliffe and Sebastian had it right, then Ned was already damned for the murders of Robyn Kydwa and his man, but at least while he lived, there could always have been hope of repentance, confession, absolution by the Church, and the saving of his soul from Hell if not his body from the law. Now both his body and soul were lost. Joliffe began to say the one prayer that seemed presently of greatest use. Christ have mercy. God have mercy. Christ have mercy. Over and over. Mercy not only on Ned Eme's soul, but on the hearts of all those whose grief would be all the worse for him dying this hopeless way.

The man who had got them into this returned with one of the bailiffs and the crowner—"We were dining together," the crowner said grumpily—and word the other bailiff was being sought.

That much explained, the crowner gave a nod to Burbage, said, "Master Burbage. I regret I can't say good evening to you, since openly it's not," and shifted his look to Joliffe. "You I don't know."

Burbage said who he was before Joliffe could answer for himself.

"Why is he here?" the crowner asked, not hostile, simply wanting what he had a right to know.

Joliffe, seeing Burbage start to wonder the same thing now that someone thought to ask it, said quickly, "We were already missing one man at rehearsal. When Master Burbage made to leave, I wanted to be sure it wouldn't be for long. Or, if it was, I could go back to tell Master Sendell the reason."

That sounded good. He could nearly believe it himself. The crowner accepted it, anyway. So did Burbage.

The bailiff, standing near at hand, staring into the shed the while, said, "The fellow looks dead from here well enough. Do we have to look closer?"

"I do," the crowner said. "Then you'll have to help take him down."

The bailiff grimaced but said nothing. The crowner went into the shed for his closer look. Joliffe approved the way he took in the place in general as he approached the body. The time he then spent looking at the body itself was short but reasonable. He even circled it although that meant squeezing against the shed's wooden wall to pass the body on that side. His foot slipped on something there and he lurched, nearly grabbed at a hanging leg for support but caught his hand back and steadied on his feet without help.

He came out of the shed, saying, "He can come down now. Best have it done before the light fails further."

His gaze went between Joliffe's and Burbage's shoulders toward the gate and sharpened in a way that made both of them look around. Burbage said, "Oh, no," and moved to head off young Hew just sliding past the barely open gate.

The boy called at him and Joliffe together, "Master Send-ell wants to know where you got yourselves away to and why you're not back yet." He had to have already taken in the gathering of men in the yard but hopefully was unable to see past them before Burbage reached him and turned him back toward the gate with a hand on his shoulder. He did not seem to know the crowner and bailiff for who they were, since he took whatever Burbage said to him and went out the gate without any backward craning of his neck for a longer look at anything.

Burbage came back saying, "Saints! That was a near thing. I told him to say we'd be there shortly." He looked to the crowner as if hoping to have that confirmed.

The crowner started, "I'll need men to carry——" He broke off as two men came into the yard and instead said to the bailiff, "Here's your fellow and the man I sent for him. With them and"——he nodded at the man who had come for Burbage——"him, there's enough to carry the body to my place. You can be the one who goes to tell the dead man's people. You know where they live?"

The bailiff granted glumly that he did.

"Then we can get back to our practice," Burbage ventured hopefully, gesturing at Joliffe and himself.

"Best you do," the crowner granted. "The inquest will be at my place tomorrow, ninth hour. You three as first finders will be there." An order, not a request. Burbage, the man who had come for him, and Joliffe all nodded their acceptance. The crowner added, "But don't talk about this anymore than need be."

"Master Sendell—he's heading our play—the Weavers

Guild's play—he has to be told," Joliffe said. "Ned Eme had a part in it."

"Blessed Saint Michael!" Burbage sounded as if he had just added a new horror to all the rest, "His brother is part of our company!"

"I leave it to you, then, whether to tell him what's happened or else just that he should get himself home," the crowner said.

Burbage and Joliffe accepted that with other bows and willingly escaped, even if it was only escape from one miserable matter to another, with now Sendell and Richard Eme to be faced and told. They split the duty. Burbage went to Richard, presently sitting in talk on one side of the yard with Master Smale and Powet. Joliffe went the other way, to Sendell who was in talk with Cecily, with Dick standing between them, his arms out-stretched while they pulled and shifted Christ's over-robe around on him.

"Like that then should keep the white robe hidden until we want it seen," Sendell was saying before he saw Joliffe. His frown was somewhere between irked and worried, as if he were ready not to be angry if Joliffe's reason for disappearing was sufficient. He finished with Cecily and Dick by saying, "It's good. You're going to look very right, Dick. Thank you, Cecily"—then turned to Joliffe with—"Well?"

Joliffe made a small beckon of his head to draw Sendell aside. Across the yard, Richard Eme had risen from the bench and was leaving, hopefully to go home rather than to the yard across the way. In no manner should any man see his brother the way Ned was now.

Looking from Joliffe to Richard Eme as he went out the

gate and back to Joliffe as they moved beyond anyone over-hearing them, Sendell demanded, with worry now definitely taking the upper hand, "What is it?" And then with the sharp-wittedness of alarm exclaimed, "It's Ned Eme, isn't it? Something has happened to him. What? How bad is it?"

Joliffe told him.

Chapter 16

The next day began gray, with low clouds and scudding rain, well suited to Joliffe's dark humour and, he did not doubt, to a number of other people's. It had been bad enough, seeing Ned Eme hanging there. Today he would have to look at his body again and did not care even for the thought of that.

Then there would be the possible wreck of the play to deal with.

After Richard Eme had left them, Sendell had perforce told everyone else why and let them all go, too, having no hope of any more rehearsing them just then. Joliffe and Burbage had stayed longer for Cecily to mark where their robes would be hemmed. Powet and Dick had waited, too, to help carry home the weighty bundles of almost finished clothing when she had done. Dick had tried to ask questions of Joliffe and Burbage. They had given him no more than shakes of their heads, refusing, until Powet told Dick to hush. Cecily had worked silently, her head bent low, and with no sign of tears. Joliffe had to suppose Ned Eme must not have been much to her, but then why should he have been? She did not know he had probably been her brother's murderer.

When she had finished, and she and Powet and Dick had left, Sendell had said dully to Joliffe and Burbage, "That was a waste of time, though, wasn't it? The play is done. No Gabriel, and likely Richard Eme will be unwilling to go on with either of his parts, and it's over-late to get anyone else who's any good to take them."

Joliffe had had no comfort to offer; he had been already thinking much the same, but Burbage said, "I think you need not count Richard out. I think that, given a few days, he'll be able to set aside whatever grief he has for his brother sufficiently to go on with the play. They never much liked each other, and you've maybe noted he does dearly love self-display."

That was harsh, but it had a true enough ring to it that Sendell had given a grudging grunt of almost-laughter. Rubbing at his face with weariness and discouragement, he had said, "Well then, we'll see. That leaves Gabriel." Only then did he give way to the despairing question that always came with any self-murder. "Why did he do such a fool thing?"

Since there was rarely a sufficient answer to that and none at all this time, neither Joliffe and Burbage had given any. Now in the gray morning Joliffe set himself to seem as ordinary and honest a citizen as he could, dressing in his soberly best doublet and unmended hosen. He let Rose straighten his collar and comb down the back of his hair for him, told Piers no, he could not come, too, and went his way to the inquest. Burbage having told Joliffe last night where the crowner lived on Hill Street, he had no trouble finding the house. Of course the finding was made easier because Burbage was standing at the front steps leading up from the street to its main door and greeted him with a glumness that matched Joliffe's own.

"I had Master Eme around to me at dawn today," he said. "He wanted what I could tell him about finding Ned's body. He wanted to come to the inquest, too. To know all, he said."

"Nobody ever truly wants to know all," Joliffe said, which was somewhat lacking in truth, given the breadth of his own curiosity at life. "Did you talk him away from it?"

"I did. I think it was his wife wanted him to come anyway."

"She'll make Richard come instead."

"You think she will?"

"He's coming along the street behind you."

Burbage looked over his shoulder and muttered something but joined Joliffe in putting the best faces to it they could as Richard Eme joined them. Properly in mourning black, he was deeply solemn and—to Joliffe's mind—altogether too aware of the moment as he accepted their condolences. He was playing "the grieving brother," Joliffe thought before he was able to curb the unkindness. Unkindness did not make it untrue, though. But neither did it mean Richard's grief was false. It was just that people whose feelings ran not very deeply often did not know the difference between the form of feeling a thing and truly feeling it. Judging from how Richard played his parts in the play, his feelings did not run deeply; they merely washed shallowly over his good opinion of himself.

"Here's Master Waldeve," Burbage said as they were joined by the man who had come for him after finding Ned. Glum greetings were exchanged all around. Then Burbage said, "Not there," as Richard made to go up the steps to the front door. "Down here." Pointing to the half dozen steps to the house's cellar.

"They put him in the cellar?" Richard said with an edge of outrage. "They put my brother in the *cellar*?"

"It was there or the stable," Burbage snapped. "Master Grevile's wife doesn't want bodies in her house. They put your brother where best they could."

"Given he can't be in any church," Master Waldeve said, low-voiced but meaning to be heard. It served; Richard Eme was instantly silent.

That was the next hard thing his family would have to face and then live with all the rest of their lives—that for self-murderers the rites of Christian funeral and burial in hallowed ground were forbidden, leaving little likelihood of salvation, no matter how many Masses might be bought for their souls, supposing a priest could be persuaded to such prayers at all. To add to the misery, in some places—but rarely in England—the body was refused any burial at all, was dragged through the town, and was thrown into a ditch or river or out with the town's rubbish; and everywhere a self-murderer's goods and property were forfeited to his overlord and lost to his family, just as for any other homicide, whether of self or someone else.

The four men went in silence down the steps. The door was standing open, a servant waiting just inside. The cellar was a series of narrow, columned bays holding up the house above it. As to be expected, it was cool and damp and dark, with shadowed shapes of stored goods along its length. Only the bay nearest the door had been kept clear, with a shroud-covered shape lying long on a trestle table in the middle of it and racks of candles set to either side. Only one candle was burning as the men came in, but the servant nodded to the nearest rack, said, "You can light them, if you will, while I fetch Master Grevile," and went away toward a patch of light marking the inside stairs.

Keeping busy lighting candles was better than standing with nothing else to do except avoid looking at the shrouded shape. Joliffe moved before the others could, but after he had lighted the first few, Burbage took one of the burning ones and went to light the other rack. They were finishing as Master Grevile joined them, the same servant with him but another man, too, who must be his clerk, given he was carrying what he needed to write down what would pass here.

"Gentlemen," the crowner said, including Joliffe in his nod. He being an officer of the crown, they all bowed in return. Straightening, Joliffe saw he was giving a long look at Richard Eme as if half-thinking to challenge why he was here. If he was, he thought other of it and only said, "Adam, take down the names of who is here. Note who are come as first finders and who is here to witness. If you will say your names, please."

They obliged. Then Master Grevile directed his servant with a silent nod to uncover the body. The man folded the shroud in even folds toward the foot of the table. Ned's body had been stripped. When the servant had done, the body lay there naked in the steady candlelight. Someone had done what could be done to better the misshapen face. Save for that and the scraped line of the rope around the neck there was nothing dreadful for Richard Eme to avoid reporting to his family. No terrible gashes. Nothing crushed and mangled. Hopefully he would have sense enough to lie about the rest to his parents and sister. Ned's parents and sister.

Master Grevile, the crowner, said, "Shall we begin? Is this the man you saw hanging in the smiths' pageant house yestereven?"

Master Waldeve, Burbage, and Joliffe confirmed that it was.

"How would you judge that he died?"

"By hanging," Master Waldeve said. Burbage and Joliffe spoke their agreement.

"You found him suspended from a beam by a rope around his neck and strangled," the crowner said.

"That's the way of it, yes," Master Waldeve agreed. Burbage and Joliffe nodded.

"Please examine the body closely to confirm there are no other wounds or signs of violence on it."

Joliffe moved to the far side of the table. Burbage and Master Waldeve stayed together. Richard Eme kept his distance. It was first finders and other immediate witnesses, if need be, who served for the crowner's jury to determine if an unexpected death was natural or by misadventure or murder. If it were natural or by misadventure, the crowner's ruling ended the matter. If it were determined to be murder, it became the sheriff's business. Here, though, the verdict would have to be self-murder and not a matter for the sheriff in the end.

No, in the end there would simply be endless grief for a son lost not just for this lifetime but for eternity, his soul damned.

But then it was already damned for the two murders he had done. Alive, he might have come to repent them, done penance, gained absolution and thereby the salvation of his soul. He could never do that now.

Always continuing to suppose he *had* done the murders. But why else, if not in despair and guilt, would he have hung himself? Surely not because Anna Deyster had not yet accepted his suit, when he could still have had hope of her.

While Master Waldeve, Burbage, and Joliffe obediently looked more closely at the body, with the crowner's servant obligingly rolling it on its side so they could see its back, too, Master Grevile asked, "Master Eme, since you are here and can be asked, perhaps sparing your parents my questions later, is there any known reason in your family why your brother should have taken his own life?"

The answer came sharp and harsh. "He thought himself in love with a woman who continued to refuse him."

"Was it marriage he offered, or—" The crowner let the question trail off discreetly.

"Marriage," Richard Eme snapped. "Marriage many times over. He gave her gifts. He implored her for her love. He must have finally despaired. It's her that brought him to this."

Burbage said back at Eme with some of Eme's own sharpness, "She learned only days ago that the man she hoped to marry was dead. Ned had no business trying for her so soon. Nor any business despairing so soon, either."

"Well, he *did* try and he *did* despair," Richard Eme snapped back. He gestured at the corpse to make his point. "He hung himself. Anyone can see it. Is there aught else for me to see or do here?"

"Can you say when you last saw your brother?" Master Grevile asked.

"At supper two nights ago. At home."

"What was his humour then?"

Richard shrugged and shook his head. "Good enough. Much as usual. Or so he made it seem."

"Thank you. We need nothing else from you at present."

"Then I'll go." He started to, as an after-thought turned back, made the sign of the cross at his brother's body, shook his head at the hopelessness of it, and left with the haste of someone glad to be away.

A slight silence stayed behind him, ended by Burbage saying, "That accords well with Ned having done it sometime in the night before last. Given how the rigor was passed off by the time he was found."

"So it's to be a verdict of self-murder then, is it?" Master Waldeve said.

"Is it?" asked the crowner.

Burbage and Master Waldeve looked at him, somewhat uncertain.

"Um," said Joliffe.

Everyone looked at him, including the clerk raising his head from the parchment on the writing board he held and the servant long since drawn back into the shadow of one of the pillars.

"You have some doubt?" Master Grevile said. His tone neither encouraged nor discouraged.

"Those." Joliffe pointed at the corpse's trunk.

"What?" Burbage asked.

Joliffe unwillingly stepped closer and pointed, without touching, at a round bruise about an inch wide, low on Ned's right rib. Then at another and another—a scatter of more than half a dozen all over his upper body. "Bruises," he said. "On his back, too."

The crowner jerked his head for his servant to roll the body sideways again. While the man did, Joliffe fetched a candle from the nearest rack and held it where it cast clear light over Ned's back. There were more of the round bruises there, a half dozen perhaps.

"Odd," said Master Waldeve unwillingly.

The servant lay the body down again and stepped back. So did Joliffe. Looking at him, the crowner asked, "So? What do you make of it?"

Joliffe looked at Burbage and Master Waldeve. They both shook their heads, frowning with uncertainty. "A pole?" Joliffe suggested. "A flat-ended, round pole about an inch thick?"

"Such as rolled under my foot in the shed when I was looking at the body," Master Grevile said evenly.

Joliffe gave him a sharp look.

Burbage said, "But that would mean—" He broke off, unwilling to say what those bruises meant.

"Look at his hands," the crowner said.

Ned's arms were laid along his sides, his hands flat on the table. Master Waldeve went forward, picked up the nearer one, exclaimed with a kind of horror, and hurriedly set it down again. "What?" Joliffe and Burbage exclaimed together, Joliffe reaching out and lifting the same hand. The wordless sound he made in his turn was more pained than horrified, although he was both. Setting it carefully down again, he said, "It's broken." He looked at the crowner. "It feels like all its bones are broken."

"If not all, then nearly all. The other one, too," the crowner said. "And the forearm on the other side."

"But there's the fingernails," said Joliffe, now making himself take closer look. "They're torn. Broken. There's dried blood on some of the tips. Like he'd—" He broke off much as Burbage had done, almost not wanting his mind to go where it was going.

"Like maybe he clawed at the wood wall there in the shed, trying to grab hold in the first moment of swinging off the wagon," the crowner said.

"But if he had changed his mind about hanging himself after he'd started," Burbage said, "the post that holds the crossbeam was in his reach. At arm's length, yes, but in reach. Or, even better, he could have reached up and grabbed the crossbeam and held on to that one-armed while loosening the noose with his—" He broke off again, this time with a wordless choking sound as the parts of it all came together in his mind.

The way they already had in Joliffe's.

Chapter 17

"Someone else was there. Someone who broke his hands so he couldn't hold to anything and save himself," Joliffe said.

Master Waldeve protested, "But still he could have wrapped his legs around the post there. The crossbeam is so short, he only had to twist his body and wrap his legs around that and hold himself up while he loosened the rope enough to call for—" His words trailed off, leaving his mouth half open as his wits caught up to the impossibility of that.

Joliffe, harsh-voiced, said it anyway. "Except he couldn't come at the post, because someone pushed him away with a pole. After breaking his hands, probably by beating on them with maybe the same pole when he surely tried to grab hold to save himself, they pushed him away from reaching it even with his legs and kept pushing at him until the rope finally throttled him."

Throttling could be a slow death or a quick. Of late Joliffe had been taught ways to kill a man quickly by throttling—silently, too, if he did it skillfully enough, he had been told. His own hope was that he never had occasion to find out how skilled he was, because he deeply doubted his willingness ever to do it. But there had likewise been a time when he had hoped never to dagger a man to death, and that hope was now a lost one. As for throttling—Ned's had surely not been quick. Hangmen who were paid to be skilled knew how to make a knot rightly, how to set it just so on a man, and what fall was sufficient when he was pushed off that his neck would break on the instant, making a quick end of him. All that took goodwill as well as skill on the hangman's part. Both the goodwill and skill being often missing, most hangings did not end easily or quickly, nor did most who came to see men hanged want it over quickly. The desperate thrash and twist of the dying man's body as it fought to stay alive against the slow strangling of the rope was what they came to see. If more than one man were being hanged at a time, wagers could be laid on which would die the first and which last the longest, with cheers and groans from the onlookers as they won or lost. Sometimes there was sufficient sympathy for the condemned man—or woman, often when it was a woman—that the hangman was allowed, even welcomed, to grab hold on the dangling legs and pull hard down, shortening the struggle, hurrying the death.

Whichever way it went, it was an ugly way to die, and by the look of it there had been no merciful shortening of it for Ned Eme.

Master Waldeve had got his mouth closed and joined Burbage in saying prayers for mercy half under their breaths. Joliffe was so choked with sickened anger at the evil of such killing he could do no more than silently cross himself. The crowner, firmly holding to business, said, "So your verdict, one and all, is that Edward Eme's death was not self-murder?"

Master Waldeve and Burbage broke off praying to join Joliffe in a ragged agreement of, "No," with Burbage adding fiercely, "Not by any means could this be self-murder."

"So let it be written down," Master Grevile said formally. As his clerk's pen scratched the words, he nodded to his waiting servant. The man came forward to draw the shroud over the body while Master Grevile told him, "Take word next to Master Fylongley and Master Purefey that they're wanted here. Do not say fully why. I'll tell them myself. I think it best we let the world still think this was self-murder for the while. Say nothing otherwise to anyone. Understand?"

The man bowed that he did and left while Master Waldeve was asking, "Are we done here?" He gestured at Burbage and himself. "We've work that's waiting for us. My forge. His shop."

"Fylongley and Purefey will be here shortly. There's no point to you going, just to be called back again before you've hardly turned around," Master Grevile said. "But we don't have to wait for them here. Upstairs will suit better."

They went, greatly willing to be out of the cellar and away from Ned Eme's body.

The parlor one storey up from the street had been readied for them, with drink and bowls set out on a table and three stools beside it. There was likewise a Franciscan friar there, seated on a bench beside the fireless hearth, telling over the beads of the rosary hung from his belt. He stood up as the men came in, his look questioning to Master Grevile who said, "Thank you for waiting, Brother. We're done for now. You're free to go pray over him."

The friar bowed his thanks in return and made to leave, only paused by the crowner's hand on his arm as he passed for Master Grevile to say something quietly in his ear. The friar gave him a startled look, crossed himself, and said, "The Virgin be praised for her mercy."

"But keep it to yourself, I pray you, until we choose to give the word out generally. For this while, the bailiffs will want it kept quiet."

"As you say, sir," the friar said and left.

"Ned's family," Burbage said. "They're beyond doubt in misery over this. They have to be thinking he's damned. His body won't even be let into a church while it's thought he did away with himself."

"They'll have a longer misery if his murderer is never found," Master Grevile returned. "They'll know soon enough it was murder. Just not yet."

He filled the waiting bowls himself and bade them sit. They did and so did he and so did his clerk who shortly joined them, although his place was out of the way in a corner where a small table would serve him for desk if need be. To fill the time Master Grevile asked about the plays, particularly drawing Joliffe out with questions. That was sharp of him, Joliffe thought. Burbage and Master Waldeve were of Coventry; there would be no trouble learning their reputations if the crowner did not already know them. Joliffe was the one from outside who had to be found out about, his part in all of this needing to be better understood. As if he did not know what the crowner was doing, he answered easily and readily about Basset's company and the play he was in and the ones he had helped with and more about Basset's company, making certain the crowner understood they had Lord Lovell for their patron. The questions and answers filled the time sufficiently until the servant who had been sent for the bailiffs appeared in the doorway, said, "I've brought Master Fylongley," and stepped aside to make way for the bailiff who had come to the yard last night.

Another man plainly a clerk, writing materials in hand, came in after him, going aside to the table where Master Grevile's clerk was willingly clearing out of his way, while Master Fylongley gave a sharp-eyed look around at all their faces, saying to Master Grevile as he did, "Master Purefey is gone to handle a fight near Spon Gate. He'll come when he can. Meantime, what's toward here? It wasn't simple self-murder, I take it?"

Master Grevile had brought another bowl to the table from a shelf along one wall and was filling it as he answered, "No. We're all agreed on that. Do you want to read what we have before going further?" He nodded at his clerk, who held up the several pages of parchment on which he had been writing this while.

"Surely." Taking the bowl and the parchment, the bailiff sat on the bench beside the hearth to read and drink. He made quick work of both, set the bowl aside, and still holding the parchment, looked at the three jurors. "Master Waldeve I know. You must be Master Burbage then, because you"— with a forward jerk of his head at Joliffe—"don't look like a townsman and must be the player."

"I am, sir," Joliffe granted respectfully. Bassett had always lessoned the players that it was better to start with respect when having to deal with anyone holding authority over them, it being easier to leave off respect if it was not warranted than crawl up out of a hole dug for oneself by ill-judged disrespect.

Maybe because the Corpus Christi plays were presently so much to the fore in Coventry, Master Fylongley gave no sign of the too-often scorn and suspicion given to players, merely nodded acceptance and turned his heed back to the matter at hand, saying, "Now. Master Waldeve, how did you happen to be there to find the body?"

"We were purposing to move the wagon into the yard today. One of the men was saying there was wear on an axle should be looked at afore we did. Guildmaster told me off to do it. To have look at it, see if it needed seeing to this year or could wait." He startled. "I haven't done it yet."

"So you went into the shed and saw—" the bailiff prompted.

"Him hanging there. I could tell he was dead. You can't mistake when they look like that."

"That was why you didn't try to bring him down?"

"Aye. I knew, too, someone else should see him. That I had to get help and someone to go for the crowner."

"Why did you go for Master Burbage?"

"He's a girdler. They have their pageant in the same yard, so we cross ways there every once in a while. He's someone I know, and I knew he was just along the way at the weavers' place, doing their play. I wanted someone as soon as might be, without I left the place too long. Didn't want to chance anyone else coming in, like."

"The rope. Is it the one that would have been used to hang Judas this year?"

"Yes. I mean, I suppose so," Master Waldeve said miserably.

"You'll need a new one now," Master Burbage muttered.

Master Waldeve sent him an ungrateful look but finished, "I mean, rope is rope. It would be hard to tell one from another if they're the same kind, but ours isn't in the box anymore. The rope we use. So I'm supposing it's the same. I looked this morning before I came."

"That was well thought to do," Master Fylongley said. "By what you say, though, the rope should have still been in its box, was not already hanging in place."

"It's kept with other things needful to the play, stored the rest of the year in someone or other's loft. The box and all was shifted to the pageant house a few days ago."

"Do you store it knotted or not?" Joliffe asked.

"Knotted. That way there's never bother about the loop's size. It's always right for going over Judas' head with slack enough to catch in the harness." Master Waldeve turned his explanation to the bailiff and crowner. "There's a harness used under Judas' doublet, so when he swings, he doesn't really hang." He went on, explaining about the harness and the demons and how it was all done safely.

"Understood," Master Fylongley said, stopping his assurances. He looked from one man to another. They all looked back at him. After a silent moment he said, "So the rope was in the shed with other things for the play, but it was not up yet. You found Eme hanging there and went for Master Burbage because he was close and had place in the same yard. He came because he knows you." The bailiff shifted his look to straight at Joliffe. "And you came—because?"

Joliffe felt like answering "Because I'm an idiot," but did not; instead he said evenly, "I'm in the same play as Master Burbage. We're at a place where everyone is needed when we practice. Last evening we were already missing Ned Eme . . ."

"He was in this play with you both?" the bailiff asked.

"Aye," said Burbage. "Although I don't know Master Waldeve knew that when he came for me."

"I didn't, no."

"Had there been any trouble with him?" the bailiff asked. "Among others in your play, I mean."

"None," Burbage and Joliffe said almost as one. Joliffe went on, "He was being the angel Gabriel." He closed off thought of what Sendell was doing about that today—desperately trying to find someone else, undoubtedly. "He did it well and made no trouble." Except sometimes goading his brother Richard, but Joliffe decided against saying aught about that because, after all, what else did brothers do?

"So when you heard Eme was found—" the bailiff prompted.

"I didn't know it was him until we were already going. I went simply because Master Burbage looked sharply upset by whatever Master Waldeve had said to him and went without telling our playmaster why. Since I'm aiding our playmaster in most things, I wanted to know what was toward. If whatever had happened meant we might be losing Master Burbage, the sooner we knew, the better. Then Master Waldeve said who it was and after that there was no going back."

That was full of enough truth to suffice, Joliffe thought. Master Fylongley seemed to accept it anyway, because he nodded, again looked at them one after another, and asked of them all, "Do any of you know of anyone with reason to have killed this Edward Eme?"

Joliffe joined Burbage and Master Waldeve in shaking their heads that they did not. That was, unfortunately, altogether true on Joliffe's side. He had no thought at all of who would have killed Ned. On the other hand, he had no doubt that Sebastian would be at him to find out. Oh, yes, Sebastian indeed would, just as soon as Sebastian heard about it.

Joliffe had some hope the bailiff was done with them then, for a time at least. As first finders and therefore jurors, their first duty had been to determine whether a death was by accident, mischance, or crime. If they had determined there had been no crime, they would have been released from further duty. Having determined otherwise, they were now charged in law with finding out all they could about the matter. Witnesses to a crime, should there be any, were supposed to testify only to what they saw and nothing more, but jurors were supposed to gather all they could and bring their knowledge with them to the trial, should the matter come to that. If it should, more than three jurors would be wanted of course, and Joliffe's present hope was that Master Fylongley would let him, Burbage, and Waldeve go for now.

But after sitting for a few moments, contemplating the floor boards in front of him, Master Fylongley looked up and said, "The morning is well along, and we need our dinners, I know, but I'd rather keep our questions going while our murderer still thinks we think Eme's death was self-murder. So . . ."

"I have one of my men waiting to bring in food and drink," Master Grevile said. "We can dine briefly and go about whatever you want next."

The bailiff beamed at him. "That's very well bethought. You'd best take care, Master Grevile, or you'll be sheriff one of these fine years."

"Mary and all the saints forbid," Master Grevile said, sounding as if he meant it, and went to the door to call his man to come.

They ate a light meal of a warm lamb pottage and fresh-baked bread. Joliffe kept warily silent throughout it, leaving the talk to men who, despite they did not all know each other, all knew other men each knew, so that all in all, Joliffe heard deeper talk about Coventry than he had yet been able to gather from anything overheard in taverns or streets.

That none of it seemed to have aught to do with anything he needed to hear and held not even passing mention of Lollards or Lollardy was pity, but who knew what would prove of use or interest to Sebastian? Burbage's trade as girdler put him nowhere so to the fore in city life as Master Waldeve's smithcraft or the crowner's or bailiff's offices had them, but he had things to say, too, when it came to talk about repairs needed to the Earls Mill bridge and whether the new spire on St. Michael's was going to prove too costly after all and especially about Corpus Christi being almost on them and how all was shaping with the plays. When Master Waldever jibed at him for being in the "Babe Jesus" play, Burbage called on Joliffe to witness with him that it was going to be far better than ever it had been, that they would not know it for the same play of other years.

Unhappily, that reminded them both that it was not even going to be the same play they had thought they had this time yesterday.

While Master Waldeve was taking a last long quaff of Master Grevile's good wine, Master Fylongley said, "We must to work, then. I must ask you three gentlemen"—graciously including Joliffe in that—"to come about my questioning with me. At least I suppose you want to."

Joliffe's acceptance came willingly enough. To his mind, there could hardly be better chance of learning more than by going with the bailiff investigating the matter. Master Waldeve's and Burbage's acceptance was more a grudging acknowledgement of the inevitable. Master Grevile, his duty done for now, bade them all an easy farewell, saying in parting to Master Fylongley, "If I hold the body here until evening, will that be long enough? Can you let his family know by then it was not self-murder and they can have him carried to church after all?"

"By then I suspect our questions will have let folk know it's murder we're asking about," Master Fylongley said. "So, aye, whenever his family sends for him, you can let them have him."

As the five of them—the bailiff's clerk coming with them—set off along the street, Master Waldeve said, "You're going to need a few more of us for jurors if it comes to trial."

"I will that," the bailiff agreed. "But it would give too much warning just yet to gather more than you three."

"Where are we bound?" Burbage asked. "Ned's family first?"

"I'm not minded to start with them, no. I have to make this seem I'm looking for the reason why he killed himself. Better to ask around to those who knew him. It almost surely must have been someone he knew who did it."

"Because how otherwise did they persuade him to put the noose around his neck if it wasn't someone he trusted," Joliffe said.

Master Fylongley gave a sharp nod. "Just so."

As if this thought was altogether new to him—and possibly it was, given the odd way people had of refusing to look straight at a thing they did not want to see—Burbage muttered, "God have mercy," and he and Master Waldeve both crossed themselves.

Master Fylongley, to whom the thought was plainly not new at all, said, "Therefore we'll begin with the woman Master Eme was wooing of late. And her family. To see what they have to say."

As they came to the corner of Much Park Street, Joliffe thought he caught glimpse of Sebastian among the flow and interweaving of folk and carts but was not certain. Given that talk of the death was probably spread widely through Coventry by now, Sebastian must know of it, but did he know yet how deeply Joliffe was wound into the business? Probably, knowing Sebastian, and Joliffe had no comfort in knowing that when the bailiff was finally done with him for the day, Sebastian was surely going to find him out and demand to be told everything he knew about Ned's death.

Chapter 18

The Byfeld household might almost have been waiting for them, but more likely they were all gathered in the kitchen and around the table only because they were just finishing the mid-day meal when Cecily, having answered Master Fylongley's heavy knock at the front door, brought him, the others, and his clerk along the passage. At either end of the table, Herry Byfeld and his mother rose together, Herry to slightly bow to the bailiff, Mistress Byfeld to slightly curtsy to him before she said to Cecily, "Bring ale for the men," at the same time Herry said to Master Fylongley, "You've come to ask us about poor Ned Eme."

"That I have, sir." And to Mistress Byfeld, "Thank you. A cup of ale won't come amiss. The day is warm for walking about."

"Clear place for the gentlemen," Powet said, giving Dick an elbow to the side and standing up from their bench along the table. On the other side, beside the empty place where probably Cecily had sat, Mistress Deyster was likewise rising, murmuring she would see to opening the shop again while they talked.

"Nay," Master Fylongley said easily. "By your leave, this won't take much time and will be quickest done if we do it all together."

She sat down again. At the bailiff's encouraging nod so did Herry and his mother. Only Powet and Dick shifted from their bench, going around to sit with Mistress Deyster, leaving their bench for the bailiff. He sat down as if there for no more than comfortable talk, crowding to one end to make room for the other men, who duly sat, except his clerk who withdrew to a joint stool beside the hearth, not far from Master Kydwa slumped in his chair and seeming to note nothing that was happening.

As Cecily, moving briskly, set out the cups of ale in front of them, Master Fylongley said, "Aye, it's about poor Master Eme I'm here. All's seen to but determining what was the set of his mind that brought him to his death. Before I trouble his parents, I thought to ask among those who knew him."

That was as well done a slide around a matter as Joliffe had ever heard. All the bailiff had said was the truth without the full truth—that he was looking for a murderer.

"You've heard he was courting Anna," Herry said in flat acceptance.

"And that she was refusing him, yes," Master Fylongley said. "There's been talk."

"There's always talk," Mistress Byfeld said bitterly. "If he was fool enough to kill himself in despair at her refusing him, that's no fault of hers. God have mercy on him," she added, crossing herself.

Everyone else did likewise before the bailiff said, still easily, "I'm not looking for fault, only for reasons. If there can be 'reason' in doing self-murder," he added as if mostly to himself before taking a sip of the ale. "This is good ale. Thank you for it. So, yes, he had been asking you to marry him, Mistress Deyster, and you have been refusing him. When was the last time you talked with him and, I presume, refused him?"

Anna Deyster looked down and aside, as if her answer had somehow escaped her wits and could be found by searching outward for it. Then she looked up again and answered, firmly enough, "Not yesterday of course." She shuddered and crossed herself. "No. Three days ago. It must have been three days since he was here. Cecily, you remember?"

Cecily, who was tending to wiping her father's chin, said without looking around, "Three days ago. Yes. In the afternoon while your mother was out."

"I remember," Dick put in. "Uncle Eustace and I came in as he was going out. You were both angry. You and him. Not Cecily. She's never angry. Only she wasn't here." He sounded momentarily confused as that came to him.

"She'd taken Master Kydwa out to the necessary," his sister said. "She came back with him as Ned was leaving, remember. And it wasn't that *I* was angry at *him*." She gave her younger brother a disgusted look. "*He* was angry at *me*."

"You'd refused him again then?" Master Fylongley asked.

"Yes," she said sharply. "But I wasn't angry. I was irked. I had told him not to ask me anymore, that it wasn't any use."

And now she was living with the thought that he had after that gone and hung himself in his despair.

"Two days ago," Herry said with the suddenness of just remembering. "You met him in the street in the morning the day before yesterday, just when you were setting out to the shops."

"Oh." His sister looked at him, startled. "Did I? Yes, of course I did. I'd forgotten. We passed greetings, nothing more. No, that's not true. He asked if he could come here again. I told him it would be best if he simply stayed away."

"It was despair," Powet said. "The young fool despaired, when what he needed was to be patient."

"Patience or none would have made no difference!" Anna snapped, glaring at her great-uncle. "I would never have married him!"

"Is that what you told him?" Master Fylongley said quietly.

She startled around to stare at him. Joliffe saw both anger and tears in her eyes in the moment before she immediately dropped her gaze to her hands in her lap and said as if smothering on the word, "Yes."

Master Fylongley nodded sagely, as if all were explained. He looked along the bench at his jurors. "Do you have any questions?"

Joliffe joined Burbage and Master Waldeve in saying they did not. Or, on Joliffe's side, not ones yet fully formed enough in his mind for asking.

The bailiff gave their thanks to everyone, and everyone rose to his and the jurors' departing, delayed only by Anna suddenly saying, "About when Ned was last here. That afternoon. Dick said we were angry, but I wasn't. Ned was, but all I wanted was for him to leave me alone. I wasn't angry."

"Very good, mistress. Thank you," Master Fylongley said with a respectful bow of his head.

Herry saw them to the outer door on his own way to open the shop for the afternoon. On the threshold, Master Fylongley paused to ask him if he could recommend who else, besides the Eme family, they might do well to ask about Ned.

Herry shrugged. "Our families have never had much to do with each other, save for Ned's interest in my sister. When we were children we ran together some, but that was long ago." Herry being all of in his middle twenties, Joliffe thought dryly. "Best you ask the Emes who his friends were, likely."

"You were at one time interested in perhaps a marriage with his sister, I believe," the bailiff said smoothly.

A tinge of pink moved up Herry's face from under his doublet's collar. "I was. But only briefly and some time ago."

"The Emes did not favor your suit? Or the young lady did not?"

"It was unsuitable on many fronts," Herry said, stiff with a dignity that made him seem much younger than a few moments ago. "I did not pursue it."

"She's quite a beauty," Master Fylongley said lightly enough to give no offense and turning away as he said it, sparing Herry any need to answer. Joliffe saw that did not keep Herry from going a deepening red as they left him.

"We're going straight to talk to Ned's family?" Master Burbage asked as they went. "You don't mean to ask more folk about Ned?"

"Afterward," Master Fylongley said. "But I've kept his family in misery long enough. I'll ask my questions there after I've told them."

They made their way through the early afternoon bustle

to Gosford Street. Master Fylongley knew the house so they did not need to ask for it. The serving man who answered the bailiff's knock at the Emes' door beside their shuttered shop started to say the family was seeing no one, but Master Fylongley said who he was and who the men with him were, and the man let them all into the passageway, then asked them to wait while he went to tell the family. "They're above," he said as he went. "In the parlor."

Accordingly, it was to the parlor he shortly led them—the bailiff, jurors, and clerk—a small procession of officialdom into the heart of the grieving for Ned's death. The parlor was a pretty room, with a wide window facing toward the street. The white-plastered walls were pargeted with swirls and cross-patterns. Cushions, some brightly embroidered, some of richly woven cloth, were on the bench beneath the window and another beside the hearth of the small fireplace. Thick rush matting covered much of the wooden floor, and a small carpet of Italian weave was laid over a square table set with well-polished pewter pitcher and goblets on a tray now splashed with wine, as if the hand pouring it had been unsteady. It was the one thing in the otherwise bright and well-kept room that went with the black-clad knot of people gathered at the hearthside bench in a grieving huddle, holding to each other for what comfort or strength they could find among themselves.

The center of it was a woman who had to be Ned's mother. She had probably once been plumply pretty, but her face in the tight surround of her wimple was now soft, sagging, and tear-marred, so that Joliffe's eyes went more readily to the girl sitting beside her, her hands clasped with her mother's in her mother's lap. She was as gowned in black as her mother but without the wimple, her golden hair pulled back but only partly hidden by a simple black veil and, yes, even reddened with weeping as she was, she was as lovely as Joliffe had gathered from talk.

Richard Eme sat on his mother's other side and was withdrawing an arm from around her shoulders and standing up as Master Fylongley and all came into the room. The man who must be Master Eme, burly in a prosperous townsman's long gown, was already on his feet behind the backed bench where the rest of his family sat, a hand resting on his wife's shoulder. He stayed there, saying only, "Master Fylongley. Gentlemen." Sounding somewhat uncertain why there were so many of them but adding, his voice heavy and weary with grieving, "Have you come to tell us we may have our son's body now?"

Master Fylongley made somewhat of a bow to the women and answered, "I've come to tell you that, yes. But also that we have determined beyond doubt that he did not die by his own will or hand. It was not self-murder. The Church will have no reason to deny him funeral rites and sanctified burial."

Mistress Eme gasped, let go one hand from her daughter's to reach up and grasp her husband's. He grasped it willingly while taking a deep, unsteady breath as he gathered himself toward the beginning of hope, gasping, "He didn't—" only to break off as he caught up to the full meaning of the bailiff's words. If his son was dead not by self-murder, then it had to be by . . .

Mistress Eme, with fresh tears running down her face past a broken, quivering smile and not yet gone as far as her husband, cried out, "I knew he had not. I knew it. Goditha, I said so, didn't I? Richard"—letting go of her husband's hand to reach out to her son—"I told you, didn't I? He was in a play. He would never have killed himself while he was in a play!"

"You did, Mother. You did. But—" Richard Eme was looking not at his mother but at Master Fylongley. "But if he didn't kill himself and yet he's dead—"

Goditha gasped, pulled one hand free from her mother's hold, and pressed it over her mouth, her eyes wide. Mistress Eme looked at her, then to Richard, and then up at her husband, her first joy going to confusion, then to horrified understanding. She brought her stare around to Master Fylongley. "You mean he was murdered?" she demanded. "My son was *murdered*?"

"I fear so, mistress," Master Fylongley said. "There is no doubt of it."

Joliffe willed him not to tell more of how her son had died. She surely knew he had hanged. She did not need to know the rest. But the bailiff seemed to be already ahead of him in wanting to avoid precisely that, because he went on quickly, "So there are questions we need to ask, the jurors and I. If you all would be so good as to answer them now, it would be a help."

"Murdered," Mistress Eme wept, now onto her daughter's shoulder while her daughter, weeping, too, held her and stared at the bailiff as if he had come from some terrible, strange world where such things as murder might happen, not from her familiar, comfortable, safe world. Yet Goditha was old enough to have clear memory of seven years ago when things had been anything but safe and sure in Coventry, especially for Lollards. Meaning for her own family as well as others. Even if, as Powet said, the Emes were "quiet Lollards," seven years ago there must have been no knowing how far the government's vengeance for the revolt would spread, how strongly the Church would demand even the least guilty be sought out and destroyed. It had not come to that, but there had to have been a frightening time until everything had settled. Had the lovely Goditha blotted all that from her mind and feelings?

More likely, Joliffe thought, was that she simply believed terrible things happened only to *other* people, not to herself or her near and dear. He had found that many people stubbornly held that common and comforting belief, but he had never been able to shelter in it. For various reasons, he had always believed terrible things *could* happen to him and to his near and dear. It meant he went through life with an almost constant twitch of wariness at the back of his mind—except for the times, more frequent of late, when the twitch was to his mind's fore, making him wary of almost everything.

Not that his deep-set wariness had been able to keep him from doing such mad things as becoming a player, let alone a spy.

"Questions?" Master Eme was saying. He sounded stunned. He moved from behind the settle, one hand groping out blindly. Richard, with somewhat more of his wits about him than the rest of his family, quickly shifted the nearby chair, turning it toward the bailiff and jurors, and guided his father to sit in it while Master Eme went on, "Yes. Of course. Anything you want to ask. We'll tell you whatever we can."

What Master Fylongley asked then were the expected questions. When had each person in the family last seen Ned? Two evenings ago, at supper. What had his humour seemed to be then? Merry. They all agreed he had been merry. No, they'd thought not much about him not coming home that night to bed or seeing him the next day.

"He has—had friends," his father said. "He wasn't wild, but there were times he'd be out and not come back right as he should have." Master Eme roused to a little fierceness. "If you found who he was with, that might tell you something about how he died, wouldn't it?"

"That's the sort of thing that can help, aye," Master Fylongley granted. Likely for whatever mercy it was, he held back from saying just how long Ned had been hanging there. Some things a family was better off not having to know, if it could be helped. He asked for the names of those with whom Ned might have been. His clerk wrote them down. Master Fylongley asked if Ned had shown unusual concern over anything of late?

"Only over Johanna Byfeld's girl," Mistress Eme said with grieving bitterness. "He wouldn't let it go. It was too soon after that other young man's death. Ned had waited for her so long, and then instead of him, she wanted that *other* man. I hope she's satisfied *now*."

"Mama!" her daughter exclaimed as Master Eme reproved, "Wife!"

Mistress Eme mopped at her eyes, tearfully admitting their reproofs with, "Yes, well, I shouldn't have said that. I shouldn't have. But there, it's said, and why couldn't she have wanted him?"

"You didn't let me want Herry Byfeld," Goditha pointed out.

"Of course not," her brother said sharply. "There would have been words said, too, if Anna had shown herself inclined to Ned, but she didn't, so it didn't matter."

"If he were alive, I wouldn't mind who he wanted to marry!" Mistress Eme sobbed.

If Ned had been still alive, she would have felt entirely

otherwise, Joliffe was sure, but no one gainsaid her. In grief people said what they needed to say, and it was wise of Master Fylongley to let them get on with it. After all, what they might say aside from his questions could be as useful as any answers made to what he asked. Now, though, he did ask, "They'd known each other a long while then, your son and Mistress Deyster?"

"The children, when they were small, used to run together, as children will," Master Eme answered. "It's only since—" He shifted what he was going to say. "Only since they grew older that they've been—less friends."

And more desirous to be lovers, Joliffe thought. But he also thought that had not been what Master Eme had first been going to say. What the draper had likely shifted from saying was "only since the rebellion," when all Lollards had become suspect because of a hot-hearted, idiot few. A quick reckoning back suggested Richard Eme and Herry Byfeld might have been just old enough to be caught up in the foolishness, but the Byfelds were not Lollards, and Joliffe suspected Master Eme kept a firmer hand on his family than to let a then-very-youthful son be drawn into treason.

Of course he had not been able to keep his second son from murdering two men.

If it was Ned who had murdered them. His own murder called that into question, didn't it?

Master Fylongley was now asking if Ned had quarreled with anyone of late or had long running trouble with anyone. As Master and Mistress Eme were saying no, Richard said, "He and Robyn Kydwa had words a while back. Just before Robyn left for—oh."

Master Fylongley caught that up quickly. "Just before

Master Kydwa left for Bristol and was killed on the way, seemingly by his servant, now fled. Is that what you were going to say?"

"Yes."

Mistress Eme looked up at her husband in dismay but left it to him to say with darkening brow, "They were to go together. Ned and Robyn. But Robyn was delayed, and Ned went on. We've all thought what ill-fortune that was, that if they had gone as they planned, Robyn Kydwa would not have been killed. But what if, instead, they had *both* been killed? What if—" He broke off, seemingly too stunned by his thought to finish.

Master Fylongley did it for him. "What if their deaths are connected? Do you have any reason to think so?"

His look invited all the Emes to answer. Master Eme slowly shook his head, and the others matched him, all looking equally bewildered. "There's nothing," Master Eme said. Then sharply questioning and demanding together, "Richard? Is there?"

Seeming startled by his father's demand, Richard declared, "No!"

There was a pause, everyone seeming to be waiting to see if he would say more, but he only looked blankly from face to face as if wondering what else was wanted from him.

It crossed Joliffe's mind that Richard Eme would do well enough in the solid life he had as his father's son and heir, but for the first time Joliffe wondered if Richard Eme chose to be in plays as a way to fill out how much of him there was not. Some people, like Powet, took to playing because there was so much in them that ordinary life was insufficient for them and they sought to set themselves free into other possibilities of being, to stretch themselves wider and deeper than called for by daily life. Other people had so little in themselves that they tried—not seeing what they were doing—to find more by playing parts in plays, as if hoping that engrafting bits of other "lives" onto their own would cure their lack. Not that anyone was ever wholly one or the other, was instead a mix of both—in unequal proportions surely, but nonetheless a mix. Joliffe had a good guess at which portion was larger in himself.

In the moment just before the silence drew out too long, Master Fylongley said, "So. That's all I need to ask presently." He looked around at his jurors. "Gentlemen, have you any questions of your own?"

Burbage and Master Waldeve seemed not to, but Joliffe asked, "Was Ned ever in the smiths' play?"

Burbage looked uncertain and Master Waldeve started to shake his head that he had not, but Mistress Eme said, "Years ago he was. He was one of the demons. He helped to—oh!"

One of the demons who helped to hang Judas. That had to be what she had been going to say, and under remembrance of then and now, she broke down in heavy weeping again. Goditha put both arms around her, and her husband, moving to join in comforting her, said distractedly, "If that's all, gentlemen, Richard will see you out."

Master Fylongley and the others all bowed and retreated to the stairs. Richard led them down and toward the front door, the sound of his mother's weeping loudly following them. Hand to the door, ready to open it, Richard paused to ask the bailiff, "What will you do next? Who else is there to question?"

"Others who knew your brother. Too, we'll try to learn if

anyone saw him going to the smith's pageant house two evenings ago. Him and anyone else."

"If he went by the back way, children may have seen him," Richard said. "That's probably how he went. We all played back there as children. They probably still do." A louder wail of weeping from overhead made all of them flinch upward looks. Richard hurriedly opened the door, asking while he did, "But we can get Ned's body now? The crowner will release it?"

"Whenever you wish," Master Fylongley assured him. "Your parish priest will likely see to it if asked."

"Yes. Thank you. That's probably the best way, yes."

Richard Eme retreated, closing the door between him and them as if escaping. Master Fylongley regarded the shut door for a moment, then shrugged and turned away to ask at Joliffe, "Why did you ask if our dead man had ever been in the smiths' play?"

Joliffe, who had been wondering how long it would be until the bailiff released them for at least a while, blinked, steered his wits this other way, and said, "Why did someone choose there to hang him? Was it the one private place he and his murderer both knew? Or was it the only place they both knew?" Which would mean his murderer was someone not familiar with Coventry. But if not familiar with Coventry, how would he know of the smiths' pageant house at all?" Joliffe set that question aside for now, going on, "Then there's why he was hung at all, rather than killed some other, more ready way."

"Stabbed," Master Waldeve offered. "Or his throat cut."

"Or bludgeoned," Burbage suggested.

"I've wondered as much," the bailiff said. "It's something you'll all have to think on, isn't it?" He heaved a sigh, shifted his belt on his hips, and said, "For now, though, you'd all like to be away to your proper work, I'm sure. I have where to find you all when needed. Learn what else you can about this Ned Eme and who might have wanted him dead, and we'll talk later. I'm away to find what's kept Master Purefoy all this while."

He left them at a brisk walk, his clerk falling into step beside him. Joliffe and the others went along the street more slowly, in unspoken agreement to let the bailiff leave them well behind, although Joliffe asked as they went, "Master Purefoy?"

"His fellow bailiff," Burbage said.

"I wish I'd never gone to the yard last night," Master Waldeve brooded.

"*I* wish you hadn't seen fit to come for me instead of haring off for one of your fellow smiths," Burbage returned, but slapped him on the shoulder in good fellowship and added, "But done is done. Just think how your wife will be pleased with all the news you can bring her when you get home."

"Think, too, how she's going to work to drag every bit of it out of me," Master Waldeve said back at him, "and then want to spread it far and wide."

Chapter 19

They parted at the corner of Much Park Street and Earl Street, Burbage saying he would be glad to get back to his proper work, Master Waldeve muttering glumly that he might as well find out a new rope before he did anything else. Joliffe said nothing but plain farewell to them both. Since Master Waldeve went rightward and Burbage cut slantwise across the street toward his own Bayley Lane, Joliffe went left. What he needed to do now was find Sebastian. Or let Sebastian find him. By now word of Ned Eme's death had to have spread wide enough through Coventry—albeit in general report still calling it self-murder—that Sebastian had almost surely heard of it.

So where was he likely to be? Not the tavern, since they had already been there together twice. St. Michael's, then, for a start, and after that a random wandering of streets, Joliffe decided.

His long-strided walk had already carried him past any direct turning to the church. He paused to buy a honey-sticky pastry at a bakeshop and retraced his way to Pepper Lane that served to swing him back toward St. Michael's. He took his time, eating as he went, half-expecting Sebastian to appear at his elbow, but Sebastian did not. A horse-watering trough in the shade of a yew tree overhanging the churchyard wall served to wash Joliffe's hands of the last of the sticky pastry before he went into the church to wander, more aware of the masons' shouts above him and the creak of the great wheel raising stones for the spire than he was of any holiness about the place.

Despite that, he lingered at St. Thomas' altar long enough to light a candle and make a silent prayer. Saint Thomas the Doubter appealed to him today: he felt full of doubts. But with the prayer said, he had equal urge to be out of the church and away and left the way he had come. For reward—if it could be called that—he found Sebastian sitting in apparent ease on the broad stone edge of the horse trough.

Joliffe stopped beside him with the idle air of a man who had nowhere in particular to go happening on another idle man doing nothing in particular. Sebastian, hands loose in his lap, one foot swinging easily, said with no ease at all or any greeting, "What's this about Eme killing himself? When? How did you get into the middle of it?"

Joliffe told him how he had got into the middle of it and all the rest. Only at the end, having deliberately saved it, did he say, "But he didn't kill himself. Someone else did for him."

Sebastian, who had been letting his gaze drift everywhere except at Joliffe, constantly making sure no one was within hearing of them, snapped his head around to stare at him. "What?"

Joliffe repeated himself and went on to tell what he, his fellow jurors, the crowner, and bailiff were all agreed on.

As if unable to contain himself, Sebastian stood up from the trough's rim, took several deep, apparently angry breaths, and sat down again. "Damnation."

"Indeed," Joliffe agreed.

They contemplated a pair of women going into the church with their market baskets on their arms and then a passing rider and horse before Sebastian said, "So how does this change how we see Kydwa's death?"

The question, although aloud, was more to himself than Joliffe, but Joliffe answered anyway. "That someone else killed them? Ned Eme suspected who, let them know it, and was killed in his turn?"

"Who?" Sebastian demanded.

Joliffe shrugged to show that not only did he not know, he had no one else to suggest for any of the murders.

"No," Sebastian said. "No, I think we should hold to it being Eme who killed Kydwa and his man. What we learned holds too well together for it to be someone else. If he didn't kill them with his own hand, he helped someone else with hiding the bodies. We can well suppose he did it because Kydwa must have found out something against Lollards here. Eme and his family being Lollards, that would give Eme reason to kill him, to protect his people. Or help someone else kill him."

"They were rivals for a woman, too," Joliffe pointed out.

"Another reason, yes. Added to the first, it would have

made killing Kydwa all the easier, I suppose." His tone laid open his low opinion of mankind as a whole, able to use such a fool's reason for murder. "So if we hold to Ned Eme having killed Kydwa or helped in killing him and hiding the body—bodies—we're left with the question of who killed him."

"And why."

"Why is easy enough. Lollards covering their tracks."

"One Lollard," Joliffe said. "Two or more would have made a better business of hanging him. It was clumsily done."

"One Lollard then."

"But why would any Lollard need to kill him, if any Lollard did? He either killed or else helped in the killing of Kydwa and his man. I think we're right about that. But no suspicion was turned toward him or toward anyone in Coventry at all. Why need him dead?"

Sebastian swung his foot, kicking his heel against the side of the trough in several dull thuds, before answering, "I don't know. There must be something else." He stood up. "So find out. I'll see you just past mid-day tomorrow at the Angel outside Spon Gate." And he strolled off like a man taking his idleness elsewhere, having used up all he could of it here.

Joliffe carefully did not watch him go, simply turned and strolled off another way in apparently matching idleness, as if he had nowhere in particular to go or anything in particular to do. Unfortunately, both were true. He did not know where to go and he had no clear thought of what he should do. He settled the first part of that by going back to the smiths' pageant wagon yard. He was somewhat surprised to find the gate still unlocked and more surprised to find no gawkers in the yard itself. The folk who always came to see where some-thing bad had happened must have already gawked their fill. After all there was not anything to see except an empty yard. Both body and rope had been taken away yesterday. There was only the empty pageant wagon to be seen in its shed and even he had no interest in that. What he wanted was to try out the way he had seen Piers and the other boys come and go from the yard, by that narrow alleyway between sheds to a rear gate.

He found the rear gate as unlocked as the fore gate. Given it was no more than a few thin boards nailed together by crosspieces and hung on rope hinges, the cost of a lock would have been wasted anyway. The gate was not even fully shut, sagging down to the dirt path outside it, leaving a boy-wide gap. Plainly the locked doors of the sheds were what mat-tered in keeping the wagons safe, and Joliffe had gathered that even those were left open as often as not this time of year.

He made to push the gate open sufficient for him to go out, but thought better of it and instead put only his head and one shoulder through and looked down at the path. The curved scrape marked in the dirt there showed that some-time lately the gate had been shoved wider open—or else been dragged, depending on which way someone had been going—to let someone larger than a boy go through. It had then been closed again as far as its sag would let it go. None of that meant anything. Joliffe pushed the gate wider open again, finding the scrape marked how far it would altogether go before it caught and stuck again about a third of the way to fully open.

He went through the gateway, onto the path. He was

willing to guess it had been a field path before Coventry grew this far to the east. On one side of it, the houses along Mill Lane backed their narrow gardens along it, except where places like the pageant wagons' yard instead had only the blank back wall of their buildings to it. On the path's other side, the trees of an orchard showed above a tall wicker fence. Going left, a little walking brought him to the river. There the path split to run both ways along the riverbank. From his wandering through and around Coventry, he could guess that a short way to his left again the path would come to the mill that gave Mill Lane its name, while to the right it would curve with the river around the orchard, the river to pass under Gosford Bridge at the end of Gosford Street, the path presumably to come out there unless it first dead-ended against someone's garden wall. He turned back to follow the path its other way, past the sagging gate and toward Gosford Street.

The houses along Gosford Street were the larger ones of merchants who had prospered enough to move somewhat out of the crowded center of Coventry. They had taken advantage of building anew to make large rear gardens, all abutting on the orchard, Joliffe presumed. A stone wall replaced the wicker fence when it came, at the pathway's end, to run along the garden-side of the house that faced onto Gosford Street. The house itself had spread its upper storeys sideways, roofing the path into a passageway. Under the overhang of those upper floors, the path opened onto Gosford Street. Joliffe stood there at the path's end for a moment, looking out and to either side along the street, busy with passersby at this early hour of the afternoon, just as it was most hours of the day. No one seemed to give him any particular heed, and he turned and went back to the gate.

For a few moments longer, he studied it and the path there but learned nothing more from it. The path was well-used. He knew boys certainly came and went along its way and without doubt other people did likewise, as a short cut away from the streets. The few inches of black thread he now bent to pluck from a rough bit of wood near the bottom of one gatepost could have come from anyone. Of itself it told him nothing, probably because it meant nothing. Most things in life seemed to mean nothing when all was said and done. Usually "meaning" came simply out of whatever passing urge people happened to put on a thing.

Except scholars. They were another matter altogether. Scholars, by what Joliffe had experienced of them, worked hard to give meaning to things no matter how great the effort needed, no matter how unlikely the meaning they devised. Then, having devised it, they began to disagree among themselves over whether that meaning was sufficient or even, after all, correct.

Joliffe looked for a long moment at the thread on the palm of his hand, but it still told him nothing, and he bent and put it back where he had found it, hooking it carefully to the wood again for no better reason than the completeness of the thing. Besides, he had no way to keep it safe, would only lose it if he took it with him, so why bother?

He went into the yard and stood a while, thinking. Ned and whoever else had come here two evenings ago had surely come by the path, not openly along the street. The bailiffs would undoubtedly ask folk hereabouts about both possibilities, but

no one was likely to remember from two days ago seeing someone turn onto the path from Gosford Street or the Mill. The
path was too used for anyone to take such note. Someone might
remember seeing Ned Eme go that way, now he was made
memorable by being dead.

Except of course he probably had not gone that way. Two
days ago he had had supper with his family, then come to
rehearse the play *and left early*. All he need have done then
was go across and a little along the lane and into the yard
here. Only his murderer need have troubled to come the
back way.

Unfortunately that still left it unlikely he would be remembered by anyone, especially if he had kept Ned waiting
and come by dark.

Well enough. To another question then, one that might
do some good to ask. Why here? Why the smiths' pageant
wagon at all?

The immediate answer that came to Joliffe was: For the
sake of hanging Ned on the Judas tree. But that brought
another question: Why had someone chosen hanging for Ned
when there were other, easier ways in plenty to kill a man?

The ready answer to that was that someone saw Ned as
some manner of Judas and had wanted him to die as Judas
had, hung on the Judas tree, that dark opposite to the Tree of
the Cross where Christ had died in self-sacrifice. But then . . .
who had seen Ned as a Judas? Who was Ned supposed to
have betrayed?

Robyn Kydwa was the obvious answer. But that supposed
someone else knew Ned had killed him and his servant.
Always supposing that Ned really had and not someone else.

Joliffe had to face that there was chance he and Sebastian

had got it wrong—that Ned Eme was not the murderer they had been seeking. But if not Ned, then who? And if someone else, then what was the why of Ned's death?

There had to be a link. There *must* be a link. Otherwise it all became too strange, too beyond hope of reckoning any sense from it.

Not that life—or death—had to make sense. All too often they seemed not to. But in this . . . Somewhere there was a link between the deaths.

Unfortunately Joliffe had only the barest of guesses at what the link was. And if Sebastian was right and all of this had to do with Lollards, then his guessed-at link was no link at all.

Chapter 20

Joliffe took his way along the streets slowly back to the Silcoks' yard, thinking as he went. Maybe Ned had been *supposed* to kill Kydwa and his servant. Maybe everything had been set and settled for it to go just as he and Sebastian had already guessed at, except Ned had backed out, not done his part, had left the ugliness to someone else and afterward been seen as a link that had to be severed. Or maybe he was never meant to do more than provide the place for the murders and the hiding of the bodies, but because that meant he knew more than the murderer was comfortable with, he had to be done away with, too.

That all made sense, in its bent way. Except it made no sense when set against the hanging on the Judas tree. Why use that complicated way to kill a man unless it meant something particular?

In the Silcoks' yard, standing beside the players' cart, he

considered going up to their room, but it was likely busy with sewing women at present. Sewing and talking. Possibly talking about the murder, so maybe there was something to be overheard and learned, but he was suddenly aware of being greatly tired, and instead of anything more ambitious, he loosed the rear flaps of the tilt, crawled in, and tied them behind him. With so much carried up to the room, there was presently place enough here for him to stretch out along the hampers that remained. He did, one arm bent under his head for cushion. He had slept in places no less uncomfortable. All that mattered was being tired enough, and it seemed he was because very shortly he went soundly asleep.

If he dreamed, his dreams were insufficient to trouble him after he awoke. Aware by the slant of sunlight against the canvas tilt that the afternoon was well along, he sat up, taking care to ease and stretch himself after his hard lying. He was still sitting, arms crossed on his up-drawn knees, when he heard Piers talking cheerfully about fishing with Tad Burbage. Not so cheerfully, Ellis answered him, "They're all a bit younger than you, by the look of them."

"Older means they're apprenticed, not free to run anymore whenever they want to," Piers said, sounding proud of his own freedom.

Ellis grunted in a doubtful way that made Joliffe wonder what he was thinking, but at the same moment Basset said, his voice slightly raised, "I'm hoping that's Joliffe in the cart."

"It is," Joliffe called back and shifted to loose the cover while Piers demanded at his grandfather, "How did you know?"

"The cover was tied from the inside, dolt," Ellis said.

"Dolt yourself," Piers shot back. "You didn't see it either until Grandfather said something."

He was ducking the cuff Ellis aimed at his head as Joliffe slid out of the cart. Seeing Piers, he exclaimed, "Boy, you're muddy to your knees and wet to the waist. Rose is going to throttle you after Ellis gets done beating on you."

"But I caught a fish!" Piers declared, knowing as well as Joliffe did that Ellis' cuffs were never hard and his mother would let no one beat him. "I left it with the cook just now. This big!" He held his hands an unlikely distance apart. Basset shook his head in silent declaration that he was not going to comment, but Ellis said, "Hah! Not nearly." Piers protested it was, and the two of them headed for the stairs in lively argument.

Basset, lingering while Joliffe tied the cart's cover closed again, asked quietly enough not to be overheard, "How goes it?"

"Oddly."

"You're done with the matter of this hanging?"

"It wasn't self-murder, so no, it's not as easily finished with as I thought it would be."

Basset paused before saying, "Not self-murder. Nor accident, I take it."

"Nor accident," Joliffe grimly agreed.

Basset took that in silently and must have decided to let it go, because as he led the way up the stairs, he asked, "How is the play doing? Is Sendell holding his own against it? All he says when I've happened to meet him is 'It's not as bad as it looked like being.'"

"He's better than holding his own. He has the thing working like a proper play instead of a limping lump of words."

"Has he found another Archangel Gabriel?"

"I haven't seen him to ask." Time enough to find out, for good or ill, when he got to practice tonight.

At that point he and Basset had to turn sideways and press against the stairway wall as Rose marched Piers down on his way to the well in the yard for a thorough washing. Piers was whining. Rose was grimly silent. Neither man presumed to say anything until they were gone. Then Joliffe said as they continued up the stairs, "Now it's your turn to tell me how things go with your play."

Basset surely knew that for the unsubtle way to turn the talk that it was, but he played up to it, saying grandly, "In a word—splendidiously." They came off the stairs in deep talk about horses for the Magi. Ellis and Gil joined in that, and except for Rose asking, when she came back with a scrubbed and chastened Piers, how things had gone with the crowner, and Joliffe answering, "Well enough. No trouble," there was nothing else said about Ned's death, which suited Joliffe more than well enough.

It was inevitably otherwise at practice that evening. Joliffe went to the yard deliberately early with the thought that if Sendell had not found someone to be Gabriel yet, his spirits would almost surely be in need of some manner of bolstering before facing the rest of the players, but he found himself forestalled. Not only were Powet and Dick already there, but a third man as well, whom Sendell announced triumphantly would be their Gabriel. As it happened, he was the Gabriel who had quit the play early on, clearing the part for Ned. "I told him the play is better beyond anything any of us had ever thought it could be," Powet said from the wagon where they were working Joseph's and Gabriel's lines together. "So he agreed. He doesn't have quite Ned's voice for the singing but he'll do well enough."

Joliffe's welcome to their new Gabriel was as whole-heartedly as his relief at the intent, calm way Sendell was getting on with things. In a while he found chance to ask Sendell in a very low voice, "Have you heard if Richard Eme will come tonight?"

"He sent word he'll be here, Saint Genesius bless him," Sendell answered, making no effort to hide his relief and never taking his eyes off his players. "And Tom will be here soon to practice as Mary with our Gabriel. Everything is holding together."

It seemed to be indeed. Leaving Sendell to it, Joliffe went to sit beside Dick, slumped glumly on one of the benches well aside from the wagon, playing cat's cradle with a long piece of string. He muttered what must have been greeting, sullen though it was, and stayed intent on his game. Joliffe ventured, "Your uncle brought you to make sure you came, and you're not happy about it?"

Dick gave twist of one wrist and a flutter of fingers, and the string between his hands took on a different pattern. "I'm not a baby, to forget where I'm supposed to be," he grumped.

Making a not-difficult guess, Joliffe said, "Things not good at home?"

Dick shot him a hard glance, then relented and said, "Rotten. First Robyn. Now Ned. But I don't see why Anna has to jaw at *me*." He took up a shrill mimicking of a woman's voice. "'Don't go blithering what you don't know anything about. Don't be a fool and talk about what you don't understand.'" He replaced the mimicking with bitterness. "It's not *my* fault if she never gets married again."

"Does she want to get married again?"

"She wanted to marry Robyn. I think she meant it when she said she didn't want to marry Ned. But she could have changed her mind. Now she can't." He missed a loop in the string and whatever he had been making fell apart into a tangle in his hands. He made an impatient sound, wadded it all together, thought better of it, and started to untangle the mess. But still aggrieved, he said, "She *was* angry at Ned the other day, no matter what she says."

"Why do you think she says she wasn't?" Joliffe asked lightly.

Dick shrugged a shoulder to show he either did not care or did not know, but after all could not resist the flattery of being asked what he thought. "Maybe she feels bad she made him feel bad enough he killed himself?" So word had not spread to the Byfeld household yet that Ned had not died of his own will, Joliffe noted. Still absently trying to untangle the string, Dick said, "I mean—" He broke off, frowning over either the string or what he meant, then went on, "I mean she sounded like she really, truly meant she was never going to forgive him. He must have believed her."

"Is that what she said?" Joliffe asked, sounding carefully barely interested. "That she was never going to forgive him?"

Dick gave a nodding shrug.

"Forgive what?" Joliffe asked.

The string fell out of its tangle into an open loop again. "Don't know." Dick started another cradle. "Maybe Uncle Eustace heard. He was ahead of me coming along the passage. But she *was* angry, no matter what she says. She went out the back door so fast she nearly knocked old Master

Kydwa off his feet. Cecily was just bringing him back in. Anna almost shoved them both over on her way out."

"And Ned? Was he angry, too?"

Dick paused, hands and fingers going still in the midst of some different twisting of his string. "I don't know," he said, sounding as if he had not thought about it before. "He just looked . . . odd?"

"Who?" said Powet. Joliffe had been too intent on Dick, and Dick too intent on his string, to see Powet had finished his work with Gabriel and crossed the yard to join them. He sat down on Dick's other side and nodded back to the wagon where Tom had taken his place with Gabriel. "He's going to be fine. Who looked odd? Not me, I hope?"

"Ned," Dick said. "The other day when Anna was angry at him in the kitchen."

Powet gave a weary, impatient sigh. "I've told you. Whatever passed between them is best left untalked of. Things are bad enough without people saying your sister drove a man to his death."

Dick made a grumpy sound and kept his heed on his string. Catching Powet's gaze across the boy's hunched shoulders, Joliffe said levelly, "She didn't drive him to his death."

"Of course she didn't," Powet said stoutly. "If he was fool enough to hang himself, it's nobody's fault but—"

Holding Powet's gaze, Joliffe made a small, denying shake of his head.

Powet broke off, held silent a moment, his stare fixed to Joliffe's. He tried again, slowly, "If he hung himself—" and stopped. Again Joliffe shook his head.

Powet's eyes widened slightly. Dick, still watching his

hands and the string and missing all their by-play, finished what he thought was his uncle's thought, saying, "Then he's damned to Hell, isn't he?"

Powet stood up and walked away. Watching him go, Joliffe said, "Yes."

He stood up and walked the other way from Powet, giving himself the look of someone practicing his lines. But of course it was not of his lines he was thinking. He had given nothing away to Powet that Powet would not hear again when Richard Eme arrived. The Emes, in their mingled grief and relief, would not be holding back in letting it be known Ned had not died by his own hand, that they were freed of the double burden of his damnation and their shame. At least until such time it came out that he had murdered two other men.

Supposing it was ever proved he had.

Supposing he had.

But that would be an entirely different shame, coming as it did with hope that prayers and Masses might save his soul after all.

So nothing had been lost by letting Powet know the truth, and something had been gained. The trouble was that Joliffe was not sure what. That Ned's death was not self-murder had meant something to Powet. Something more than simple surprise. Dismay? Fear? Alarm? So many different feelings might be read into that widening of the eyes and abrupt moving away, but what was the why of any of them?

Powet had been very quiet through all the bailiff's questioning of his family today. Because he had nothing to add to what was being said? Or because he knew something he was taking care not to say?

Joliffe stopped circling and made himself ask the question at the center of all that wondering.

What reason could Powet have had to kill Ned Eme?

The ready answer to that was: none.

Then Joliffe had to ask how willing was he to accept that ready answer, and the answer to that was: not at all.

So . . .

Where that "so" might have gone was broken off by most of the other players arriving in a clump, followed by much relieved welcoming of their new Gabriel and some muted jeering at him that he had chosen to come back now he had heard they had a good play on their hands. Too much aware-ness of the dark why behind him being there kept much true merriment from their jeering, but their relief and welcome were real enough, although even those broke off when Rich-ard Eme came into the yard a few moments later, alone and all in mourning black.

A part of Joliffe's mind dryly assessed how Richard Eme's late entering was well-timed, drawing every set of eyes in the yard to him as it did. Another part of Joliffe's mind promptly chided him for so uncharitable a thought. Making his entering notable was probably the last thing from Richard Eme's mind.

Or maybe it was not. Watching him cross the yard toward the others clustered at the wagon, Joliffe shifted his thought. He would not deny Richard Eme was grieving, but at the same time there was that about him that told he was very aware of being a dead man's brother and of the heed that brought him. As with his playing, there was insufficient heart under it to make it feel true. The trouble was not that he did not feel: the trouble was that he did not feel deeply—that his feelings stayed comfortably within shallow depths that never tore and tossed him, even in grief for a dead brother.

Joliffe, well aware of how he himself too often felt things far too deeply for any comfort—as if he had one layer of skin too few between him and the world—had never been able to decide whether he was the better or the worse for that. There were assuredly times he could have done with feeling less, but if he had, he would not be who he was, and did he want that?

Only sometimes.

Richard Eme had been accepting everyone's first awkward sympathies with becoming gratitude, but now looked at Burbage and around to Joliffe lingering on the edge of it all and exclaimed, surprised, "You haven't told them?"

"There's not been chance," said Burbage. "We've only all just come and there's been—" He waved a hand at Gabriel.

Richard Eme took a step back, spread his arms halfway out like a priest about to give benediction, and said, "Ned didn't die by his own hand! He can have funeral and be buried in holy ground. The bailiff told us. He didn't kill himself. It was murder."

What had been murmured sympathies turned to exclaims, fairly evenly divided between relief that Ned's soul was safe and startlement at thought of murder. Joliffe, unsure of the first and no longer startled by the latter, kept silent. He only answered the questions turned to him for why Richard Eme had expected him to have given them the news that it was murder, then was saved from questions about the murder itself by Sendell saying, "Enough for now. We need to set to work. Master Eme, since you're here, we'll run from the beginning."

Chapter 21

This being their first time on the pageant wagon itself, with stairs to consider and the need to pattern people's going out of and into the stage house—the place being small enough to make such considerations very necessary—the practice went unevenly, with more thought on how and when and where to move than on what was being said. That was as it should be, and Sendell kept all going along well, given against what he had to work. Sometime during the while Joliffe was watching Powet as Joseph forget most of his lines with Mary, Cecily Kydwa came quietly into the yard, her arms laden with the players' garb. She slipped along the wall to a bench where she busied herself with laying out the clothing, each set of garb in a carefully folded pile of its own. That done, she sat down to sew on Mary's blue gown.

Leaving Powet and Tom to struggle onward without him for a few minutes, Sendell went aside to speak with her, apparently only about the garb because Joliffe, watching, did not see her demeanor change at all. When Sendell started back to the wagon, Joliffe went over, cleared a space beside her by carefully moving a folded robe, and sat down. She gave a sideways shift of her eyes toward him without faltering in her stitching and said, a little questioning, "Master Joliffe?"

"I wanted to tell you, since Master Powet likely won't have first chance, that the crowner and bailiff have determined Ned Eme's death was not by his own hand. He did not kill himself."

"I know," she said softly. "A neighbor was spreading word along the street. We heard not long after Master Powet came away. But he knows now?"

"He learned it here."

She nodded, accepting that, and kept sewing. Given her silence, Joliffe saw no way to ease toward anything more, so he simply asked outright, "Three days ago, when Mistress Deyster quarreled with Ned in the kitchen, did you hear anything at all of what it was about?"

Cecily did not pause in her sewing and her voice was as steady as her stitches. "It had to do with my brother, I think. I heard his name. Nothing else."

"Nothing else at all? You were right there in the kitchen with them."

"When Master Eme set again to persuading her to marry him, it seemed a good time to take my father out. She told you I did that. We went out. What they said to each other while I was gone I don't know."

"What did you hear when you came back?"

"That's when I heard my brother's name."

"From whom? From Mistress Deyster or Master Eme?"

"I couldn't tell."

She had not ceased her sewing but her stitches had become quicker and now were uneven. At a guess, she was lying, but about what—about hearing only that, or about what she had heard, or simply about who had said her brother's name? All of that? None of that, but something else as yet unasked that she feared might be? What?

And why?

Richard Eme joined them. "Master Sendell says we're to try on our Prophets' garb if it's ready."

Cecily settled her needle firmly into the blue cloth, set it carefully aside, and rose to take up one of the folded piles. She handed it to him and another to Joliffe. They took off their doublets but needed to strip no further: the Prophets' robes were loose, full, and reached from neck to heels, easily hiding shirts and hosen.

"I think they're finished," Cecily said softly as the men shook out the folds around their ankles and stretched their arms to try the sleeve lengths. "If I've done the hems rightly."

She had, but Richard Eme, looking down at his robe's hem, began in the tone of someone about to assert his superiority by making complaint, "I think this could be . . ."

"Not possibly bettered," said Joliffe cheerfully. "Look how we match." He stood beside the other man. "No, look down without bending. See? When we stand together, the hems are the same length. That will look very good." Before Richard Eme could think to point out they stood together on the stage hardly any time at all, what with being up and down the stairs and rarely ever side by side, Joliffe surged on, "Mistress Kydwa, you've done very well by us indeed."

Faint color touched her cheeks. She murmured thanks.

Leaving Richard Eme no chance to spoil it, Joliffe took him by the arm and turned him back toward the wagon, saying, "We must needs show Master Sendell."

Sendell was pleased. Richard Eme accepted that as if the approval were merely his own due, then said with a nod toward the wagon where Powet and their new Gabriel were settling their parts, "As I was saying, Master Sendell, if you want me to take him aside and tell him how my brother was playing Gabriel . . ."

As much to save Sendell as for his own purpose, Joliffe took Eme by the arm again, this time saying, "Since you've brought up your brother, there's something I want to ask," and walked him away from the wagon and aside from anyone else in the yard, adding as they went, "As one of the crowner's jurymen, you understand."

Richard Eme's face had fallen immediately into linea-ments of grief at mention of his brother. Now his voice had a sorrowful tremble tinged with anger as he said, "Anything. Anything that can help to find who did this to him *and* tried to shame our family."

That gave Joliffe a thread to try and he said, "Is there someone who would want to do that—make such trouble for your family, even if it meant killing your brother?"

"We're nobody!" He thought better of that; changed it to, "My father is high among the drapers, has been on the guild council, will likely be on the city's council one of these years soon. There's nothing in any of that. He's made no enemies. He doesn't have the push to make enemies. We live quietly."

"What of Ned? I know he traveled for your father."

"Because I'm needed more here at the heart of things."

"Certainly. So it was your brother who went to Bristol and saw to the family holdings outside of Coventry, yes?"

Joliffe had carefully linked the first, which was something he could be assumed to know from Ned's talk of it after Robyn Kydwa's body was found, to the second, which was unlikely for him to know. As he had hoped, Eme accepted him knowing both and readily answered. "Yes. Ned was ever happier than when out and about. *Doing* something, as he liked to say. As if sitting at the center of everything, seeing that all goes as it should, isn't *doing* something." The words were bitter, the grievance seemingly a long one between the brothers. But probably remembering he was after all speaking of someone now dead, Eme shifted back to his grieving voice. "He was good at that side of things. He's going to be missed that way."

But any other way? Joliffe wondered. Still, a vast difference between brothers did not mean a lack of affection, and he said evenly, "It did give him more chance to get into some manner of trouble without his family knowing of it."

"It might, but I don't see that he did. There's no sign of it. The books and money all tally as they should, both with each other and with reports from our factor in Bristol and the steward at the manor."

So, for all the talk of confidence placed in him, a close watch had been kept on the younger son. Not close enough, if he had indeed killed Kydwa and his servant, but close enough, it seemed, that any large pattern of trouble would have been found out. But, "What of here in Coventry?" Joliffe persisted. "Was he ever in trouble with gambling or drinking or anything else that could have made him an enemy?"

Eme had begun shaking his head while Joliffe was speaking, was still shaking it as he answered, "Nothing like that. He wasn't given to gambling or drinking or anything like that."

"What of the Byfelds? Was there particular close friendship there?"

"No. Nothing particular. Less than with some other families. The most we ever had to do with them was when all of us were small and played together. A whole band of children, I mean, not simply us and Herry and her. Then it was grammar school for the boys and dame school for the girls, and our ways parted. We were too grown."

"By 'her' you mean Mistress Deyster."

Eme's face stiffened with some in-held feeling, then twisted with the pain of giving way as he exclaimed with raw regret, "I mocked him. About her. Saint Michael, judge of souls, forgive me. I meant nothing by it. I swear I meant nothing. When we thought he'd hung himself, I thought—" He broke off, unable to say what he had thought. He pressed a hand over his mouth to stop its trembling and mumbled past it, "I thought I'd goaded him to killing himself."

That was the most open, honest feeling Joliffe had ever seen from him. To see there was honest grief somewhere in the man bettered Joliffe's thoughts toward him but did not stop him saying, "It's known Herry Byfeld wanted to marry your sister."

Eme's hand and open grief both dropped away. Stiffly, he declared, "That would never have been allowed."

"Why not? It would seem a very reasonable marriage between two prospering families."

"It wouldn't have been." Firm-voiced until then, Eme went

to a mutter. "It was two years ago and nothing to do with Ned's death."

"Yet your family would have countenanced him marrying Anna Deyster?"

"Not happily, no. But Ned was less to be bid the right way than Goditha is."

Joliffe was forestalled from asking more by Hew coming to say Cecily wanted their Prophets' robes and the Doctors were to try their gowns.

The play and its attendant matters took up the rest of the time in the yard, giving Joliffe no other chance for questions. It was just as well that garb and growing used to the wagon took up most of the time, because his lines as Prophet and Ane were not to the fore of his mind though he tried, not very successfully, to take refuge in the work, away from all his questions and the few answers he had. None of the latter told him enough, not even somewhere else to look than just at the Emes and Byfelds. There had to have been more to Ned's life than only a narrow living between the two families and working on the play. If so, Sebastian might be finding it out. Or it might be that for these few weeks that mattered, those *had* been the bounds of Ned's life. If that were so and the reason for his death came from somewhere outside those bounds, answers would be harder to find. As yet there was not even hint of such a thread. Would Sebastian have to find it out in Bristol? Was that where the murderer had come from? Was Ned's death for something he had done—or not done—in Bristol?

But if Ned had been meeting someone from Bristol, the smiths' pageant house would have to have been Ned's choice. Joliffe could come up with various reasons both for and against Ned choosing the pageant wagon yard for that, and the hanging remained troublesome. Had it been a thing of the moment, with the rope and Judas tree simply to hand in a burst of anger? But nearly every man wore a dagger most of the time. A burst of anger was more likely to lead to a drawn dagger and a quick stabbing than to the more difficult business of hanging. No. There was something deliberate and intended in the choice of hanging, and that the Judas tree was used strongly suggested the choice had been someone's of Coventry rather than anyone's from Bristol. There might be something that ran between Ned's death here and Bristol, but one end of that something was surely deeply rooted here in Coventry. What Sebastian might be finding out, Joliffe was not even going to guess at.

What most frustrated him presently was that tomorrow was Sunday. There would be no practice and therefore no chance of questioning anyone as easily as he had done this evening. He thought that taking Dick and Cecily and Richard Eme almost unawares had helped in having answers from them he might not otherwise have had. Like chance would probably not come again, since after Sunday there were only three days to go through until Corpus Christi. For those days, practice would be intense with polishing the play to its highest and best, with no time for "idle" talk around the edges.

Awareness of that may have been why Joliffe was less than subtle at practice's end, when finally, in the blue gloaming of deep twilight, Sendell said they were done for now. Simeon and the two Angels were already gone, released earlier when their part of the play had been run. Joliffe could have gone then, too, but had hung about to watch. Now Tom dropped from being Mary and left, whistling, while the Doctors in the Temple were taking off their robes. They had worn them though their part of the play tonight because, being cut very full, the robes' hanging sleeves were in constant danger of tangling with each other as the Doctors moved around on the wagon's limited space, and Burbage, Eme, and Master Smale had wanted more time to grow used to them. Because of that, Cecily was still there, too, unable to sew in the faded light but waiting to take the Doctors' robes away for finishing.

Richard Eme was fastest out of his, stripping it off and tossing it onto the bench near Cecily, taking up his doublet in the same motion and putting it on as he headed for the gate and away. Burbage and Master Smale took off theirs with somewhat greater care, aware some of the stitching was only loose basting. While Cecily helped them, Joliffe went to see to Eme's, shaking it out carefully, folding it, setting it down beside the other carefully piled garb. Powet was already stacking an armload on Dick to help in carrying home, telling him, "You wait and go with us."

Burbage, hooking his doublet closed and his back to everyone else, said quietly as Joliffe came to him, "Did you learn anything new?"

"Ah." Joliffe could not quite keep his mingled amusement and guilt out of his voice. "You noted what I was doing."

"You saved me doing it. Did you learn anything of use?"

"Nothing. No one knows any reason why someone would want to kill Ned."

"We'll have to see what gossip my wife turns up," Burbage said. "I told her to ask freely. She said all she'd probably need do is listen."

"That will probably prove of more use than anything.

Here, I'll put your robe with the rest. You'll be wanting to hie home."

Burbage handed over the robe with thanks and went, a prosperous man with home and family mattering more in his life than murder. Joliffe, taking their robes to Cecily, was all too sharply aware how wide was the gap between Burbage's life and his. Their shared effort in the play and their easy talk together was a bridge between them but a frail one. Joliffe felt a momentary sadness for that, then let it go as he handed Cecily the gown and asked her, after she had thanked him, "Have you remembered anything else you might have heard said between Ned Eme and Mistress Deyster?"

Cecily froze, stricken, staring up at him.

"The thing he said that made her so angry at him," Joliffe prompted.

Powet shoved past him, one shoulder hitting his for no better reason than Powet meant it to as Powet said angrily, "Leave her be." He took the three heavy Doctors' robes from her arms. "Go on with Dick," he said to her. "I'll bring the rest. Go on."

Cecily went, snatching up her sewing basket on the way and not looking back as she followed Dick toward the gate. Sendell was still at the wagon, circling it, staring at it, probably considering possibilities and giving no heed to Powet and Joliffe across the yard. To keep it that way, Powet held his voice low despite his open anger as he said at Joliffe, "The girl has enough woe without you badgering her. Leave her be."

Nothing loathe to use Powet's anger since it was there, Joliffe said back almost as fiercely, "I'm supposed to believe she was right outside the door and heard nothing?"

"All she would have heard was Anna being angry at Ned."

"There had to have been words said. She was right there at the rear door."

"She was coming in the same moment Dick and I were. The most she could have heard was Anna say 'If he was, what of it? You and yours are clean, aren't you?'"

"Why didn't you tell that when Master Fylongley was questioning you?"

"Because we thought Ned had killed himself then, didn't we? Why make it seem even more Anna's fault than folk were going to think it? Ned must have said something against Robyn. Nothing else was likely to make her that angry. I thought she must have finally made Ned understand he had no hope of her, and that's why he'd hung himself. Only—" Powet's anger faltered. "Only he didn't, did he?"

Hoping to drive him a little further, Joliffe prodded, "What did she mean by 'clean'?"

But Powet's anger was fading rapidly. He shook his head, sighed, shifted the weight of the robes in his arms, and said, "I don't know. Clean of Robyn's death, I suppose. How would I know what? What matters is that Ned shouldn't have been fool enough to speak ill of the dead at all. Nor should I be now. Pray pardon my anger at you. It was seeing Cecily in pain. She has enough to bear as it is. I know you're only doing what you must."

"I'd rather that I didn't," Joliffe half-lied, making his own apology in answer and acceptance of Powet's.

Powet nodded sadly. He looked suddenly weighted down by more than his armload of clothing. "I know," he repeated, turned away, and left, quite plainly not wanting Joliffe's company.

Nor did Joliffe want his just now and went to join Sendell

in contemplation of the wagon, on the chance Sendell might want to talk of what more might be done with the play in the few days they had left, but also with hope that good, clear talk like that might help to cleanse the confusions in his own mind.

Chapter 22

The shadow of the stone-towered gateway had barely crept out from the tower's foot when Joliffe strolled through it the next day, following Spon Street out of Coventry. Sebastian had said to meet him just past mid-day at the Angel. This was as "just past" mid-day as was possible by Joliffe's reckoning. What he had not known was how far it was to this Angel, but a few hundred yards sufficed for him to see its sign of Saint Michael with his spread wings and spear. The tavern itself was set somewhat back from the road, with a rowan tree to one side throwing a little shade toward the benches set about the yard to take advantage of the warm, fair weather. The ale must be good here, and maybe the food, too: a number of men of various crafts, to guess by their clothing, were sharing benches, with both drink and food in hand. The warm buzz of their talk was all about Joliffe as he threaded through to Sebastian sitting on a short bench in the sun against one corner of the building, a drink in his own hands and a place kept for Joliffe beside him by way of a pitcher, a drinking bowl, and fat cuts of bread and cheese on a wooden plate set there.

Joliffe took up the bowl and plate, shifted the pitcher to be between him and Sebastian, and sat down. "Much thanks," he said with a nod at the bread and cheese. "More thanks," he added as Sebastian lifted the pitcher and filled his bowl for him, and asked before taking a large bite of cheese, "So. Learned anything of use?"

Sebastian, who seemed to have finished eating and was doing no more with the ale in his own bowl than swirling it a little, said, "Our Ned Eme seems to have led a singularly blameless life. Except for the odd murder now and again, if we hold to the thought he did for Kydwa and his man."

"Do we hold to that thought?" Joliffe ask thickly around the cheese.

"So far, yes. I've found no reason to shift our thinking there."

"Yet."

Sebastian gave him a sharp look. "Have you?"

Joliffe shook his head that, no, he had not.

"Well then," Sebastian said with something of a glower. "There was talk in plenty to be heard yesterday and last night. Tavern talk and all. You heard none, I suppose?"

"There was practice all the evening, and then I was to bed before curfew." Joliffe paused a beat to let Sebastian take that for a "no" before going on, "I asked some questions at the practice, though. His brother was there."

"Despite his brother being dead?" Sebastian asked sharply.

"It was for the play," Joliffe said evenly, with no hope Sebastian would understand. "The play is all of us. Is more than any one of us. If there's any way at all you can keep going, you don't fail the others."

Sebastian frowned over that for a silent moment, then said, surprising Joliffe, "As with us who serve our lord master the way we do. Mostly we don't know the others, but we don't fail them even so. If we can help it."

"And Kydwa was one of us," Joliffe said.

"He was. Not by much and among the least but one of us even so. Since you say you've found nothing that says Ned Eme didn't kill him, that leaves us only need to find out who murdered our murderer, because that will lead us to whoever set him on to murder Kydwa, and that will be our link to whatever the Lollards are up to hereabouts."

"Do we have any proof that they're up to anything at all?"

"They still have their gatherings. That I found out for certain. The signs and spoor are there to be found if you look for them." A small current of blame ran under the words. Sebastian had taught Joliffe those "signs and spoor" but knew full well that Joliffe made little, if any, use of them. "The Emes are part of it all. Our Ned was, too."

"Part of all what?" Joliffe asked.

"Lollard meetings. To do their readings, then talk big against everyone who isn't them and make complots toward whatever new trouble they next intend."

"Is there sign"—Joliffe managed to hold off from adding "and spoor"—"that they're plotting any new trouble?"

Sebastian's face pinched in, probably with disappointment and regret at having to admit, "Not that I've found out yet. But three murders have to mean something is being desperately kept secret."

Joliffe could not deny the likelihood of that and held silent, chewing steadily at the bread.

"What more have you learned on your side of things?" Sebastian asked.

Joliffe swallowed. "I didn't say much to you about the Eme and Byfeld families when we last talked. We centered then on what seemed immediate to Ned Eme's death. I've thought more about them since then."

Sebastian nodded for him to continue.

"Although they're not friendly with each other, there are links of somewhat long standing among them. A few years ago the Byfeld eldest son was interested in wedding the Eme daughter. Neither family seems to have been pleased at that, the Emes least of all, and his suit went nowhere. On the other side, Ned Eme had wanted the Byfeld daughter even before her first marriage and had hope of winning her in her widowhood, only to lose her to Robyn Kydwa. With Kydwa dead, he had renewed his suit and was pushing it hard."

"What did the families think of that?"

"From what they say, I think his family was tired of listening to him, would have accepted the marriage if the woman had accepted him. Or maybe they knew they didn't have to worry, that she would go on rejecting him."

"That wouldn't have lasted," Sebastian said with the glum certainty of someone who had suffered from women's ways. "She'd have given in later if not sooner."

"I have to doubt that. Even with him dead, she's doing none of the usual moaning of 'if only.' That's despite she was heard being very angry at him two days before he—" Joliffe's mind stumbled on a thought. He fell silent, following it.

"Before he was killed?" Sebastian said.

"Yes." Joliffe said it slowly, still following his thought. Then he shook his head and said, still caught into his thought, "No."

"Yes? No? What?" Sebastian prodded.

Joliffe regrouped his wits, stopped staring into the empty air in front of him, and said, heedful again, "Yes. She was heard being very angry at him and admits she was and shows no regret for it. No maidenly pining."

"What was the quarrel for?"

"She says she was simply refusing him again. Someone else says he heard her say 'If he was, what of it? You and yours are clean, aren't you?' Only it could have been more of a challenge, I suppose, now I come to say it aloud. It might have been 'You and yours are clean. *Aren't you?*' I'll ask Master Powet about that, now he's chosen to remember it was said at all."

"He didn't tell you that at first? Hiding something, is he?"

"He said he kept it to himself when he thought Ned had killed himself because it might make his niece seem somehow at fault in Ned's death. Now that's no worry anymore, he talked of it. Said Ned must have said something against Robyn Kydwa because nothing else was likely to have made her as angry as she was."

"What did she mean by 'clean'? Clean of what?"

"I asked Master Powet the same. He said he didn't know."

"But they're not clean. The Emes. They're Lollards."

Joliffe suspected that was a hare that would not run, but Sebastian would go on prodding it with a stick until it dropped over dead. Yes, the Emes were Lollards, it seemed, but Joliffe very much doubted they were of the wilder kind. They would believe what they believed and go about their business, would pay their tithes to the Church and speak respectfully to the priest and believe both Church and priest were damned for their ways but leave them to it, satisfied with seeing to their own souls, willing to leave others alone and hoping to be left the same. What Joliffe wanted was to follow the thought that had come to him, not get caught into debate, and he answered Sebastian with a silent nod around a mouthful of cheese and bread.

They talked only a little longer together, to no gain. Least gain came when Joliffe asked what he had wanted to ask for some time. "What of our bishop's other man here in Coventry? Has he found out anything of use?"

Sebastian returned him a blank face and empty stare and nothing more.

"Ah," said Joliffe, accepting that was all he would be told. Very probably not even Robyn Kydwa had known who was his fellow spy in Coventry. As Sebastian had said early in his dealing with Joliffe: what you did not know, you could not tell—or sell. So he was not ready even to admit for certain there was another of their fellows here in Coventry. They parted company soon after that, Joliffe leaving Sebastian still sitting there and himself sauntering away as if on his way to waste a Sunday afternoon as easefully as he could.

There was nothing easeful in his thoughts, though, as he betook himself to the riverside path he had followed in his earlier wandering around Coventry. It being a Sunday, there were couples and families strolling there in the warm summer's day but no one that he knew or who knew him. That left him free while he strolled to sort and shift the pieces of possibility his new thought had brought him. By the time the riverside path had circled him slowly around to come back into Coventry through the Gosford Gate he had decided what he would try. If he was wrong, he would look a fool but at least the matter would be cleared from his mind, leaving room to find another answer.

A better answer than the one he thought he had and did not much want.

By way of his earlier wandering, he knew that not far from the Emes' house there was a lane that ran south off Gosford Street. Not far from it, on the street's other side, was the passageway leading to the path that ran behind the smiths' pageant house and to the river, but while that path was simply a path, the lane that Joliffe now turned into was a proper and paved street, albeit narrow and shadowed under the overhang of its houses. At its other end it came to the White Friars' monastery, where a turn to the right along the street there headed Joliffe toward Much Park Street with the monastery's wall on his left and on his right another town orchard like the one the other side of Gosford Street. He was come around two sides of a rectangle: if he turned right again when he reached Much Park Street, he would be on the rectangle's third side and shortly pass the Byfelds' house.

Before he came to that corner, though, he found what he expected. On his right, running behind the rear yards of the houses facing onto Much Park Street, was a cart-wide track between those rear yards and the orchard. Surely most used in autumn at orchard harvest time, it would be useful any time to go somewhere more privately than by the street, from neighbor's to neighbor's rear doors or farther. Such as around the way Joliffe had just come. At twilight-time or after dark there would be small likelihood of being known while going out this way and around by way of the White Friars' lane to Gosford Street. There the chance of being seen and known was somewhat more but still slight in the few moments it would take to cross it and disappear into shadows and the path past the smiths' pageant house.

Joliffe followed the track. He had no way to tell which of the rear yards he passed belonged to the Byfeld house. He had to be satisfied with finding the track ended at the far corner of the orchard, did not go through to Gosford Street but went far enough that one of the yards it passed had to be the Byfelds'.

So now he knew how . . . someone . . . might have gone a long way round to the smiths' pageant house without the near neighbors remarking on the lateness of the hour for a walk. It made what he had guessed a little possible and opened the next step he would have to take. The problem was how to take that step. He saw no way to it this afternoon.

Or was it that he did not want to see a way to it?

He shook he head against that as he went back the way he had come. No. This was something that had to be seen through to the end, no matter how much more grief that end was going to bring if he were right. For now, though, the only thing to do was wait, and he went off to join in whatever Basset, Rose, and the others were doing with their day.

Chapter 23

As it happened, Basset and the others were taking the afternoon at their ease. Against all likelihood, Rose had yesterday declared the garb for Basset's play was done, so even she was having a restful day. She had seen to them all going together to morning Mass at Holy Trinity, that being the Silcoks' church, but was not pushing their devotion further than that. When Joliffe came up the stairs into their chamber, he found all signs of sewing had been tidied away. The garb, carefully folded, was set out in piles along the work table, and the players' sleeping pallets and floor cushions were scattered over the floor, with Ellis lain out on one of them, snoring slightly in pleasant sleep. Rose and Piers were sitting on cushions in the patch of sunlight through the far window, playing at something on the game board set between them. Basset, Gil, and—somewhat to Joliffe's surprise—Will Sendell were sprawled at ease at the room's other end, talking in apparent good cheer, with cups in hand and a pitcher set in their midst.

They all waved for Joliffe to join them. He did willingly and for the rest of the afternoon lost himself in the rich and satisfying talk of their shared world of plays and fellow players present and past, roads traveled and places seen, good times and bad. Their laughter over how, years ago, their playing of Noah and the Flood was washed out by a thunderburst and downpour at the very moment Noah welcomed his wife into the boat wakened Ellis sufficiently for him to growl without opening his eyes, "It wasn't that laughable at the time."

"It wasn't," Basset agreed, his smile nonetheless unabated.

"But then there was the time," Ellis went on, sitting up, "when—" and he was away on one of his own favorite stories that had them wiping the laughter-tears from their eyes by the time he finished.

All in all, it was a better afternoon than Joliffe had had in a long while, and at the end they all—Rose and Piers, too, of course—went out to supper together, with Rose reminding them as they went of how they had tried to use the infant Piers as the Infant Jesus and how that had turned out.

"I remember," Will Sendell laughed. "He kept wiggling out of the swaddling bands. I didn't know babies *could* wiggle out of swaddling bands."

"They shouldn't be able to," Rose said with a dryness only Joliffe could have matched. "But he did."

"Looking back, I can see it was done for kindness on his part," Joliffe offered. "He didn't want us ever mistakenly having hope he was sweet and biddable."

"Hai!" Piers protested. "I'm biddable. You can bid me all

you want." His most mischievous grin spread over his face. "I just won't do it if I don't want to."

A chorus of general agreement answered him, and Ellis tousled his hair in the way Piers claimed to most dislike. That was become a more perilous deed now that Piers was so well grown, but this time Piers only ducked out from under Ellis' hand and punched his shoulder in friendly fashion, and afterward went along the street with Ellis holding Rose by the hand on one side and his arm over Piers' shoulders on the other, plainly well-content in each other's company.

They dined in a good inn on the marketplace. Basset insisted Sendell was their guest. Sendell insisted back that he would at least buy a pitcher of wine for them to share. That turned into several pitchers of wine, with Joliffe buying the second and Ellis the third, while Basset said he would pay for the meal. It was altogether as good an afternoon-into-evening as Joliffe had spent in a long, long while. Their players' talk went on, continuing to call up the mischances and bon-chances that had come along their way. "Or that we've tripped on and fallen sprawling over," Ellis mock-grumbled.

They all laughed, Ellis, too. All in all there was a great deal of laughter. Will's lost company was not forgotten, nor some mischances over which there could be no laughter even now. But likewise there was the continuing thought under it all, in Joliffe's mind at least, that all things pass and that, come what may, the present moment is when he and everyone lived. All the rest was past or to come, and if now was very good, it should be enjoyed to the full.

When time came he had to leave them, Joliffe's regret was real and deep. He was jibed at for going, with laughing demands to know where he would have better time than with them. He jibed back that change gave life its savour. Piers declared he had found himself a girl somewhere in Coventry. Joliffe laid a finger along his nose and said as if imparting a deep secret, "The less said, the less pestered, youngling," and sauntered out.

The long almost mid-summer afterglow of sunset still filled the western sky. Reportedly, curfew would not be very closely kept these last few days before Corpus Christi as the town filled with outside folk come for the festival and plays, when it was wanted they have as many hours as possible to spend their money. The long twilight at this time of the year aided that. Would aid him, too, with what he purposed. Supposing he was right in his guesses, of course. Supposing . . . supposing . . . supposing.

He had been supposing much through yesterday and today. Now he would find how much of his supposing was true.

She was already there, walking in the orchard, just as he had . . . supposed she might be. There were not many ways or chances to be alone from a house over-full of people. The orchard was there, just beyond the back gate, and no reason why she should not, as other people did, walk there in the last daylight, for ease after the day's work. Given all her present grief, no one would refuse her that small solace nor force their company on her when she said she wanted to walk alone. It would be only kindness to let her do so, as well as perhaps a relief to everyone else in the house to have her away for a while, taking the weight of her grief with her.

Because there were others—not all of them couples— strolling along the paths wound through the orchard, she took no immediate heed of Joliffe until he came directly in her way and stayed there. Forced to halt, she lifted her gaze from the ground and for a moment openly did not know him.

"Mistress Deyster," he said.

Anna Deyster rearranged her face from whatever stark place her thoughts had been. "My uncle is at home, I think," she said, dropped her gaze again, and made to go around him.

Joliffe let her, but turned and fell into step beside her, saying, "It's you I meant to see here."

Her step faltered, then went steady again. Her gaze stayed down, and with taut dismissal in her tone, she said, "I don't want to be seen."

Everything about her, not just her voice, was taut. Joliffe thought she was like a tightly twisted rope that if released would go whipping wildly out of control, lashing around and around until finally limp. Watching her from the side of his eyes but carefully keeping only quietness in his own voice, Joliffe said, "My guess is that you've taken to walking alone in the orchard most evenings."

"Yes," she all but snapped. But since it seemed he was not going to go away, she made an attempt at easing her voice and said with strained lightness, "I think my mother worries that I hope to meet Robyn's ghost here in the twilight."

"Do you?"

"Do I what? Meet him? Or hope to meet him?"

"Either. Both."

"No." She bit down on the word as if she meant it to be her last, then said as if bitterly unable to hold it in, "Hope is gone out of everything."

Joliffe waited three paces. He could feel her, in the darkness of her thoughts, begin to forget he was there. Into her darkness he said quietly, "I should think you'd be afraid it was another ghost you might meet here."

Her look at him questioned what he meant, as if she truly did not seem to understand. Joliffe felt a qualm that he was very much gone the wrong way, but he finished his thought. "Ned Eme's ghost."

Anna Deyster jerked to a stop and turned on him. Even in the blue shadowing of the evening he could see the tightening of fury take her face. "Ned?" she spat out. "His ghost? His soul went surely straight to Hell the instant he was dead. There'll be no coming back by him, nor ever prayers enough to shift his damned soul to Heaven. He died damned and he'll stay that way."

Joliffe waited the length of a slow-drawn breath before saying quietly into the evening darkness, "You made certain sure of that."

Her rage against Ned had burned up her awareness of what she should and should not say. Remembering now, too late, she seemed to shrink. Even as Joliffe looked at her, she dwindled from a woman furyed enough to have killed a man to simply a woman very tired and ready to be done with it.

"Yes," she said, matching his quietness. "I made certain sure." Still quietly, almost inevitably, she asked, "How do you know?"

"When Master Fylongley was questioning you and your family, nothing was said about when Ned had supposedly hung himself. Everyone seemed to be taking it he had done it the day he was found. We hadn't said otherwise. But when Master Fylongley asked when each of you had last seen Ned, you shivered and crossed yourself and said not yesterday of course. The 'of course' was because you knew he had been hanging there all that day *and* the night before it, too, not merely for a few hours before he was found."

She said, "Ah," and moved on.

Joliffe moved with her, matching her slow walk, saying, "It was a little strange, too, that you didn't remember when you last saw him. It's usually the first thing someone remembers when they hear of a death: the last time I saw him was . . . But your brother had to remind you."

"Ah," she said again.

"Was it then, in the street that morning, that you asked him to meet you in the smiths' pageant house that evening?"

Her eyes still on the path in front of them, she said, "Yes. We'd played there—all around there—as children. We both knew how to go there by the back way without drawing heed. I let him think I wanted to talk with him where we'd likely be unbothered by anyone. He didn't think about the Judas tree being there."

The anger and force of will that had let her do what she had done was again in her voice and the clutch of her hands together. Joliffe, keeping his own voice even and low, said, "But you thought of it."

When she did not answer that, he asked his own inevitable question. "Why?"

She twisted her head from one side to the other, refusing an answer.

"He said something to you the day before that made you angry at him," Joliffe pushed, his voice still quiet. "Made you angry enough to kill him. What was it? Did he tell you he'd killed Robyn Kydwa?"

Anna Deyster drew the harsh breath of someone struck a painful blow. She stopped, swaying a little where she stood.

Joliffe held back from reaching out to steady her. This was not a woman ready to be touched.

"Yes," she hissed. "He was at me again to marry him. He said he had waited so long to have me. He said Robyn wasn't worth mourning over. He said Robyn was . . . was . . ."

She could not get the word out, was choking on it. Joliffe said it for her. "A spy."

"Yes." This time she spat the word. "He said Robyn was a spy against Lollards here in Coventry and that he killed him to protect his family and others."

"Do they need protecting?"

"No! There's no one needs protecting here! That was just Ned's excuse. Ned's *lie!*"

Not entirely Ned's lie. Robyn Kydwa *had* been spying. But Joliffe could also believe Ned had used that for excuse to do what he wanted to do—rid himself of a rival for a woman he meant to have. Either way, at the last it did not much matter what was true in the layers of why Ned Eme had murdered two men, or what Anna Deyster believed or refused to believe. The end and sum of it all was that between them, she and Ned had killed three men in brutal, ugly ways. But Joliffe still had a question and now was the time for it, while she was still talking, before she maybe wound herself tightly closed again, not understanding that it was too late for silence to do her any good now.

"How did you do it? How were you able to hang Ned? He can't have simply let you."

She stopped walking and laughed, a bitter, ugly, terrible sound. Joliffe was almost glad the twilight had deepened enough he could no longer clearly see her face as she said with scorn and bitterness, "It was so easy. I was there first, to ready things. When he came, I was standing on the wagon, waiting for him just where I needed to be. I told him I was weakening toward him, that I hadn't wanted to meet somewhere we'd be seen because it was too soon to be seen I was giving up Robyn, but still I was weakening. He believed that. He tried to put his arms around me. I backed away, said I was still torn over it all, asked him to turn away from me while I gathered myself to part from memory of Robyn forever." Everything except contempt left her voice. "He truly believed I was that weak and a fool. He turned his back on me. The rope and the noose had been already up when I came there. I'd only had to make sure the noose was in reach when he turned away from me. I threw it over his head, jerked it tight while he was still too startled to do anything, and pushed him off the wagon to swing and choke. To swing and choke," she repeated viciously, then choked herself on what sounded like her own anger and triumph and sickened memory all together.

His voice kept carefully empty, Joliffe said, "Except it wasn't that easy. You had to keep him from grabbing hold of something to save himself even then."

Anna Deyster lurched forward into a rapid walk. Keeping pace with her, Joliffe insisted, "Didn't you?"

"I had to. I had to." Her hands, that had been folded tightly together at her waist, were now fists pressed between her breasts. She began to beat them against herself, lightly at first, then with increasing force. "He made Robyn suffer. I made him suffer in his turn. It took him longer to die than I thought it would, but he finally did. He couldn't even pray for pardon with the rope choking him. He died unshriven and damned. Damned forever!"

That she had given Ned no chance of salvation plainly mattered greatly to her. Did it matter at all to her that her own salvation was in doubt if she could not come to remorse, confession, and penance for what she had done?

Her walking had brought them to the orchard's edge, to where a gate stood open into the rear yard of what Joliffe guessed was her own home by the way she came to a sudden stop and stood staring the length of the yard toward the house at its far end. Then she abruptly turned aside and sat down on a bench there beside the gate. "I can't go in there again," she said.

Joliffe stayed on his feet in front of her. "Are you ready to go to the bailiffs, then?" As if it were something she had choice in. She might, of course, go back on all she had said, deny she had ever said it, but he did not think so. It had all been weighing on her so heavily that the slight added weight of his questions had been too much. Words and truth had broken out of her. He did not think she would mend enough to take up lying again.

But she went on sitting there, not ready yet for what must come next, and what Joliffe had supposed would happen happened: someone came looking for her down the length of the yard from the house, carrying a horn-sided lantern. To the good, it was Powet. When he was near enough for the lantern light to show him Joliffe standing just outside the gate, he said with open surprise, "Master Joliffe? Have you seen—" He reached the gate then, saw his niece on the bench, and changed that to, "Ah, there you are. Your mother is fretting. You said you'd not stay out like this again after the other night. You could have brought Master Joliffe into the house."

There was half a question behind that last and in his look

at Joliffe. Well might he question finding her out so late and alone with a man, but Joliffe had his own question and asked, "When was she out so late before?"

One hand out to urge his unresponding niece to her feet, Powet said, "Um? When? When was it, Anna? Four nights ago, wasn't it? Herry and Dick have a wager laid you'd do it again, no matter what you said. I think Herry has won. Now . . ."

"Uncle Eustace." Anna Deyster lifted her aged and ravaged face to the lantern light. "I killed Ned."

Powet's hand fell back to his side. He stared at her, then looked sharply aside at Joliffe who nodded agreement to her words. Powet looked desperately back to her and said, begging her to unsay it, "Anna, no."

She stood up from the bench. Her back was straight. Her voice was firm. "Yes. Now I have to go to the bailiffs and tell them so." In an echo of her uncle's gesture, she put out a hand to him and asked in a voice gone momentarily small, "Please, will you come with me?"

Chapter 24

Word of Anna Deyster's confession and arrest burned through Coventry the next day with something like the speed of fire through dry stubble. More than once it overtook the slower-spreading word that Ned Eme's death had not been by his own hand, making momentary confusion for those unable to re-sort the pieces quickly enough. Joliffe heard more than he wanted to of the gabble-talk as he paced the streets, waiting for Sebastian to find him. He supposed Sebastian would, rather than wait for when they had settled to next meet, and surely enough as Joliffe walked through the marketplace in early afternoon, Sebastian's hand came down on his shoulder.

They made play of having chance-met, so that if anyone heeded them it should look like two acquaintances briefly meeting, making an exchange of greetings, and soon parting. What actually passed between them was Sebastian saying, falsely smiling, "Out Bishop Gate. First street to the left. Second alehouse along it," and Joliffe answering with as false a wide smile, "I'll go long way round, shall I?" so that he and Sebastian would not go along Cross Cheaping and out the Bishop Gate at too much the same time. Sebastian gave an agreeing, smiling nod to that and they slapped hands and parted company.

A half hour later they were facing each other along a bench in a dark, slovenly den of an alehouse that looked to sell second-hand clothing as well, and Sebastian was not smiling at all as he said in a low-voiced growl and with a glower, "That's it, then? That's all she told you about it? She killed the fellow because he stupidly told her he'd killed Kydwa to have her? That she doesn't believe what he said about Kydwa being a spy because *she* says there's nothing to find out about Lollards here?"

"That's the sum of it."

"There has to be more. What a fool of a grieving woman thinks is true or not is worth nothing," Sebastian grumbled.

"If there is, it will have to be for someone else to find." Joliffe stood up, spreading his hands to show that was all he had. "I'm done for this while."

Staying seated, looking up at him, Sebastian said, "Not if I give the word otherwise."

"It won't matter what word you give. I'm a player. Much of my value to our lord lies in my being a player. A good one. From now until after Corpus Christi all I am is a player. What you and any Lollards get up to in that while is your business and theirs, not mine. Not"—he added as he started to leave—"that we've found sign of any Lollards getting up to anything here. So I'm not going to worry overmuch about it."

To Joliffe's surprise, Sebastian lifted his cup in gesture of farewell and said with his rat-toothed grin, "The Lollards for me. Playing for you. Fair enough for now."

Joliffe grinned back and went out.

The next few days were not that simple, of course. The talk and scandal of it all likely added to the pleasures of the hundreds of out-folk flowing into Coventry for the week, and Joliffe could not help hearing far more than he wanted to hear, more especially since it followed him straight to the last practices for his own play.

His worry the first day was over what they would do if Powet decided he was too distracted to go on with Joseph. Will Sendell could probably take up the part, but what if, instead of Powet being unable to go on, Richard Eme declared he could not work with the uncle of his brother's murderer? At this late in the practices there was only so much patching could be done before the play suffered in the playing.

So he was relieved that first afternoon's end when everyone came, gathering to the yard at the expected hour. By the look of them, they all were as unsure as he was how things would go from there. Powet was gray-faced and haggard with strain and grief. Dick was little better, half-hiding, huddle-shouldered, behind his uncle as if unsure he wanted to see or be seen. Richard Eme for once had nothing to say, simply stood looking as if he had been blindsided out of all reckoning of how the world should be. No one else seemed to know what to say to them or to each other and sat or stood around in awkward silence. But they were all there, and Sendell stood in front of them, the roll of the script in his hands like a marshal's staff of office, and said, "We know what's happened and

it's terrible all around. There's nothing good to be said"—
here he looked at Powet, who had drawn Dick to his side with
a steadying hand on his shoulder, and then at Richard
Eme—"beyond how sorry we all are."

Murmurs from everyone else and a general nodding of
heads agreed with that. Powet and Richard Eme nodded
back in thanks and acceptance. Dick looked as if he wanted
to bolt, but with his uncle's hand on his shoulder, he managed his own awkward nod.

"That said," Sendell went on, "we still have a play to do.
It's a fine play. We've made it that. Better than any of us
thought we could when we started." As he surely meant it to,
that won a shaky laugh among them all, and he said more
strongly, "I doubt any of us want to fail it now. So, into your
garb and up on the wagon and everyone to their beginning
places. We'll run it as if we mean it. Prophets, let's set it
going, and mind you keep the pace fast to the forward."

Joliffe, knowing from experience how possible it was to
lose oneself in the necessity of a play no matter what was
happening—or waiting to happen—in life beyond it, threw
himself full strength at his Prophet, willing Richard Eme to
match him because the drive they brought to the beginning
might lift and carry everyone else forward in their turn. It
worked. Or something did. From the Prophets onward, the
play flowed like a thing with a life of its own, carrying them
all with it. Their new Gabriel fitted in like he had been there
all along. Joseph was sincere and comical in deft proportions.
Mary remembered to move like a girl and held the bundle
that was supposed to be the infant Christ as if it were a real
child, not a wad of cloth. Even Dick, by the time he had to
come from the stage house as Christ, had moved beyond his

immediate misery into feigning the mix of wisdom and merriment that Sendell had been working him toward.

The only moment that nearly undid them all was Simeon's Nunc Dimittis that he sang so much from the heart that it seemed to be for all the passing away there was in the world. Joliffe saw the tears rising in more eyes than his own among those on the stage and took up his next lines as the prophetess Ane more quickly than he might have, to move everyone onward from where their thoughts should not go just now. His own included.

At the end everyone came back onto the stage. Joliffe, looking around at them, saw they were all as lifted up and worn out as he was, and he started to clap, both for himself and them. Sendell, beaming at them from the yard below the wagon's edge, joined in, and then everyone in a burst of relief and triumph was clapping for each other.

"We can only hope," said Sendell when they had done, "that the next two practices go badly."

Those among them who knew the old adage that a bad last practice meant a good performance when it counted explained it to those who looked either puzzled or alarmed at Sendell's words. That made for more laughter before Sendell held up a hand and finished, "Word is we're to play at five sites this year. If you haven't heard, those will be in Gosford Street, then along to the meeting of Greyfriars and Earl Street, onward to the corner of Smithford and West Orchard, around to where West Orchard meets Cross Cheaping, and lastly at St. Michael's churchyard. The weavers have promised us plenty of apprentices and journeymen to pull the wagon, so all we have to do is be there. And play our hearts out, of course."

They cheered him for that, and he dismissed them for the night. Only to Joliffe, lingering behind everyone else, did he show how tired he was, sagging down on a bench to sit staring at the pageant wagon across the yard. In the evening shadows the bold colors of its red and blue painted sides and the green and yellow curtains of the stage house were muted, the emptiness of the stage profound after all that had been there so short a time before. Joliffe sat down beside him, guessing he needed to talk. Not taking his eyes from the stage, Sendell said, "It's going to work. I truly think it's going to work."

"If they could do this well tonight," Joliffe said, "they'll be fine come the day."

Sendell gave him a wry, sideways look. "Yes. Tonight. You couldn't have waited until after Corpus Christi to make all this trouble, could you?"

The question was mostly in jest, but Joliffe answered it straight because it was something he had already thought on. "If she had had more time for what she had done to wear a familiar groove into her thoughts, into her feelings, I might not have been able to jar her so easily—if ever—into open guilt."

"No," Sendell agreed. "I don't suppose you could have." He slapped his hands down on his thighs and said in lighter humour. "Still, we have a play and that's what counts. I'm going to bed. I'm so tired I can hardly walk straight. You?"

"I'll sit here a while, while it's quiet. It's been a long few days and I could do with doing nothing for a time."

Sendell nodded to that and strolled away to the stairs. Joliffe stayed where he was, but the "nothing" that he hoped for did not come. Instead, his mind turned yet again to what he supposed he would never be able to answer: Had Anna

Deyster confessed—first to him and then as freely to Master Fylongley, and after him to the other bailiff—because she could no longer stand the pain she was in? Or did she do it from a need for penance for her deed mixed with a confused hope that the law would make an end of her, ending her struggle through a life that seemed to have betrayed her at every turn?

Those questions had come as he listened to her readily confessing again and again to bailiffs and sheriff, but there was no way that he could ask her for answer. Supposing she even knew herself.

The curfew bell began to ring and he left the yard, closing the gate carefully behind him, heading back through the streets to his bed, tired enough now to sleep no matter what his thoughts.

Against what he had supposed, through the next two days he had some answer of what Anna Deyster's fate was likely to be. Along with all the other talk about the murders, word spread that Mistress Byfeld was swearing she would buy a pardon for her daughter no matter what the cost. Pardons were not always possible, but whereas a wife killing her husband was treason and execution for that hard to avoid, murdering a murderer was another matter altogether, and there was not much doubt left of Ned's guilt after someone—it was supposed a villager not wanting to chance being pulled onto a jury—sent a boy to the crowner with a message of where Kydwa's servant's body could be found under a stream bank. That ended all possibility the man had killed his master and run away. It likewise must have stripped from Ned's family what hope they might have held that after all he had not done what Anna Deyster claimed. It also meant that Anna Deyster had as many people on her side as blaming her, and although she would perforce be found guilty of Ned's murder since she continued to insist on it, the odds were strong that Mistress Byfeld would succeed in a petition and payment for a pardon from the crown.

Such a pardon would suffice to save her daughter's life but not much else, because the law would strip Anna Deyster, proven a criminal, of everything she owned.

It was Powet, meeting Joliffe outside the gate to the pageant yard as they went to their final practice, who told him something more. They had said nothing directly to each other since they had taken Anna Deyster to the bailiffs. Joliffe was leaving it to Powet as to when—or if—they ever spoke together again and felt a spasm mixed with relief and wariness when Powet held out a hand to stop him going into the yard.

The wariness was dispelled when Powet said quietly, "I know you did what needed to be done. There's no blame to you in it. You've heard her mother means to get her pardon?"

"Yes. It's likely she will, from what I've heard. I'm glad." He was not sure if he was truly glad or not—it was a brutal death and damnation she had given Ned Eme—but he supposed "glad" was what Powet needed to hear and therefore said it.

"There's something more that you're not likely to hear. The day she . . ." Powet had to stop, look away, swallow, regain himself before going on. "That day, after she set Ned to meet her, before she killed him, she went to a lawyer. Anna did. We only found out today. She enfeoffed all her property to Cecily. There's nothing for the law to take from her. I thought—I thought it might matter to you to know everything isn't lost."

Oddly enough, it mattered deeply. Robyn Kydwa's death had surely ended what small hopes beyond bare survival Cecily Kydwa might have had for her life. Now Anna Deyster, giving up hope herself, had given hope back to Cecily. It was, in its odd way, a kind of fair exchange and, "That means that maybe your nephew Herry will have more interest now in marrying her after all," Joliffe said.

Powet looked momentarily startled. Then thoughtful. "I hadn't gone that far with it yet," he said. "But—yes. Yes. Very possibly."

Corpus Christi day came beautifully, with weather as perfect as June could offer. The early morning procession of guildsmen, churchmen, mayor, and city officers through the streets was splendid with all the ceremony a prosperous town could give in honor of the Lord. The trains of each guild and church and every monastery in Coventry bore banners and crucifixes, while at the heart of it all was the Sacrament in golden vessels carried by priests in the full glory of their embroidered copes, with over them a canopy of crimson silk on silver-gilded poles held by four of the richest burgesses in their finest furred robes and jeweled collars. As display of Coventry's faith and the city's dignity and pride and power, the procession could not have been bettered.

When it was over, the rest of the day was for eating, drinking, general merriment through the streets, and—*the plays.*

All the pageant wagons of the various guilds had been

rolled out of their yards before dawn by the journeymen and apprentices of their guilds, and hauled into order of their plays in a crowded line along Gosford Street just inside the gateway. Now there was a jumbled time while people streaming back from either being in or watching the procession searched out their own wagons—"Dolt! You're in the Crucifixion. It comes *after* the Nativity. You're farther along."— and began the changing of clothing and doing whatever painting or masking their parts might need.

The Master of the Pageants was a tall, pale man who sensibly rode a tall horse back and forth along the line as he oversaw it all, his helpers trotting at his side until sent hither and yon with whatever orders were needed. He and they would be wearied to the bone by day's end because on him would depend the smooth forward going of the plays from one playing site to another. Still, he must have done the business before because he was handling it deftly and calmly, by what Joliffe saw of him, and that boded well for the rest of the day.

Piers had disappeared farther along the line to join the other demons at the Harrowing of Hell, but Joliffe caught glimpses of Basset herding and arranging his players at the wagon just ahead of where Sendell was doing the same with his. Gil and his fellow shepherds were practicing ducking behind the cloth hanging to the ground on both sides of the wagon and coming out quickly. Ellis and the other two Kings in their royal gowns and shining crowns were sitting on their horses, calmly above it all. He caught Joliffe looking at him and gave a kingly inclination of his head. Joliffe, robed as First Prophet, raised one hand and waggled rude fingers at him. Ellis looked away and did not look back.

And then, suddenly it seemed, everything went quiet. From away along Gosford Street where the crowd was gathered at the first playing site there was the formless sound of many people talking, but for just that moment there was stillness along the line of wagons. The Master came riding from the rear of the line, the clop of his horse's hoofs loud on the paving, and drew rein beside Basset standing on his pageant wagon. He looked ahead, then looked at Basset. He said something and Basset answered. The Master nodded and rode a few more yards forward, abreast of the twenty men waiting to pull the wagon. He said something to them. Their leader nodded. The Master turned in his saddle to face back along the line, raised his voice, and gave the order all were waiting for.

"Let the wagons roll!"

Author's Note

I was already at work on this book when I went to the symposium "Drama and Religion 1555–1575: The Chester Cycle in Context" at the University of Toronto in May 2010. Besides the scholarly papers that were given, the entire cycle of twenty-three medieval plays from Chester, England, were performed out of doors on wagons moved from site to site on the campus over three half-days. The plays began with the Creation of the World and followed through Old and New Testaments to Judgment Day. Each was done by a different group from schools in Canada and the United States, with no attempt to unify their styles; all were done according to the individual group's own imagination and resources, their styles widely diverging.

As someone who has seen much theater, both from the audience side and while performing on stages, I was as fascinated by the onlookers' delight as by the productions themselves. And by "onlookers' delight" I mean my own as well as what I saw and heard around me. People watched in riveted delight as the Temptress in the Garden of Eden changed into a slithering serpent; cheered when Moses pulled the tablets of the law from the rocky cliff behind him; laughed ourselves silly at the southern hillbilly shepherds settling down for a night of watching their sheep with their coolers of beer and snacks beside them—and were nonetheless deeply moved by their so-humble but sincere gifts to the Christ child. Nor is anyone likely to forget Herod on his high throne, sneeringly throwing the occasional grape at the audience—or the silence as we watched the Crucifixion. And I'm here to tell you that when the demons burst from Hellmouth, to prowl and snarl only a few yards from our faces, we were truly taken momentarily aback. Some plays were stronger productions than others, but at end the overall feeling left was that we had gone a wonderful journey. You did not have to be Christian in that audience to be carried along on the mythic strength of the story.

In short—brought alive by theatrical imagination, these medieval plays *work*.

Which pleased me no end, since that was what I was imagining and trying to do with the plays in *A Play of Heresy*. Unfortunately, unlike the cycle of plays played in Chester and York, only two of the cycles done in Coventry remain—that of the Shearmen and Taylors and that of the Weavers. If you should happen on a book titled *Ludus Coventriae or the Plaie Called Corpus Christi*, full of plays, take note this was published under the misconception that what are now called the N-Town plays were the lost ones of Coventry. Instead, the book I used the most while writing this story was *The Corpus Christi Plays*, edited by Pamela M. King and Clifford Davidson, from Medieval Institute Publications, Western Michigan University. Where occasionally things diverge in my story from the facts given in the book, pray remember that nothing is static and what is recorded of plays and pageant houses in the 1500s is not necessarily exactly how things were in the 1400s, a time for which we have less documentation about the plays.

What is intriguing, besides the surviving plays themselves, are the odd bits of information scattered through the town records, such as where some of the guilds had their pageant houses, and the cost for painting Herod's face and mending the Devil's garment. These are winnowed out and gathered together in the delight-filled *Records of Early English Drama: Coventry.*

A more immediately available experience of drama in medieval Coventry is that staple of Christmas carols—"The Coventry Carol." It's the lullaby that the mothers of Bethlehem sing to their doomed children at the Massacre of the Innocents in the play that, in this book, Basset is directing—one of the two plays that somehow survived when most of the Coventry plays vanished. Listening to the song's delicate, sorrowing beauty makes one wonder how much of all too perishable grace and beauty is lost from medieval times.

Now for Coventry itself. Again I feel obliged to ask readers to move with me past the clichés about medieval towns, lest it be thought I write too rosy a picture of them. Much of what we "know" about them (such as all their streets were narrow and dark and deep in filth, with people throwing rude things out of upper windows) dates from later centuries, when the shifting economics led to the over-population of towns and cities and the accompanying breakdown of their governmental and social structures. Citizens of medieval towns— quarrelsome and ambitious among themselves though they might be (and the records show they definitely could be)— tended to be very proud and protective of their towns. Sponsoring fine civic events such as the Corpus Christi plays was one way of showing it, mixing piety and civic promotion in a combination very common throughout medieval England. The Tudor economics and their Reformation tore much of that to shreds. For an in-depth look at the inner workings of medieval Coventry, there is *The Coventry Leet Book,* published by the Early English Text Society.

A number of records exist from medieval Coventry. Out of them, I have amused myself by using names of some actual citizens in this story. There was an actual John Burbage listed in the Coventry subsidy of 1434, when John Burbage of Bayley Lane paid 1s. 8d., sign of a prosperous man. Whether he was in any way an ancestor of Shakespeare's Richard Burbage, I don't know, but it's diverting to know that Stratford-upon-Avon is not far from Coventry and that scholars love to speculate the young Shakespeare may have seen the last performance of these plays in Coventry before the Protestants shut them altogether down. (Turns out it was not, in the long run, the Lollards whom folk had to worry about.) So, if we are speculating, let us speculate that the young Shakespeare perhaps met the young Richard Burbage, descendant of John Burbage, then. But, no, I am not going to write that story.

Johanna Byfeld of Much Park Street is likewise in the records. And in the town records for 1441 is the order that "Richard Eme and all others, who play in the Corpus Christi pageant, shall play well and sufficiently, so that no impediment may arise in any play, on pain of 20s. to the town wall."

Less happily, the 1431 Lollard uprising and its aftermath are also real, as are the executions, among others, of a Thomas Kydwa and of Alice Garton, just as told here. For this background, "Lollardy in Coventry and the Revolt of 1431" by

Maureen Jurkowski in *The Fifteenth Century, vol. 6: Identity and Insurgency in the Late Middle Ages*, edited by Linda Clark, was invaluable.

Of course, should you go looking for medieval places in Coventry mentioned and used in this story, you will find little. The German bombing of 1940 burned out what was left of the medieval heart of the city, including St. Michael's church (become, by then, St. Michael's Cathedral) whose shell remains next to the new and glorious cathedral put up in its place for reminder of the great cruelties of mankind and of the grace of forgiveness and mercy.

For a wonderful site for "seeing" Coventry as it was and is, go to http://www.historiccoventry.co.uk. There are maps of Coventry at different times over the centuries, and photographs from the late 1800s into the 21st century. A journey in time both delightful and sad.

For a clearer understanding of how suicide—a word not used until centuries later—was seen and responded to in medieval times, Alexander Murray's three-volume *Suicide in the Middle Ages* was extremely useful.

Biblical quotations are from the Bible in English—now known as the Wycliffe Bible—available in England in the 1400s. Bibles in English were not completely forbidden. Copies are known to have been owned by several kings, and license from a bishop could be had for lesser people to own one. The Church's principal objection to the Bible being in English was the abuse some people made of it, taking from it what they wanted in order to justify what they wanted to do. It has always sounded better (at least to the perpetrator) to say, "The Bible made me do it."

By the by, yes, there were organs in medieval England at

the time, including portative ones. Yet again I feel obliged to insist that, despite the tedious media clichés, medieval times should not be summed up as nothing but ignorant, ugly, and brutal, existing under a perpetually overcast sky with plague and warfare every day from the fall of Rome to the Renaissance. The surviving art and literature and music from the time show a love of complexity, order, and beauty. Study of the legal structure and the bureaucracy that supported it evidence a society striving to create and maintain an ordered life. There were of course ugliness and injustices and outbreaks of violence—but those are not exclusive to medieval times and it is grossly unfair to characterize the period as if they were. Almost needless to say, the simplistic willfulness of those who continue to portray the time as "nothing but nasty," ignoring everything to the good that the medieval world has to offer, annoys the hell out of me.

Not to mention those who can't trouble themselves to figure out that how things were in 1250 are not likely to match how things were in 1450. Think: 1750 versus 1950. Change happens—in clothing, attitudes, and societal structure. "Even" in the medieval world.

More cheerfully, for those who also read the Dame Frevisse series and happen to remember a rat-faced spy Joliffe encounters when finding excuse to befriend Arteys in *The Bastard's Tale*, you may find that scene plays differently now you have met Sebastian in *A Play of Heresy*.